TEMPTED BY THE WOLF

ALSO BY ALICIA MONTGOMERY

Shadow Wolf

A Touch of Magic

Heart of the Wolf

THE BLACKSTONE MOUNTAIN SERIES

The Blackstone Dragon Heir

The Blackstone Bad Dragon

The Blackstone Bear

The Blackstone Wolf

The Blackstone Lion

The Blackstone She-Wolf

The Blackstone She-Bear

The Blackstone She-Dragon

TEMPTED BY THE WOLF

BOOK 6 OF THE TRUE MATES SERIES

ALICIA MONTGOMERY

ABOUT THE AUTHOR

Alicia Montgomery has always dreamed of becoming a romance novel writer. She started writing down her stories in now long-forgotten diaries and notebooks, never thinking that her dream would come true. After taking the well-worn path to a stable career, she is now plunging into the world of self-publishing.

 facebook.com/aliciamontgomeryauthor

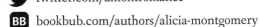 twitter.com/amontromance

BB bookbub.com/authors/alicia-montgomery

PROLOGUE

13 YEARS AGO...

The hunger pains were back. She tried to ignore them, but they were gnawing at her insides. When was the last time she had food—real food? The small creatures the she-wolf hunted were disgusting, but they kept the pangs at bay. But she wanted an actual meal today. A hot meal. Or a sandwich. But she needed money for that.

She hunched in on herself, wrapping the too-big jacket around her. Clothes were hard to come by, especially in her size, so she made do with what the she-wolf found. Eyes scanned the busy pedestrian street, looking for an easy mark. The woman with the baby stroller. Naw, she didn't look like she carried cash. The man in the headphones? Hmmm, based on his ratty shoes, he probably didn't have money either.

Ah, there he was.

The old man wearing a hat. He just left the cafe, paper cup in one hand and a newspaper under his arm. And a fat bulge in his back pocket meant a wallet full of cash. He seemed distracted, too, as he stopped at almost every window display on the shopping street, looking at all the holiday displays. Was it almost

Christmas? She didn't know. The air was much colder, but there was no snow yet.

A rush of people went by, and she used the crowd to blend in, slowly making her way to the old man. She followed him, staying a good distance away. Finally, he stopped at a display outside a toy store, his eyes glued to the window. Picking up her pace, she drew nearer, until she was just close enough.

She brushed past him, bumping slightly against the man's pants. Deft fingers slipped inside, liberating the wallet from the back pocket. Prize in tow, she ran, her oversized shoes clomping on the concrete. Her heart was pounding, and she looked back, just to make sure he didn't see her or was following her. A quick glance told her he wasn't on her tail, but he was gone from his spot in front of the toy store. Seemed strange, for a man his age to move so quickly, but she didn't care. She could probably get a couple of hot meals from the bills in the wallet.

"Ow!" she cried as she bumped into something. "Watch where you're—" She stopped short when she looked up and saw who she bumped into.

Brown eyes looked down at her, the corners wrinkly and turned up. "Watch what, little she-wolf?" the old man in the hat said.

Her eyes widened, she pivoted to run away, but he was inhumanly quick and grabbed her by the collar of her jacket. She struggled to get away, but he hauled her into a back alley and then shoved her against the wall.

"I believe you have something of mine," he said, putting his hand out. When she tried to protest, he clucked his tongue. "C'mon now, little she-wolf, hand it over."

She grumbled and fished the wallet out of her jacket and slapped it on his palm. "Now get out of my way, old man," she rasped, as she tried to get around him.

"Tsk, tsk," he said, blocking her as she tried to sidestep

around him. "Hmmm...your technique wasn't too bad, and your hands were pretty light, but I supposed that has to do with their size. But, you were too sloppy. Not only did you look suspicious when you walked away, but you also fell for my trap."

"T-t-trap?" she stuttered.

"Why, yes," he chuckled. He opened the wallet and tossed out the wadded pieces of blank paper from the inside. "Doddering old man, big fat wallet in the pocket. You must learn that sometimes, the easiest pickings aren't always what they seem. And you need to challenge yourself to improve continuously."

"Oh yeah, old man?" she asked, puffing up to her full stature, at least as full as a 12-year-old girl could get. "Who's gonna teach me?"

He sighed. "I suppose I will have to tutor you. I did go to all this trouble to chase you down."

Her big brown eyes, much too big for her face, widened. "What?"

"Come along now," the old man gestured for her to follow him. "We have much work to do."

———

Present Day

The three Lycan Alphas sat around the conference table, waiting for the large projector screen in front of them to turn on.

"Do you have any idea what they want to talk to us about, Grant?" Liam Henney, the Alpha of San Francisco asked the man in the middle.

Grant Anderson, New York Alpha, shook his head. "I'm afraid not."

"The Lycan High Council calling all three of us for a

meeting can't be good news," the woman to his left said. Francesca "Frankie" Anderson (née Muccino) shook her head, her lovely mismatched blue and green eyes turned dark. She was Alpha to New Jersey, but as Grant's wife, she was also his consort and the Lupa of New York.

Jared, Grant Anderson's faithful admin, called their attention. "Alphas, Switzerland is online."

"Put them up on the screen, Jared," Grant said.

The screen flickered to life. Five people showed up on the screen, all of them sitting around an oval table.

"Alphas," the woman in the middle greeted. "I trust you are all doing well?" Lljuffa Suitdottir was the oldest member of the council and their de facto leader. She wore her white hair in a severe bun and wore a crisp white suit jacket.

"Lljuffa, Council," Grant addressed them. "Under the circumstances, I supposed we are all well. So, to what do we owe this honor?"

Lljuffa's lips curled into a smile that didn't reach her piercing light blue eyes. "Straight to the point, Grant?"

Grant's hands curled into fists under the conference table. "We're all very busy, as I assume you all are as well."

"Fine," the Lycan woman said. "We're here to discuss all the events in the past year."

"And which events might those be?"

"Let's not be glib, Grant," Lljuffa replied.

"Ah, are we finally going to discuss the mages and Stefan?" Grant asked, referring to their enemies and their leader. "Well, we've been talking about them and our alliance with the witches for the past few months now and yet nothing's moved on that front. So, I naturally assumed this was about something else."

Lljuffa's eyes narrowed. Behind her, the four other council members looked at each other.

"Yes, well, Alpha," Rodrigo Baeles, the youngest member of

the Council spoke up. He was a handsome man, with dark hair and olive skin. "There are other matters, as you know."

"The Creed Dragon," Jun Park interjected as his eyebrows drew together into a frown. "Are you in control of him? Has he pledged to your clan?"

Grant let out a laugh. "Sebastian Creed will never allow himself to be under anyone's control."

"But he could expose all of us! Or kill us all," Oded Khan protested, shaking her head and sending her her dark curls bobbing around her pretty face. "You must have him pledge to your clan."

"I cannot force anyone to pledge to me," Grant said.

"Ah, but you didn't stop the warlock from pledging to you," Adama Amuyaga countered. The African council member was the second-oldest of the group, and also one of the fiercest opponents of the alliance with the witches. "And you accepted his oath of allegiance. A warlock pledged to the Alpha of a Lycan clan! No one's heard of such a thing."

"I'll take care of the warlock," Grant said. "But, I suppose you have other reasons why you wanted all three of us here?"

"Alphas," Lljuffa began. "There's been a lot of...talk."

"Talk about what?" Frankie interjected.

Lljuffa's light blue eyes trained on Frankie. "Well, for one, two Alphas marrying?"

"There aren't any rules against that, are there?" Grant inquired.

"No," Lljuffa said. "But, there have been a few rumors going around that the two of you are planning to merge your clans and possible claim more territory."

"And if we were?" Frankie challenged, her voice raising. "Look, I've got less than 50 Lycans under me, many of them retirees or young families. If anything, joining my clan with New York would be more of a burden on them."

"Your close ties with San Francisco could be suspect."

"Could or are?" Liam spoke up. "We have a few thousand miles between us. I doubt we could take over the entire United States."

"But you are married to a witch, no?" Lljuffa said. "And your child...do you know if it will be a witch or a Lycan?"

Liam's face remained calm. "As you know, we can't determine that yet. Lara is my True Mate," he reminded them.

"And that's the problem." Lljuffa shook her head. "Do you know how many other True Mate pairings there have been around the world?"

"How many?" Grant asked.

"None," Park answered. "Nowhere in Asia, Europe, Africa...nowhere else except New York, New Jersey, and San Francisco."

"Surely that's a coincidence," Frankie said. "And maybe more will be popping up soon."

"And why would this be a concern anyway?" Liam asked. "Shouldn't you be happy that we are reproducing easily now? Five pairings, all in all, two full Lycan children already born." The San Francisco Alpha remained cool and collected, but he seemed to struggle for control, especially since Lljuffa mentioned Lara and his child.

"It is not a concern. Yet." The Council leader straightened in her chair and she squared her shoulders. "But, going back to the warlock. You must turn him over to us."

"Daric is not a piece of property to be bartered or sold," Grant said.

"But you keep him detained at Fenrir," Lljuffa countered.

"We are keeping him here now to help him recover from his injuries," Grant corrected.

"And after?"

"The crimes he committed were against us, and now he is

also pledged to me. As his Alpha, he is my responsibility, and that includes punishment for his crimes. But, seeing as he is not a Lycan, you cannot order him to make atonements or serve us, nor do you have jurisdiction over him."

Lljuffa's eyes narrowed. "Very well." She turned to the other council members. "We will talk this over and contact you again. Good day, Alphas." She turned away, and the screen went black.

"So, what do we do?" Liam asked as soon as Jared disconnected the call. "We have the mages trying to kill us, and now we have to worry about the Council too?"

Grant let out a deep sigh, and Frankie took his hand in hers, giving it a squeeze. "Well, Sebastian shouldn't be a problem. He says he can control the dragon and he's very careful now. He won't risk anything, not with Jade being pregnant and all."

"And Daric?"

"Well, that's the wild card here. But I have a plan. Daric is our greatest asset right now. With what he knows, surely we can use it to defeat Stefan."

"But you would need him to cooperate. Are you going to use his mother?"

Grant shook his head. "I can't. I mean, I could, and I've thought about it, but we all know doing that would make us all just as bad as Stefan." Frankie nodded in agreement.

"Then what are you going to do?"

"I haven't figured out that part of the plan, yet," Grant said. "But, I suppose we could strike a bargain. Get him to trust us. Help us defeat Stefan. Daric wants the same thing we do."

"As far as we know," Liam added. "You'd trust him not to betray you?"

"Of course not," Grant said. "Daric will have to be kept on a tight leash."

"How are you going to do that without using his mother against him?"

Grant shrugged. "We'll keep an eye on him."

"That still doesn't answer how you're going to get him to work with you," Liam pointed out.

"The only thing I can do is give him our proposition. I'll need your support in this, Liam."

The San Francisco Alpha nodded. "Of course, whatever you need."

"Good. I'll speak with Daric today and let you know what he says."

CHAPTER ONE

Meredith sighed for the 137th time that hour. She shifted her stance, finding a comfortable position to stand. Here she was, wasting her talents by playing babysitter to a warlock. This wasn't what she signed up for. Of course, forced servitude to the New York Lycan clan wasn't part of her life plans either, but she made her bed and now had to lie in it.

She thought she had it all figured out. Fenrir Corporation was a target ripe for the taking. The conglomerate was worth billions of dollars, and they wouldn't miss a couple of million here and there, right? Meredith was trained by one of the world's top cat burglars, and this is what she did. Steal things and sell them for money. Lots of it, as her secret bank account in the Cayman Islands, could attest. Never mind that its CEO, Grant Anderson, was also the Alpha of the East Coast's most powerful Lycan clan. It should have had her own she-wolf running the other direction. Actually, the bitch did warn her, but she couldn't help it.

Fenrir was the ultimate prize, and she spent six months of

her life staking out the place, finding weak spots and then springing into action. Months spent planning the perfect heist, only to be ruined by a little witch and a brainy little Lycan scientist. She thought the 33rd-floor research facility would be empty and she broke in one night after she was sure its two primary occupants were gone. How was she supposed to know that they'd come back—after office hours— to check on something? They caught Meredith in the act of stealing a few pieces of tech and had her detained. The nerve! Of course, said witch, Lara Chatraine and Lycan scientist, Jade Cross, were now her best friends, but that wasn't the point.

The Alpha of New York's sister offered her a deal—ten years of serving the clan instead of rotting in a jail cell in the ice desert. The choice should have been obvious, although, for a Lone Wolf like her who'd never been part of any clan, it was a tough decision. All her life, she'd been independent and never had to be under an Alpha's thumb, and frankly, she preferred it that way. But then she also preferred not freezing her ass off, so she took their offer.

Ten years of serving the clan. Meredith already had a couple of months under her belt, but the rest of her time seemed to loom overhead. Her she-wolf was also dying to break out of her skin. The New York clan had outfitted her with a tracking device that could not only track her across the planet but would explode if she tried to remove it. Shifting into her wolf form would mean breaking the ankle monitor, and she wasn't sure if Lycan healing could regrow a limb.

Patience, she told the wolf.

I didn't get us into this mess. Why should I have to suffer?

Oh, shut up, bitch.

Stop calling me a bitch!

Well, technically, you are one, so...

The she-wolf whined, then lay down and pouted.

Meredith knew her relationship with her she-wolf was special. According to the other Lycans she talked to, none of their wolves spoke in complete sentences, nor conversed with them. Lucky them. Some days, she couldn't get the animal to shut the fuck up.

A low moan caught her attention, and her head snapped towards the figure in the bed. Daric, the prisoner she'd been guarding for the last two days. The warlock had been injured badly in their last confrontation with the mages, the Lycans' enemies. Daric couldn't use any of his powers, so he had apparently tried to stab the mages' leader, Stefan, with a knife. That didn't go so well, and Daric ended up getting hurt.

Meredith sighed again. Witches and warlocks were biologically human, and thus didn't have the same speedy healing and metabolism Lycans did. She didn't know how the hell they ended up being the dominant species on this planet, seeing as they were all practically like walking bags of organs wrapped in a balloon.

Daric let out another moan and twisted his body, the white sheet covering him slipping lower. Meredith felt her mouth go dry at the sight of his chest—broad and muscled, with a sprinkling of dark blonde hair. His shoulders were wide, nearly taking up the entire width of the small twin bed. His arms were thick and muscled, like tree trunks. His torso was covered in bandages, but she was pretty sure he'd have a rockin' set of six-pack abs. Daric was about half a foot taller than her 5'10 frame, and probably outweighed her by over a hundred pounds. He could probably pick her up and slam her against the wall and—

The she-wolf growled in appreciation.

Oh, stop it.

Meredith quickly looked away, trying to ignore the rush of

heat and desire. She would not go there. Again. The first time she got near Daric, he had attacked Jade, and she pulled him off her. The shock of electricity that shot up her arms surprised her, and she nearly let go of him. Even in his powerless state, he managed to pin her to the ground. The heat of his body was something she could never forget, and some nights she woke up wanting and horny, wishing that—

Fuck this shit; she needed to get laid. It had been too long. Almost two years. But, she didn't exactly have the opportunity now. She didn't shit where she ate, and she couldn't go anywhere else except the Fenrir Corp building. Now that Jade had a *motherfucking dragon* for a mate, who also owned a security firm, the Lycan scientist didn't need her as a full-time bodyguard, and thus, Meredith was trapped in the basement, guarding their warlock prisoner.

"Stefan. Mother!"

Daric's scratchy groan had Meredith scrambling to the side of the bed. This was the first time in two days the warlock had been conscious enough to say anything. Dr. Faulkner, the Lycans' resident physician, had been by regularly to check on him. Daric had suffered a few bruised ribs, but no internal injuries. Still, he needed time to recover and rest.

"Daric," she called softly. "Do you need Dr. Faulkner?"

Blue-green eyes flew open and a large hand wrapped around her wrist. Meredith struggled to break free, but his grip was like steel, and his touch sent tingles across her arm.

"Let go, warlock!" she hissed.

He loosened his grip as surprise flashed briefly on his face. "Where am I?"

"You're back in your cell in Fenrir," Meredith sneered.

Daric struggled to sit up, his fingers massaging his temple. "Stefan..."

"He got away, unfortunately," she explained.

"My mother?" His eyes zeroed in on her. "Where is she?"

"She's safe, with the New York coven."

He relaxed visibly, the tension leaving his shoulders. "I've been hurt."

"Yes, well that's what happens when you try to kill a master mage with a butter knife," she said sarcastically. "What the hell were you thinking anyway? Going up against Stefan without your powers?"

"I had no choice," Daric replied. "It was our only chance to kill Stefan."

"Well, it was a stupid choice," Meredith muttered. "You could have died."

"It almost sounds like you care, Lycan," Daric countered.

"I don't, warlock," she spat, hoping the nervousness in her voice didn't come out. "I was just afraid I'd have to clean up the smear your pathetic little body would have left. I hate getting blood on me."

Daric swung his long legs over the side of the bed and attempted to get up. He stumbled, and Meredith pushed him back down.

"What are you trying to do? You've been in bed for two days!"

"And thus, I'm in need of the facilities." Daric looked meaningfully at the door leading to the small bathroom.

"Ah, well I guess you gotta drain the snake, right?" As soon as the words left her lips, she slapped her hand over her mouth. God, she even surprised herself sometimes. *Don't think about his snake. Don't think about his snake.* And there it was—a mental image of Daric's penis stuck in her mind. Thick, veiny, erect and—Fuck, this would be a long day.

Daric struggled again but got to his feet. He towered over her, but he was still weak, so she could probably give him a gentle push, and he'd fall over.

"Do you need help?"

"Not to drain my snake," he replied.

Meredith turned bright red. God, she was turning into Jade, who blushed at the mere mention of sex or penises.

"I could use some help with this," he said, rubbing the thick, scraggly beard on his lower face. "Could I bother you for some razors?" His voice was less raspy, but his strange accent was more pronounced than usual. When she first heard his voice, she thought he sounded vaguely European with a touch of a refined British accent.

"I'll see what I can do," Meredith grumbled. As Daric disappeared into the bathroom, Meredith left the cell. She walked out of the main detention area and into the small hallway leading to the elevators.

"Hey, Tank," Meredith said to the burly Lycan guard standing outside.

"Yo, Meredith," he greeted back. "How's the prisoner?"

"Up and about. Say," she began. "Any chance you can get me some razors?"

"You ready to slit his throat already?" Tank chuckled.

"Ha! Tempting, but no." She shook her head. "He's tired of the hobo Jesus look, I guess."

Tank shook his head. "I don't think the Beta will allow that, but let me see what I can do." The Lycan guard picked up the telephone next to him. He said a few words and then put the phone back into the receiver. "Sorry," Tank said, shaking his head. "Mr. Vrost said he doesn't want to leave the warlock alone with anything sharp. You can offer to shave him if you want. But the Beta was pretty clear about not leavin' him alone with anything he could use as a weapon."

"Fine," Meredith shrugged. "Have someone send the stuff. I'll take care of it." She really shouldn't, but she couldn't help it. She had been held as a prisoner in this same facility, so she felt some sympathy for Daric. God knows, she had needed some grooming herself by the time she had some contact with the outside world.

Tank nodded and picked up the phone again. A few minutes later, one of the Lycan security guys, Heath Pearson, came down with a small paper bag.

"You need help, Meredith?"

She shook her head. "I think I can handle one injured warlock with no powers. Thanks, Heath."

Meredith strode back into the main detention. By the time she got to Daric's cell, he was already sitting on the bed. He was wearing a fresh pair of loose pants, and from the dampness of his hair and the droplets of water on his skin, he probably took some time to freshen up. A small towel hung around his neck.

"Nick Vrost said not to give you anything sharp," Meredith said, holding up the paper bag. "But I got the short end of the stick, so I'm volunteering myself as your personal barber today."

Daric stood up and sat on one of the chairs in the middle of the room. "Then I leave myself in your capable hands."

Meredith smiled wryly and walked over to him. She opened the bag and took out the razor, a can of shaving cream, and a pair of scissors. "I've never done this before, so you need to tell me what you want."

A pregnant pause hung in the air. "What I want," he began. "Is...Just take it all off, I suppose. Unless you have a preference?"

She shrugged. "I'm not Vidal Sassoon here, mister."

He looked at her like she was speaking another language.

"Right." Daric was raised in a remote village before he was kidnapped by an evil, egomaniac mage. He probably didn't know who the iconic hairdresser was or watched that comedy about the assassin who wanted to become a hairstylist.

Meredith began by using the scissors to trim the scraggly

beard, then picked up the shaving cream and squirted a dollop onto her palms. Working it onto his jaw, she ignored the warmth of his skin and the way the hair tickled her fingers. Satisfied with the amount of foam on his face, she wiped her hands on her pants and picked up the razor.

Daric leaned back on the chair to give Meredith a better angle. She leaned down close enough, placing the razor on his cheek. As she took a deep breath, his scent filled her nostrils. Hmmm...she didn't know warlocks could have a scent. This one certainly did and it was one she knew instantly. Chocolate. Rich and creamy chocolate. The smell was driving her she-wolf wild, and the little slut was rolling around, howling with delight.

Shut the fuck up, bitch!

"Are you going to start before my beard grows any longer?" Daric asked, his eyebrow raised.

Swallowing a gulp, she pushed the desire away, hoping he didn't notice anything. "Um, yeah." She thought she had some snappy comeback, but her brain somehow froze. With a deep breath, she began to shave his beard, working methodically and slowly, trying to calm her shaky hands. But she was so close to him she could feel the heat emanating from his body and his wonderful scent wrapping around her, making her panties flood with her wetness. Thank fuck he wasn't a Lycan, or he would have smelled how horny she was right now. She steadied herself by reaching for the back of the chair, but instead, grabbed his shoulder by accident. Fuck, it was like pure stone, hard and unyielding. Meredith had the urge to withdraw her hand. She wasn't sure what possessed her, but she dug her fingers into his shoulder instead. She thought she felt his breath hitch. Maybe it was just her imagination.

With a last downward stroke of the razor, she finished with her task. She took the towel draped around his neck and used it to wipe away the remaining foam. Sweet baby Jesus, had he always been this handsome? She had glanced at him once before when they first caught him but didn't give it a single thought. A few weeks later, when he had the beard, he looked like that homeless guy who pushed his cart down 3rd Avenue. And now, clean-shaven and looking refreshed, Daric was heart-stopping, drop-dead gorgeous.

As her hands rubbed the towel over his jaw, his fingers traced over the back of her palms. They wrapped around her wrists gently, holding them still. Blue-green eyes looked up at her, not with hate or passion, but expectantly. Like he was waiting for something to happen.

"I don't understand," he whispered, shaking his head.

"Understand what?" she asked. His gaze was hypnotic, and she struggled to break free. But all she wanted was to get lost in them.

The sound of someone clearing his throat made Meredith jump away from Daric.

"Am I interrupting anything?" Grant Anderson, Alpha of New York, stood in the doorway, arms crossed over his chest, a bemused look on his face.

Meredith shook her head and then grabbed the paper bag on the table, stuffing all the items back inside. "No, we're done here," she said, straightening her shoulders.

"I've come to discuss terms, Daric," Grant said as he strode toward the warlock.

Meredith walked towards the door. "I'll be outside," she muttered. She didn't even spare a last backward glance before the door closed behind her.

———

Daric watched the Lycan's retreating back and the door slam behind her. Her perfume of wildflowers lingered in the air after she left, as did that strange feeling in the pit of his stomach.

"Daric?" Grant asked, shaking him out of his trance.

"What do you want?" Daric asked, then added, "Alpha." Pledging to the New York clan was not his smartest move, but it was the only one he had at the time. "Where is my mother?" He could feel her, she was alive, for sure. Their link was strong, stronger than it had ever been now that Stefan was far away from them, but they couldn't use it to communicate.

"The New York witch coven had taken her to their compound," Grant explained. "Their leader, Vivianne Chatraine, is taking good care of her, I assure you."

"It can't be worse than what Stefan did to her," Daric said bitterly. The master mage had kept his mother locked up for over eighteen years. Stefan used Signe to control him, but no more. Thanks to the Lycans, Signe was safe. But her rescue had come at a price, namely, his pledge to the New York clan and his freedom. "When will I see her?"

"We'll arrange it, but Vivianne says that Signe needs time to heal," Grant said. "Now, let's discuss terms."

Daric let out a sardonic laugh. "Terms? I assumed that you would keep me here, of course." He crossed his arms over his chest. "It would be worth it, to know my mother is out of Stefan's clutches."

"Didn't you have a plan for what you wanted to do after you rescued your mother?"

The warlock shrugged. "I never thought I would survive," he confessed. "My plan was to kill Stefan, and if I had died, then that was what my fate would be."

"You can't see your own fate?" Grant asked. "I thought you were a seer."

"That's not how it works, I'm afraid," Daric began. "The only person whose fate I can't see is my own."

"Well, if you have your destiny in your hands, then why would you want to stay in here for the rest of your life?"

"What do you want with me, Alpha? Not satisfied with keeping me a prisoner for the rest of my life?"

"What do you want, Daric?"

"I want to kill Stefan." The hate in his heart was still there. He thought it would have gone when he got his mother back, but it remained rooted in place. After all, the master mage had killed his father to get his powers, before he took Daric and Signe away from their little village in Norway.

"Then help us defeat him," the Alpha stated. "You know you can't do it alone."

"Not with this." Daric raised his arm, showing off the metal band around his wrist. It was a special bracelet the Lycans had developed to dampen his active powers. "Take it off and he will die by my hands."

"Do you know where he is? Can you trace him and kill him?"

Daric was tempted to lie. "I cannot. But I know most of his hiding places."

"And why would he go back to any of those places, knowing you betrayed him? What makes you think he's not prepared for you to come? He could be preparing to capture you again or kill you."

Daric opened his mouth to speak, then realized the Alpha had a point. Eighteen years had taught him that Stefan was no fool. He also had many hiding places that Daric didn't know about. Whenever he had the chance, Daric searched for where Stefan was hiding his mother, but never even got close. He and Stefan had the same powers, that of changing and moving matter, but Stefan had also stolen the powers of many other blessed warlocks and witches, plus he had a whole army of human slaves to do his bidding.

Grant waited for his answer patiently, never betraying any emotion or thought. He wasn't Alpha for nothing.

"What do you propose, Alpha?" Daric finally said.

"An alliance of sorts," Grant said. "You help us, we'll help you."

Daric's eyes narrowed. "Servitude from one master to another? I don't think so."

"You're technically pledged to me, and so you must obey me," Grant began. "But, I don't make my people do anything they don't want."

"And my other choice is to rot in here?" Daric asked. "Not much of a choice, Alpha."

"And you don't deserve that for all you've done?" Grant countered. "Your mother is safe; I'll guarantee she'll be comfortable for the rest of her life, if you want. That's more than generous."

Daric paused. "What would you have me do?"

"Help us. Help us find Stefan and defeat him. Work with Dr. Cross so we can finally stop the mages."

"And once you do get Stefan, what do you plan to do with him?" Daric asked. "Will you keep him in this cell for the rest of his life?"

"If we capture him alive, yes," Grant answered. "But we will use any means necessary to stop him."

Daric gritted his teeth. No, Stefan was his. Vengeance was his. The master mage would die by his hands and his alone. But the Alpha didn't have to know that now.

Grant cleared his throat. "I'll give you time to think about it. And, once I hear from Vivianne, I'll let you know if Signe is ready to come for a visit." He gave Daric a last nod and then left the room.

As the metal door slid closed, Daric remained seated on his bed. The silence in the room was deafening. Was he destined to spend the rest of his days trapped in this cell? He supposed Grant was right. He should be punished for the crimes he committed over the last few years, even if they were things Stefan made him do. Daric told himself his mother's life was on the line and he did those things to save her, if only to prevent the guilt from crushing him. No, there would only be one way to wipe the blood off his hands, and that was to kill Stefan.

He stood up, and looked up at the camera in the corner. Someone would be watching for sure, if not the Alpha himself. "I've made my decision," he said.

A few minutes later, the door slid open, and Grant walked back inside. This time, Daric was seated at the small table in the middle of the room. He motioned for the Alpha to sit.

"Well?" Grant asked, leaning back on the chair.

"Fine, I will share my knowledge with you. But only if you promise me I will be there when you try to capture Stefan."

"Done."

"Now take this off me," Daric demanded, waving his arm with the bracelet.

Grant shook his head. "You know I can't. You could dematerialize at any time, and I wouldn't be able to find you."

"Then we have no deal. You've seen what Stefan can do, what he did to me without my powers," he said, motioning to the bandages on his torso. "Stefan will kill me with a wave of his hand."

"If you were in my position, would you remove the bracelet?"

The warlock remained silent.

"Daric, I promise you, when the time comes, you will be there when we get Stefan. But for now, you've got to trust me."

"But trust goes both ways, right?" the warlock asked.

Grant uncrossed his arms and leaned forward. "I suppose, but then it's also earned."

"Then we will have to see what happens," Daric said cryptically.

"Fine," Grant said. "I'll inform the team and see what we can do. But, to show you my trust in you, I'll hold you to your word and your pledge to me on your father's grave and your mother's life that you won't try to escape."

"And how would you do that?"

"I won't have you outfitted with a tracking device. I'll only have your word that you won't run away."

"How can I run away when I'm in this cell?"

"You won't be for long. I'll have you transferred to our security team barracks on the 16th floor. You might like communal living, but you'll be free to stay in your room, if you prefer."

Daric shrugged. "As you wish."

The Alpha continued, "You'll have the freedom to go to certain areas and have some privacy," Grant said. "I will, however, assign someone to escort you when you're around the building or if you need to go outside. I do have my people here, and some of them don't know who you are or what you're doing here."

"Fair enough," Daric said.

"Someone will be by to bring you upstairs," Grant said, getting to his feet. "By the way, you know Nick Vrost will not be happy with this arrangement. Do not cross him. I'll talk to you soon, Daric."

"Alpha," he nodded. As soon as Grant left, Daric lay back down on the bed. His ribs were still sore, but he didn't want to show his weakness. Trust the Alpha? Trust the Lycans? Years of brainwashing from Stefan had conditioned him to hate the Lycans. Could he learn to trust them? Could they trust him? For one thing, he'd already lied to the Alpha. No, not about wanting to kill Stefan. But about his powers. As a seer, he couldn't see his own destiny, but there was another who left him drawing a blank.

The Lycan woman. Meredith.

Aside from seeing flashes of the future here and there, when he touched another person, he'd get visions about them, both past and future. Some good, mostly bad. He learned to live with it. He had to or it would have driven him mad and prevented him from touching anyone. It became difficult when he needed the company of a woman, but he managed. For one thing, he mostly went back to the same half a dozen lovers he'd had over the years. Women who he knew had happy or even boring lives.

The first time he held Meredith when she was under him, and he pinned her arms over her head, he flinched and prepared himself for the visions that usually took him over. But there was nothing. Complete silence and merciful blackness. He was so surprised that he could do nothing but stare into her dark amber eyes and her flushed face.

Daric thought it was a fluke. He wanted to test it again. She had been so close he could smell her perfume—it reminded him of the wildflowers that used to grow in his mother's garden. Her hands were on his face and he reached up to touch them. Again, nothing. No flashes or images from her past.

What did it mean? He shook his head. He wasn't sure. Was it possible the bracelet was also dampening his seer powers? No, he could still feel the link to his mother.

It didn't help that he desired her, and could see the bold wanting in her eyes that time he pinned her down with his body. It had been a while since he'd wanted a woman. He only sought out female company to relieve the biological need. But with Meredith...He often wondered if her lips would feel soft against his or what her breasts would feel like in his hands. How her bare skin would feel against his. She was intoxicating. And all wrong for him. She was brash, loud, crude, and his enemy.

Or at least, she was a Lycan, and she stood in his way. No, this was one path he wouldn't go down. He had to control himself and make sure she stayed away from him. Stefan's demise was his singular goal. Nothing would stop him, no matter how lush or desirable the temptation.

CHAPTER TWO

"Did you do what I asked, Victoria?" Stefan said to the woman in front of him.

"Of course, Master," she answered. "But, if you would allow me to speak—"

"About what?" Stefan's voice grew angry. "Do you have a problem with what I'm doing?"

"Of course not, Master!" The witch shook her head. "I'm just thinking, perhaps we are moving too fast! The mages aren't getting the proper training and they're getting sloppy! And the humans we've been taking to amass our armies! Why, they're not trained, many of them were half starved when we picked them up off the street!"

"You dare question my tactics, Victoria?" the master mage asked. He raised his hand, and a ball of blue fire began to form.

"No! Of course not," she bowed her head and cowered back. "I know our defeat and the loss of Daric—"

"Do not say that traitor's name out loud!" Stefan raged. "He is dead to me! He tried to kill me and he can rot in that Lycan jail for all I care."

"As you wish, Master," she said, cowering back.

Their last defeat at the hands of the Lycans had deeply affected the master mage. While their previous skirmishes with them kept revealing Stefan's cleverness, cunning, and the deeper layers of his plans, this time, it seemed to unravel him. Victoria wasn't sure if it was the betrayal of his protégé or the loss of the Creed dragon that did it, but Stefan had changed. Instead of careful plans, he was getting careless. And Victoria was at a loss. She hated the Lycans as much as Stefan did, but it was as if her master was taking a last stand—the last battle to be fought to end the war, and she wasn't sure if they were on the winning side.

Stefan turned to her, his face drawn into a pensive mask. "Do not fret, Victoria," he assured her, his lips curling into a smile. "I still have many cards to play. In fact, perhaps it's time to use my most important one yet."

"What is it, Master?" Victoria asked curiously.

He laughed. "Rome wasn't built in a day, my dear. And so I've been working for decades."

"Working on what, Master?"

Stefan let out of laugh. "My dear, what did you think this was all about? Just destroying the Lycans?"

"Isn't it?" Victoria gritted her teeth. "Those filthy creatures should be wiped off the face of the earth!"

"Ah, your hatred does fuel you well, my dear," Stefan commented. "But, no."

"What? You don't want to get rid of them? But why—"

"Shush, my dear, have you no faith in me?" Stefan asked. "I want to crush them as much as you do. I hate them all. But, death would be too good for them. Don't you want them to suffer?"

"What are you saying, Master?"

"The Lycans are an untapped resource. You don't think the spell control to the humans was the final goal, do you? No. I've also been working to modify it. To control the Lycans and take over the world."

Victoria gasped.

"With an unstoppable army—both human and Lycan—I will rule this wretched world!"

"So, you do have a spell to control the Lycans? But how would that work?" Victoria shook her head. "The Lycans are programmed to obey their Alpha—it's ingrained deep in their DNA, which is why our spell wouldn't work on them in the first place."

"With some modifications, the spell will work."

"And the Alpha? Would you have to break a Lycan's pledge to their Alpha?"

"Something like that," Stefan said mysteriously. "And I still have our biggest ally working behind the scenes."

"An ally?" Victoria asked. "Who?"

"Someone who you and the Lycans would never suspect."

CHAPTER THREE

Meredith walked—no, she practically ran back to her room on the 16th floor. She closed the door behind her and sat on her bed, breathing deeply. Was Daric putting some sort of spell on her? She could hardly tear herself away from his gaze. No. It must have been her imagination. Daric and his damn sexy chocolate scent and his muscles and stupid handsome face and his yummy abs and...

Grreeowwrl.

Ugh. She would have told the she-wolf to shut up, but it would only encourage the damn animal.

"Arrggghhh!" she moaned, throwing herself on the bed and placing her pillow over her head. Stop it, she told herself. Why was she acting like some teenager? She had to stay away from Daric. Throwing the pillow aside, she sat up.

After the last skirmish with the mages, Meredith was transferred from her cell in the Fenrir Corporation basement detention level to the security barracks on the 16th floor. Alynna Westbrooke, who took charge of Meredith after she was detained, said that she had earned it. Meredith had, at that point, risked her life several times for the New York Lycans.

The room in the Fenrir security training facilities was spartan, but it was certainly an improvement from her cell. At least here she had a window, along with a great view of the Manhattan skyline. She started to put her own touches in the room to make it homey.

Meredith also joined the new batch of recruits for the New York clan's Lycan security force. She supposed she had to do something with her time. And most of the people in the security team weren't bad, but they were definitely in the "hazing the new girl" stage. Or at least she hoped it was, and it wasn't just because she kicked some of their asses the first time she encountered them.

A knock on the door interrupted her thoughts. "Come in," she called.

The door creaked open, and Grant walked in.

"Hey, what's up?" she asked.

"You know, most Lycans here would call me Alpha or Primul," he said wryly.

"Well, you're not my Alpha, are you?" Meredith retorted.

"I suppose you're right," Grant smirked. "May I?" he asked, motioning to the chair in the corner of the room.

"Go right ahead," she shrugged.

Grant took the chair and moved it closer to the bed. He looked up and squinted at the large poster hanging over Meredith's head. "Wow...that is..." It was a picture of a unicorn in screaming shades of purple and pink on a lime green background.

"Fabulous?" Meredith supplied.

"I was going to say headache-inducing," Grant said, shaking his head.

"So, to what do I owe this visit? I don't think you're here to comment on my interior design skills."

"Right." Grant cleared his throat. "I have a job for you."

"A job?" Meredith asked. "You know, you can just tell me what to do, right? You don't have to make it sound like I have a choice."

"But you do," Grant said. "This is entirely voluntary. But it could be beneficial to you."

Meredith was intrigued. "All right, you have my attention. What is it?"

"Daric has agreed to help us find Stefan and stop him. I need you to keep a close eye on him."

Nuh-uh. No way. She just resolved to stay away from Daric, and now Grant wanted her to spend more time with him?

"I can see you're not crazy about the idea," Grant said. "So, why don't you think about the next part of my deal? I'll shorten your sentence to 5 years if you do it."

"What?" Meredith shot up to her feet. Five years was a lot. That meant she'd be out of here soon (or soon-ish) and sunbathing on a beach in Bora-bora in no time. It was certainly better than a decade. All she had to do was babysit the warlock? "What's the catch?"

"It wouldn't be any different from guarding Dr. Cross," Grant said.

"Then why not offer it to any other of your security guys?" Meredith countered. "Is it because I'm dispensable? You know, he'll try to escape the first chance he gets and get rid of anything that stands in his way."

"Not at all," Grant replied. "In fact, the reason I want you to do this is that I don't think he'd hurt you."

Meredith remained quiet. What did Grant mean?

"Is there something wrong, Meredith? Why don't you want to be assigned to Daric? Did I walk in on something this morning?"

"What?" the blonde Lycan gasped. "That was...it wasn't...I

was just being nice because I know what it's like to be locked up for weeks without any company."

"Then is it because you don't think you can guard Daric?" Grant challenged.

"No!" Meredith protested. "Fine. I mean, yes, I can babysit the warlock."

"Good," Grant stood up. "Because he's moving into the room next to yours."

Before Meredith could protest, Grant stood up and left the room.

"Oh, fuck me," she moaned and fell back on the bed.

CHAPTER FOUR

The following morning, Meredith received orders from the Alpha that she was to escort Daric from the 16th floor barracks to Jade's lab on the 33rd floor. She was finishing her morning workout, practicing her martial arts floor exercises by herself when one of the assistants from the executive floor handed her an envelope. Inside were instructions, including a schedule for Daric, which basically just consisted of three hours a day working with Jade and then back to the barracks. Seeing as she only had about an hour to go before she had to pick up the warlock from his room, Meredith headed to her room, took a shower, and got dressed for the day.

Her current clothing options were quite limited, seeing as she didn't exactly earn a salary. She put on a pair of dark jeans, a pink t-shirt, and sneakers then pulled her long, blonde hair back into a ponytail. After checking her reflection in the mirror and swiping some lipgloss on (which, she told herself, was not to impress anyone), she walked over to the room next to hers and knocked on the door.

"Yo, warlock, time to get up!" she said, rapping her fingers on the wood. "I don't have all day, you know."

The door slid open. "I've been ready for the past hour," Daric retorted.

Meredith stood still, her eyes roaming over Daric. The warlock was dressed casually in a pair of blue jeans, boots, and a tight, dark green t-shirt with the Fenrir logo that stretched across his expansive chest and showed off his muscular arms. His long blonde hair was freshly washed and pulled back in a messy man bun. There was already a light stubble on his face and she suddenly found herself wondering how it would feel against her inner thighs.

"Well? Are we going or not?" Daric asked, his blue-green eyes peering down at her, a haughty look on his face. Scratch that last thought; now she wanted to wipe the floor with that handsome, arrogant mug.

"Right," Meredith muttered. "Follow me." She turned around, not even bothering to check if he was following, because, where else would he go?

They took the elevator up to the 33rd floor. Meredith's handprint and retina scans were already programmed in, and they entered Jade's lab with no problem. The clean and modern laboratory was large and looked like any scientific research facility. Meredith had no idea what most of the equipment in there was for, but she knew they were probably expensive. In the middle of the room was a staircase that led to an upper level which housed Jade's office and inner lab. As they entered, Daric looked around in wonder. "So, this is where you Lycans study magic?"

"Yeah. Sorry, no cauldrons or pointy hats here," she quipped.

"And where is Dr. Cross?"

A loud crash from the inner office interrupted Meredith before she could answer. Daric tensed visibly, his brows knitting. Then, a faint feminine moan resonated from the inner lab followed by the rhythmic banging of furniture against the wall.

"Goddamnit Jade!" Meredith slapped her hand on her forehead.

"Is that...Dr. Cross and her mate..."

"Going to Pound Town?" Meredith finished.

"That's rather crude," Daric said pointedly.

"Just be glad you don't have enhanced hearing," she groaned, sticking her fingers in her ears. She was happy that Jade and Sebastian were True Mates and all, but Jesus, someone needed to take a hose to them.

She sighed. Meredith was still trying to wrap her head around the concept of True Mates. She had never even heard of or knew what True Mates were about until she came to New York. Lara and Jade had explained it when the witch had found her own True Mate in the San Francisco Alpha.

Lycan couples had trouble conceiving, and the couples who do have children hardly have more than one. Lycans who marry non-Lycans also don't conceive shifter kids, only fully human ones. The one exception was True Mate pairings. It was some type of Lycan magic/biological mojo that made two people so compatible that they immediately conceived a shifter baby the first time they had sex. Apparently, it also made the mother invulnerable to most things, including poisoning, stabbing, bullets, and falling a hundred feet off a cliff. While she thought it would be cool to be invincible like Superman, growing a magical bun in her oven didn't sound appealing. *No.* A family wasn't in her future. She was too fucked up to even think about being a mom.

They stood there awkwardly for a few more minutes until the sounds finally stopped. Another minute later and the door to the office opened.

"...And you better not forget it," came Sebastian Creed's low growl.

"Oh, you bet I won't forget it," Jade huffed, smoothing down her skirt. Her hair was in disarray and her lipstick smeared. "I can't believe that you would...Meredith?" The Lycan scientist's light green eyes widened in surprise when they landed on the other Lycan. "What are you...D-d-daric?" Her face went entirely red and she turned to the man behind her. "You said there was no one outside!"

The handsome man beside her frowned and glared at the intruders. "There wasn't anyone here when I came in, darlin'," Sebastian said. "How the fuck did you two get in here?"

"Sorry to rain on your sex parade," Meredith said dryly. "You guys need to put a sock or tie on the door or something when you're banging in there."

"We won't be doing anything in there anymore," Jade said as she stomped down the stairs.

"Fine, we'll just bang in my office next time," Sebastian muttered as he followed her. He gave her ass a soft slap, which made the tiny scientist yelp.

Meredith rolled her eyes. "Oh please, tone it down in front of the guest, lovebirds."

As soon as they reached the main lab floor, Sebastian stood protectively in front of Jade and stretched to his full height, crossing his arms over his chest. "What the hell are you doing here?"

"I'm here to assist Dr. Cross," Daric replied, his face remaining calm. Though not as wide as Sebastian, Daric was easily an inch or two taller than the dragon shifter.

"Jade?" Sebastian turned to his mate. "Is this true?"

"Um, yeah, Grant told me this morning," Jade replied nonchalantly. "Daric's knowledge and assistance could help us defeat the mages."

"But he's one of them!" Sebastian bellowed. "Why the fuck didn't Grant tell me this?"

"Calm down, baby-daddy," Meredith said, which earned her an "I'm-gonna-set-you-on-fire" look from Sebastian.

"First of all, this is my work," Jade retorted. "And he probably didn't say anything because you'd overreact. Just like you're doing now."

"I am not a mage," Daric interrupted. "I am still whole. I have not used blood magic and therefore, am still a warlock, albeit a powerless one, thanks to your mate," he said, waving his arm and showing off the bracelet. "In exchange for some freedom and other concessions from the Alpha, I've agreed to help Dr. Cross learn more about magic and how we can stop Stefan."

"Oh yeah? You can bet I'll be talking to Grant about this." Sebastian's eyes turned gold, the beast inside him simmering at the surface.

"Sebastian, please," Jade soothed, rubbing a hand over his arm. "It'll be okay. He doesn't have any magic, the lab's monitored, and Meredith's here."

That seemed to ease some of Sebastian's anger, and his eyes turned back to their usual gray color. "I'm still going to see Grant."

"Whatever you want," Jade said, pressing a kiss on his arm. "Now, I'll see you later, okay?"

"Fine," Sebastian said gruffly. He wrapped an arm around her waist and kissed her hard. "I'll be by at five. Be ready to go by then. No staying late, okay?"

The Lycan shook her head. "We'll leave at five on the dot."

With one last glare at Daric, he left.

"Really, Jade?" Meredith admonished. "In your office? I eat lunch there. Gross."

"Not on my desk!" Jade countered. "It's the hormones. I can't help it."

"Uh-huh. Well, I supposed if my baby-daddy looked like that..."

"Stop calling him that, he hates it."

"Well, what should I call him? Your lover? True Mate? If he wants to be called something respectable, then he better put a ring on it, girl," Meredith pointed to Jade's left hand.

"I don't need—"

Daric cleared his throat. "I'm sure your personal life is fascinating, Dr. Cross, but perhaps we can get on with our business first?"

Jade's face went red. "Right, well, let's start then." She motioned to the large table in the middle of the lab. "Please, have a seat."

The warlock nodded and parked himself on one of the chairs by the table, while Jade sat across from him.

"I'll be in my corner," Meredith said, walking over to her usual chair. She was bored one day and found some pink glitter and markers and wrote "Princess chair" on one of the office chairs that was lying around the lab. She sat down and started perusing the stack of new gossip magazines on the table. Though she tried to concentrate on the dirty divorce details of some Hollywood celebrity couple, she couldn't help but tune her ears to Jade and Daric's conversation.

"...And now that we have time, tell me more about your powers," Jade said. "Transmogrification. Or the power to change matter. How does it work? Can you change anything into anything else? What are the limits? You can also transport yourself and others, right? How-"

"Too many questions, dear Doctor," Daric interrupted. "Maybe we can start with the basics. I can change the form of matter into almost anything, with some limits. First, I need to know how something works or what it is made of for me to change its properties. I can't simply turn water into wine without knowing how wine is made in the first place."

"Ah, so you need knowledge...how do you gain it?"

"The old-fashioned way, I'm afraid," the warlock continued. "Study. Lots of it. When I was younger, my father and I would spend hours reading books on science, biology, botany, chemistry and other subjects."

"So, you can't just, let's say, change a cat into a mouse without knowing the biology of both animals?"

"Correct. If I did such a transformation and it was not successful, well...you don't want to know. But, that's why I stick to simple things. Non-living things. For example, if I knew the ingredients of your favorite shampoo or your mother's recipe for chocolate cake, I could recreate them using other materials."

"But what about transporting yourself and others? Moving things around? Don't you need to study human biology for that?"

"Moving things around is simpler, as I simply bend the matter to my will, making it move from here to there. As for transporting myself and other people, to some extent, yes, I would need to study human biology, if only to make sure I don't accidentally put your spleen where your heart is. That is why one of the first things I learned about was the workings of the human body. Finally, I would also need to know the place where I need to go, so I don't materialize inside a wall or a tree. Which is why I can only transport to places I have been to or make sure I'm going in and out of open spaces. I can use satellite imagery to see the place I need to go and materialize there."

"Oh, so you use computers and GPS to help you locate the right places?"

He gave a short laugh. "Of course. We have Wi-Fi. We're not savages."

Meredith gave a snort. Daric and Jade looked over at her. "What?" she asked. "Enhanced hearing, remember?" She flipped her hair and turned her attention back to her magazine. Biting her lip to stop from laughing, she secretly wondered if Stefan had other uses for an Internet connection in his various hideouts. Did he have a Facebook profile? What type of updates did he make? "Maimed another Lycan, score! #DieLycansDie" or maybe "Defeated by the Lycans again. #FML".

Jade and Daric continued their discussion, with Meredith half listening.

"The best way to understand would be to see my powers in action," Daric said.

"I wasn't born yesterday, Daric," Jade pointed out.

Good girl, Jade, Meredith thought.

"I'm under explicit orders from the Alpha. Under no circumstance am I to remove the bracelet," Jade continued. "But, you said that the bracelet didn't dampen your innate powers. Tell me, how can you see the future? Could you show me mine?"

"Ah, curious little Doctor," Daric said in a low voice. "Some people think knowing the future is a gift, but those who can see it know it is a curse. Are you sure you want to know what lies ahead for the daughter of the dragon?" There was a pause. "I didn't think so."

"Is it...bad?" Jade asked hesitatingly.

"I can tell you that it's not bad. I've seen a great destiny for her, one that no one should alter, even if it saves her from hardship and heartache."

The Lycan let out a sigh of relief. "Is the future set?"

"No, it is not," Daric replied. "Everything I see is merely one possible future, one that could change based on what happens now. However, I mostly see a person's past and share visions with my mother, and to some extent, Stefan."

"But can Stefan see you now? Can he know what we're planning?"

"I've been blocking him out. I couldn't before, not when he had my mother. The only time I tried to block him out...well...it didn't go well for me. Or for her."

Meredith's hands tightened into a fist, her fingernails leaving half-moon marks on her palms. God, Stefan was such a fucking dick!

"And what do you think Stefan is planning to do now?" Jade asked.

"He'll be amassing his army of human slaves," Daric said. "He will find a way to strike back."

"You said there was a counterspell to stop him from controlling humans. Could we find a way to discover it?"

"I suppose, with time we could. But killing Stefan would be the simplest way."

"If we can get through his human slave army in the first place," Jade pointed out. "If he gathers a lot of people, then there might not even be enough Lycans in the world to stop him."

"Yes," was all Daric said.

Jade's keen eyes narrowed. "Could he possibly control the Lycans, too?"

"It would be difficult," Daric said. "It's already difficult to control humans, but to control both a human and an animal at the same time? It would be challenging."

"But not impossible?"

"Technically, no. But, wolves are pack animals. You need to have a semblance of order, an Alpha to follow. Not only would the spell have to control both the human and animal side, but fight the Alpha bond."

"Hmmmm," Jade said thoughtfully. "I've never thought of it that way. But it makes sense. When we pledge to our Alpha and clan once we come of age, there's this natural tendency to follow the Alpha's orders, as well as protect the clan."

They continued their conversation about magic, with Jade asking questions and Daric answering them as best he could. Meredith continued to half listen, but if she was being honest, she couldn't help but keep them in the corner of her eye. Or rather, a certain handsome warlock. She wasn't even looking at him and yet, couldn't pull her attention away. The low timbre of his voice sent heat pooling in her middle, and it was distracting. Get it together, Meredith, she thought, giving herself a pep talk.

Yummy.

Oh, not you again.

C'mon. Just one taste. Don't you want to know if he tastes as good as he smells?

"Leave me alone, bitch!" Meredith cried, jumping up from her chair.

"Mer, are you ok?" Jade asked, concern marring her face.

Daric, on the other hand, frowned. "Can you not control what comes out of your mouth, woman?"

"What? How dare you!" Meredith felt the anger rising inside her. "I have a name. Maybe you can use it sometime."

"All right, all right," Jade said, standing up. "I think we're good for today. I have to log in what we've learned and do some more research." She walked towards the other Lycan. "What's wrong, Meredith? Are you feeling all right?"

"Yeah, I'm fine," she muttered, giving Daric a dirty look. "It's going to be a long...life. He's roomed next to me, too, you know."

Jade gave her a sympathetic look. "I'm sorry. Look, at least we get to spend more time with each other. And I'm glad you're not in the basement anymore."

"Yeah, bright side, right?" Meredith smiled. "Aww, you do

miss me!" She hugged Jade, wrapping her arms around the other Lycan.

"Of course," Jade choked, pulling away. "Who else would keep me on my toes?"

"Well, when you get a chance and Lara comes back from San Francisco, let's go hang out in my room. I've made some improvements since I moved in."

Jade laughed. "I'm sure it'll be interesting."

Meredith threw another sour look at Daric. "Well, I should get our prisoner, er, guest back to his quarters. Plus, I got training after lunch. Vrost'll have my ass if I'm late again."

"I'll see you tomorrow morning," Jade said.

"Let's go, warlock," Meredith called.

"And you shout at me for not using your name?" Daric countered.

"Oh, just move your ass, I don't have patience for this right now."

The two of them left the lab and went into the elevator. Meredith pressed her palm on the sensor and then mashed the button to the 16th floor repeatedly, willing it to go faster.

"Is that helping at all?" Daric asked sarcastically. "Perhaps hitting it with a club might make it come quicker?"

"Oh yeah, why don't you wave your hand and get us out of here?" Meredith retorted. "Oh wait, you can't!"

Daric's back stiffened, his face turning hard and expressionless. "Why the Alpha thought you were competent enough to watch over me, I'll never know."

"A monkey could stand watch over you, warlock."

"Oh, so he did make the right decision."

Meredith gritted her teeth and as soon as the doors opened to their floor, she stomped out. "You already know the way to your room, but I can write you directions if you need them and make sure I use simple words."

"I'll find my own way. Besides, I would not want you to use up all your crayons."

Anger and rage boiled in her, but she tamped it down. "Drop dead, warlock," she hissed and stomped away from him.

———

Meredith groaned as her body hit the padded mat. She stared up at the ceiling of the Fenrir Security Team training facility, slightly dazed and the wind knocked out of her.

"What's wrong, Lone Wolf?" Luke Carter said, grinning at Meredith. "Not feeling well today? Is it that time of the month?"

There was a chorus of guffaws behind her, but Meredith ignored them and stood up. "I can wipe the floor clean with you any time of the month, Carter," she spat. Goddamnit, how could she have fallen for that one? She wasn't paying attention, that's why. *Pull your head out of your ass and concentrate! Stop thinking about the warlock.*

"Less talking," Nick Vrost, Fenrir's Head of Security and Beta to the New York clan, barked.

Vrost was tough but fair. He didn't give her or Faith Greer, the only other woman on the trainee squad, any special treatment, but didn't coddle them either. They were all equals, and they equally got an ass reaming when they didn't perform well.

Meredith crouched low into her fighting stance, moving into a position that was pure instinct at this point. Her body was an instrument, one that was honed and trained at an early age. By the time she was fifteen, she could easily overpower men (Lycans included) over a hundred pounds heavier than her. Training in three different martial arts, physical conditioning, and just plain old hard work, not to mention, getting her ass kicked, made her efficient and effective at taking down her enemies.

Being part of the New York clan's security trainee team was a privilege she didn't earn, but her skills made her a natural fit. The people on the squad weren't exactly friendly to her, and they all hazed her since she was the new girl, but Carter especially seemed to have had a chip on his shoulder. It was probably because she knocked him flat on his ass on the first day she was there. He'd been trying to get under her skin since then.

Find his weak spot, a familiar voice inside her head told her. *Use it against him.*

Carter was over six feet tall and had more than seventy pounds on her. His upper body was pure muscle, but like an upside-down pyramid, he was clumsy on his feet. Sure, he had the reach advantage, and if he ever hit her with his meaty fists, she'd probably get the wind knocked out of her. But Meredith was quick, well-trained, and smart. The other Lycan had immediately underestimated her the first time they had trained. Of course, it looked like he had been learning a few tricks of his own. After all, to make it this far, one had to be smart and strong. The New York clan only employed the best and the brightest to be part of their Lycan security team, the elite guards that protected the Alpha and the clan. Grant and Nick chose trainees based on skill and not connections and if a trainee survived the year-long probation period, they could become a member of the team and move up in the clan hierarchy.

"Are you two just going to stand there?" Nick said impatiently.

Hoping to impress the Beta, Carter lunged forward. Big mistake. Meredith was ready, reading his body language in half a second. She twisted around and let him think he'd caught her, but kept her arms up. In one smooth motion, she broke free of his grasp, then bent down to sweep him off his feet. He landed on the mat with a heavy thud.

Meredith gave him a sweet smile. "Aww, what's wrong, Carter? Is it that time of the month?"

Carter said nothing, but quickly rose up, his face red with anger.

"Step back, Carter," Nick ordered.

Not wanting to disobey Nick, he nodded and slinked back to his corner.

John Patrick, one of the more senior members of the team, walked up to her and slapped her on the shoulder. "That was awesome, Meredith, I knew you could do it."

Out of all the guys, Patrick was the nicest and the one who didn't haze her too much. In fact, on her first day, he approached her and welcomed her. He was also the one who warned her about the ribbing and the practical jokes, as it was something all the newbies went through.

"Nice form," Tate Miller said, flashing her a bright smile and gave her a pat on the back.

"Yeah, I know you appreciate my form," she said dryly. Tate Miller was six-feet-two-inches of All American hotness. Blonde and blue-eyed, he could have any girl's panties melting, including her own. At least he did when she first saw him. He did fill out that white shirt nicely, with his tanned and muscled arms and broad chest. She'd flirted with him a few times, but stopped the other day when he took it too seriously. After an evening workout, Tate cornered her outside the female locker room, where he pushed her against the wall and tried to kiss her, but she turned away. God, she was so tempted, but he worked at Fenrir. She couldn't. It was awkward between them at first, but he quickly apologized for his behavior, and things more or less went back to the way they were - heavy flirting, but no follow-through.

"It is a nice form," Miller said and winked at her.

Meredith looked over at Carter triumphantly, but when she opened her mouth to deliver an insult, Nick gave her a warning look.

"I need less talking from you," the Beta said.

"I couldn't agree more," came a voice from behind.

Nick's ice blue eyes suddenly turned frosty. "What are you doing here, warlock?" The hate from the Lycan was evident, and the air in the room grew thick with tension.

"The Alpha said I might enjoy communal living," Daric answered. He was dressed in the same T-shirt, but he had changed into loose black pants. "And so, I thought I might join the rest of the occupants of this floor in exercise."

"I told the Alpha that this was a mistake," Nick said. "But he wouldn't listen. Seems to think you could be of some use to us. I think you'd only be useful locked up in your cell. Preferably for the rest of your life."

"It's an unconventional arrangement, but even you'd agree it was an offer I couldn't refuse." Daric walked closer, onto the mats. "I was thinking it's been far too long since I've had some exercise."

All the Lycans in the room turned to the warlock, their distaste and hate visible.

"You want to train with us?" Nick asked. "Not that I would ever allow it, but what can you do? You have no powers, warlock."

"I know how to fight, Lycan," Daric said. "I've had other training aside from magical. Perhaps one of your pups could pose a challenge."

His head snapped towards Meredith's direction, but he wasn't looking at her. His eyes were trained on Patrick and Miller. The two men tensed beside her.

"If the warlock wants a challenge," Tate began as he cracked his knuckles. "I'm sure I'd be up for it."

"No one is challenging anyone today," Nick began. "Warlock, you are to stay in the common rooms only. The training area is for members of the Lycan security team and trainees only."

"As you wish," Daric said, giving him a small nod. "I should, perhaps, have my escort to make sure I stay in the correct areas?"

Meredith gritted her teeth, but Nick turned to her and motioned to Daric. "Meredith, show the warlock which places he's allowed in the security barracks. The common room, gym, kitchens, and dining only."

"Yeah, yeah," Meredith muttered. As she passed Daric, she cocked her head. "Let's go, warlock."

"Whatever you say," Daric replied, following her out.

The training area took up the entire floor beneath the living quarters. From there, they had to walk through the long hallway past the showers and therapy room, all the way to the set of stairs that led to the upper floor.

"What the heck were you thinking, going down there?" Meredith suddenly asked. "You know there's a room full of Lycan shifters in there who all want you dead. Are you suicidal or something?"

"Do you actually care about what happens to me, Lycan?" Daric asked.

"Only because it's my job," Meredith muttered as she stomped up the stairs, Daric right behind her.

"I'm sorry to be taking up your time, especially since you seem to prefer the company of—"

Meredith whipped around, but before she could say anything, the sound of rushing footsteps caught their attention.

"Meredith!" Alynna Westbrooke, Grant's sister, called out as soon as she saw the other Lycan. "Thank God, I found you!"

"Alynna?" Meredith's brows wrinkled. "What is it?"

"You have to come with me," Alynna said, taking her by the arm. "We have a couple of people detained in the basement level."

"What does that have to do with me?"

"Well, they said that they're your brothers."

Meredith felt her stomach drop. "My brothers? They're here?"

"So, you do have brothers?" the brunette asked.

"Um, sort of. Three of them? One of them a big guy with a scar down his face?"

"Yeah! That's him. Scary, that one," Alynna confirmed. "I didn't know you had brothers."

"I don't," Meredith replied. What were they...this wasn't good. Her heart began to pound, and her gut told her there was something wrong. "I mean...it's a long story. But I need to see them. Now."

"Okay." Alynna looked at Daric. "Let's get Daric back to his room."

"No!" Meredith gripped Alynna's arm. "Please, can't we...I just need to see them now. If it was Grant, could you wait?"

Alynna hesitated, then narrowed her eyes at Daric. "Fine, but you do as I say and keep quiet."

Daric shrugged. "If I must. I don't care either way."

Alynna looked at Meredith. "Let's go."

CHAPTER FIVE

Daric followed behind the two women as they entered the elevator. He wasn't sure what was going on, but curiosity definitely pricked at him.

He knew he had been mean to Meredith today, and on purpose. But with every insult he hurled at her, the ache in his middle grew. He tried to stay in his room and read some of the books they had provided him, but he couldn't concentrate. Not when all he could think of was the scent of wildflowers and dark amber eyes flashing in anger. His plan was to make her hate him, and it seemed to work, too well almost.

Unable to do anything else, he went out to the common rooms. There was no one around, so he decided to explore. He found the staircase that led to the connected lower level, which housed the training room and gym. Voices led him to the main exercise room and when he walked in, he could feel an ugly, unfamiliar feeling rise up in him.

Meredith was in the middle of a training exercise, and while she easily outmaneuvered and outwitted her opponent, he didn't like the way he had his arms around her. And then there were the two men who came forward to greet her victory. The one man, the tall one with the blonde hair, looked and touched her with familiarity, his eyes roving her her body. He wanted nothing more than to obliterate every atom in his body.

"We're here," Alynna announced.

They walked into the secure area, which was not the same as the detention levels were he had been kept, but the security was just as tight. Alynna led them into a dark room, which had a one-way mirror on one side.

Meredith gasped when she saw the occupants of the other room. Three men were inside, one of them casually sitting on one of the chairs in the middle of the room, another beside him. Leaning against the wall, partially hidden in the shadows, was another figure.

"Meredith?" Alynna asked. "Do you know them?"

The blonde Lycan nodded. "Yes. Can I see them?"

"Wait," Alynna said. She grabbed the phone hanging on the wall and spoke into the receiver. "Confirmed, Grant. Go ahead."

The small door to the side of the room opened and Grant walked in.

"Gentlemen," he greeted. Grant's stride was confident, his air that of an Alpha. He stopped in front of the table, looking down at the two men expectantly.

"Alpha," the dark-haired one greeted. He stood up and tugged at the sleeve of his shirt, revealing a wolf's head tattoo on his forearm. "My name is Killian."

The one beside him grabbed the neck of his shirt and pulled it aside. "Alpha," he acknowledged. A similar tattoo was on the right side of his chest.

Grant looked at the third man in the shadows, who didn't move an inch.

"Believe me, he has one too."

"He still needs to show it to me," Grant answered.

With a sigh, Killian turned to the third guy. "Connor. Do it."

The man moved into the light. He was tall, probably as tall as Daric, but had reddish blonde hair and a beard. Tattoos ran down both arms and curled out from the neck of his shirt. He would have been handsome, were it not for the long scar that ran down his right eye and cheek, which made him look dangerous. He continued to walk towards Grant, lifting the side of his shirt to show off the tattoo on his rib cage.

"Well, Lone Wolves," Grant began. "What are you doing in my territory? And why would you cause a ruckus in the lobby of a public place and risk exposing our secret?"

"We know you have her," Killian said. "Meredith. Our sister."

"Sister? She never said she had brothers," Grant replied. "If you were her brothers, then you would still have a clan."

"We're not her biological brothers," Killian explained. "But we grew up together."

"Lone Wolves banding together? You know that's not allowed," Grant said with a frown. "There's a reason you were designated as such."

Behind the one-way mirror, Meredith was wringing her hands, her face drawn into a deep frown. "What happened? What did they do?" Meredith asked Alynna.

The other Lycan sighed. "The three of them came into the lobby of the building this morning, and demanded to see the Alpha of New York and their sister."

"In front of all the humans?" Meredith asked.

Alynna nodded. "Yes. That's why we had to detain them."

"Idiots!" Meredith muttered. "I told them not to come after me!"

"Hold on," Alynna frowned. "You told them...how?"

Meredith shrugged. "I have my ways. Anyway, that doesn't matter."

"We need to find her and talk to her," Killian continued.

"Your sister was caught breaking into our offices. Do you know what kind of punishment that holds? She was lucky she only got 10 years of servitude to the clan," Grant explained.

"And you have my thanks, Alpha, for not sending her to the Lycan Siberian Detention Facility," Killian replied. "But we need to see her now."

"Why should I let you see her? Especially after you risked exposing our secret?"

"Because we are desperate, Alpha," Killian explained. "I ask for your leniency one more time. Let us deliver the news to Meredith."

"What news?"

"That our father is dead."

The air in the observation room grew so heavy even Daric could feel it. He turned to Meredith, who remained still. Not a word or reaction, not even a flicker of emotion in her eyes. In fact, they remained cold and emotionless. He longed to reach out to her, touch her, and make sure she was all right.

"Meredith?" Alynna asked in a small voice. "Mer, I'm so sor—"

"Take me to them, now," Meredith said in an eerily calm voice. "I need to see them."

"I can't—"

"Alynna," Daric spoke. "She should be in there, with her brothers."

Alynna's eyes darted from Daric to Meredith, and then she let out a sigh. "Grant will kill me, but fine." She looked at Daric. "You stay in here. If you move an inch, I'm gonna eat you for dinner, you hear?"

He nodded.

"Let's go."

Daric watched them go, Meredith's retreating back as stiff as a board. He thought of his own father, and how he watched him die at the hands of Stefan. He knew the feeling, the cold numbness and denial, and the grief afterwards. His chest tightened, and the need to comfort her grew. No, he couldn't do this. He needed to harden his emotions, if he was going to succeed in killing Stefan, and he definitely needed to stay away from Meredith.

———

"Killian!" Meredith cried as she burst through the door to the room.

"What the hell?" Grant exclaimed. "Alynna, I told you not to bring her here."

"Grant, c'mon!" Alynna admonished. "She just found out she lost her dad."

The three men gathered around Meredith, who stood quietly in front of them.

"Is it true?" Meredith asked, her eyes searching their faces.

The blonde one, Quinn, nodded. "Yes, it is. Archie's gone."

Her breath hitched. "How...when...I..." She sank down on the chair, her face draining of color. "When did you find out?"

"A few days ago," Killian said. "I mean, the NYPD called us in Portland. We went and identified him today."

"What happened?" Alynna asked. "Did they tell you anything?"

Killian shook his head. "They don't know yet. They just said they found him in an alleyway. Said it looked like he had jumped from a building."

"No!" Meredith protested. "He wouldn't!"

"We'll find out more tomorrow," Quinn supplied. "We're going to see the detectives at the police station to get more info."

"I don't understand," Meredith said, taking a deep breath. "He can't...it's not true..." She stood up quickly, nearly knocking the chair over.

"It was him, Mer," Killian said, taking her hands in his. "I'm sorry. It was Archie."

"Can someone please explain what's going on?" Grant said. "Who is Archie? Was he your father?"

"Archibald Leacham or Archie to us. He wasn't our biological father, but he was the closest thing any of us had to one," Killian began. "He found us all. We all lost our clans and families or," he looked at Connor, "worse, and he took us in."

"He knew you were Lycans?" Alynna asked.

Quinn nodded. "Yes. He was married to a Lycan, but she died a few years after they got married. He's properly registered with the Portland clan."

"He was able to gather you all together? He found you?"

Killian gave a nostalgic smile. "Kind of. Or we found him. We were all underage when he found us. We lived in his house outside Portland and as soon as we all turned eighteen, made us register as Lone Wolves so that we wouldn't have any problems if we traveled to other territories."

"He took in four strays?" Grant asked. "Just like that?"

"Archie was also a master thief," Quinn explained. "Taught us everything we know."

"Wait, you're all...I mean, like Meredith?" Alynna asked.

Quinn laughed. "Kind of. The three of us," he motioned to the two other men. "We all have our specialties. Killian can pick any lock, break into any safe, and escape from any situation you can think of."

"And Quinn's our master hacker," Killian finished. "Archie sent him to Stanford and Caltech."

"And you?" Alynna asked Connor.

The man huffed and said nothing.

"Connor has a very particular set of skills," Killian said with a mysterious smile. "But he taught us all how to fight and defend ourselves."

"So, Meredith," Alynna said. "You kind of do all the things they do?"

She nodded. "A little bit of everything."

"How did you get in with these guys?" Grant asked.

"I was..." Meredith took a deep breath.

"Archie took her in," Killian finished. "We had all been under Archie's guardianship for a few years. Meredith was the youngest and last one he adopted."

"Our baby sister," Quinn joked.

"Ugh, I hate it when you say that!" Meredith pouted. "I'm not a baby!"

"Alpha," Killian continued. "I'm sorry for causing trouble. We're not here to break out Meredith."

"Yeah, that's what she gets for getting caught," Quinn said, which earned him a slap on the head from Meredith. "Ow, Mer! Stop it!"

"Shut up, keyboard warrior!"

Killian rolled his eyes, apparently used to the banter of the two. "As I said, we just wanted to let her know the news."

Meredith sank back into her chair. "Archie...it's just not him. He wouldn't do that."

Killian frowned. "We know. We think we found a connection with the mages."

Grant suddenly stood from his chair. "How do you know about the mages?"

"Calm down, Alpha," Killian said nonchalantly. "Just because the Council's trying to keep a lid on the whole mage thing, doesn't mean news can't get out. If anything, we know you've been trying to rally the clans together to stop the mages."

"What did you find out?" Meredith asked.

"Well, we're not sure yet," Killian said. "But Archie came to New York to meet with someone. We found his datebook and there was a flight number, an address, a time and then next to it, he wrote 'mages?'."

"From that point, it only took a little bit of digging," Quinn continued.

"But how could he get mixed up in all of this?" Meredith asked, a confused look on her face.

The three men looked at each other and grew quiet.

"What?" Meredith asked. "What happened?"

It was Connor who spoke, the first words anyone ever heard from the gigantic man. "It's not important. We just need to figure out what happened to him and make them pay."

Meredith frowned. They were keeping something from her, and she was going to find out what.

Grant sighed. "Seeing as this is an unusual circumstance...I grant you permission to stay in New York to investigate what happened to your father."

"Thank you, Alpha," Killian said with a grateful nod. "We'll stay out of trouble, I promise."

Grant shook his head. "We have a few rooms open in our security barracks. If you don't mind bunking together, you all can stay for a few days. Meredith's staying there, too."

"That's very generous of you, Alpha," Killian replied.

"I'll show them upstairs then," Alynna said.

Grant massaged his temple with his fingers. "And I'll brief Nick. He's not going to be happy about this."

CHAPTER SIX

As Alynna led the men down the hallway of the 16th floor barracks, Meredith muttered to herself and walked straight to her room, the door closing behind her with a soft thud.

Archie...

Her she-wolf let out a pained howl. Of course, her animal was mourning the loss, too. After all, it was Archie who encouraged her to talk to her she-wolf and nurture it.

You need to make friends with her, Meredith, he would always say. *She's strong. She didn't break, but you can't let her break you.*

Despite what happened when she was a child, the she-wolf stayed whole. Meredith, too, grew stronger under Archie's care, plus she had a warm bed, food, and people she could consider family, not one by blood, but by choice.

Guilt and pain stabbed through her. She and Archie did not part ways on good terms. When she left 8 months ago, she had been so angry at Archie. God, the last things she said to him...

A sob escaped from her mouth and finally, the tears she'd been keeping inside began to flow. She sat on the bed, gazing at the wall. The sadness gripping her heart was making it difficult to breathe.

Suddenly, the door opened and she quickly wiped the tears from her eyes. "Who's— what the fuck are you doing here? Don't you know how to knock or did the mages forget to teach you manners?"

Daric strode in, his face an unreadable mask. "You didn't come back to escort me to my room."

"Yeah, well, I'm done for the day," she stood up and walked over to him. "And I'm done with you! Get the fuck out." When he didn't move, she slapped her hands on his chest and gave him a shove, but he remained rooted to the spot. "Don't you know what 'get the fuck out' means?" She began to beat at his chest, pounding as hard as she could, despite the fact that he didn't even flinch. Anger and rage filled her, bubbling to the surface, forcing more hot tears down her cheeks. When she slowed down, Daric wrapped his hands around her wrists.

"Feel better?" he asked.

Meredith choked and a deep, guttural sound tore from her chest. She tried to pull away from him, but he only drew her closer, pulling her to his chest. The warmth of his skin emanated through the thin T-shirt, and she inhaled his delicious cocoa scent. She sobbed against him, and he put his arms around her in a tight embrace. Not caring one bit who he was and the things that happened between them that morning, she slipped her arms around his waist, trying to get as close to him as possible. His presence, his scent, and his hands soothing her back was comforting, and he let her cry for a few more minutes.

Finally, she pulled away, letting out a hiccup as she frowned. "I ruined your shirt with my snot," she sniffed.

He stared down at the wet patch on his chest. "It's only a shirt. Now," he looked down at her with his intense blue-green eyes. "How are you feeling?"

Reluctantly, she pulled away and took a deep breath. God, what just happened? One moment, she hated Daric and then the next...he was hugging her like he was her best friend. Or a lover giving comfort. "A little better," she said before walking back to her bed and sitting down. She had to put as much distance between her and the warlock as possible.

"I, too, have lost my father," he said.

"He wasn't my father," she replied quickly.

"Well, perhaps he's the closest thing you have had to a father figure," Daric pointed out. "I'm sure his loss is comparable to that of losing your biological father."

She shrugged. "I wouldn't know. I don't remember my real father."

"Did he abandon you?" he asked, his voice edgy.

"No, he died when I was young," Meredith confessed. "I was born in North Carolina, to the Charleston clan," she said. "My dad died when I was four and my mother raised me. When she died five years later, there was no one in the clan who wanted to take me in, so they sent me to my dad's closest relatives in Alabama - his human cousin and his wife."

"Was that Archie?"

She shook her head. "No." Jedd and Marie Simmons were fully human. They were also human pieces of shit. "I...I ran away when I was eleven. They probably never reported me missing because they wanted to keep the money the Charleston Alpha was giving them to take care of me." Bitter memories flooded her brain, threatening to overwhelm her. Pushing them deep down inside, she continued. "I made my way across the country and Archie had found me roaming the streets of Portland a year later."

"How did you manage to get there?"

She ignored his question and continued with her story. "I was hungry. I saw Archie and stole his wallet. Actually," she let out a small laugh. "He let me steal his wallet. And then he found me, then took me in. He had already formed his little pack and I was the newest addition."

"So, he found abandoned Lycans like you and took care of them?"

"Yeah...I guess. I mean, he did teach us to be criminals," she pointed out. "I'm not sure that qualifies as fatherly advice."

"He taught you his trade," Daric said. "Perhaps the only thing of himself he could give you, since you were not blood related."

"Why the hell am I talking to you about this anyway?" She stood up and faced him. "Don't you dare tell anyone about this, warlock."

"My lips are sealed," he said, giving her a slight smile that made him seem even more handsome.

Her eyes were immediately drawn to the strong line of his lips and Meredith felt a flash of attraction and heat. It dawned on her that they were alone. In her room. With a bed. An image of them tangled between the sheets imprinted in her mind and she stared up at him. The intense look in his eyes made her wonder if he was thinking of the same thing. The room suddenly was too small and the air became heavy with his scent and something she didn't want to say out loud.

He moved closer, slowly, like a curious cat. His hand moved to her face, touching her cheek carefully like he was handling delicate glass.

The sound of the door opening made him immediately drop his hand and his face slipped back into his usual cold, haughty look.

"Meredith, I wanted...Daric?" Alynna asked. "What are you doing here? I thought Grant told you to go back to your room and stay there."

"I thought this was my room," he explained, quickly walking

towards the door. "I'm still getting to know the layout of the floor. My apologies."

Alynna's eyes narrowed. "Uh-huh. Right." The warlock quickly left without another glance and the two women were alone. "Are you okay, Meredith?"

She shrugged. "Yeah, I'm fine."

"You know...if you need to talk..."

"I said, I'm fine," she insisted. "Are Killian and the others settled in?"

"Yeah, they're a couple doors down," Alynna said.

"I want...I need to find out what happened to Archie," Meredith said.

"Don't worry, Grant has given you permission to help your brothers investigate Archie's death, as long as you don't try to escape and you continue with your current assignment."

"What?" Meredith asked. "He did? But why?"

"Meredith, you may not have pledged to the clan, but you're one of us now," Alynna explained. "You've helped us so many times, risking your own life in the process. And this is what clans do. Protect our own."

She shook her head. Did Grant really trust her? What did he want in return?

"I do hope you'd consider joining the New York Clan."

"What?" Her head snapped up. Alynna's statement suddenly came out of left field and left Meredith stunned. Join the clan? No, she was a Lone Wolf. It was a mark she would wear for life. Clan life wasn't for her. Besides, it wasn't any form of freedom. If she pledged to New York, yes, her 10 years of servitude would be forgiven, but that meant she had to do whatever Grant told her to do. It would be exchanging a decade of servitude for a lifetime of being under the clan's thumb.

"Think about it, okay?" Alynna said. "Now, tomorrow, you'll be heading to the police station downtown to talk to the detectives working on the case. I'm not sure all of you will fit in a town car, so maybe you can just take one of the Escalades."

Meredith frowned. "I know my brothers are big, but we can all probably fit in a cab or something." It wouldn't be the first time she'd be squished in the backseat of a car with Quinn and Connor.

Alynna laughed. "With Connor and Daric in tow, I'm not sure any cabbie'll be willing to take you anywhere and I really can't see that warlock taking the subway, though I'd pay good money to see that."

"Daric?" Meredith asked. "Can't you get someone else to guard him for a bit? Just until I wrap things up?"

Alynna shook her head. "Oh no. He insisted in helping you. After we left, he apparently talked to Grant. He said he wanted to help and that if the mages were involved, then he would be the perfect person to assist you."

"What?" Meredith asked incredulously. "He asked Grant if he could come along to help us?"

"Yes," the other Lycan confirmed. "Is everything okay with you guys? I mean, if something's bothering you—"

"No," Meredith replied quickly. "I mean...yeah, whatever floats his boat." She gave a shrug like she didn't care. But it did bother her. First, Daric comes into the room and she pours her heart out to him. Then he acts all weird and for a second she thought he was going to...no, it was all her imagination. The warlock wandered into her room by accident, saw her crying and then it was too late for him to make a graceful exit. That was all.

"All right then, goodnight Meredith," Alynna said before leaving her room.

Meredith sighed and plopped down on her bed, thinking about what had just happened. She'd made many mistakes in her life, but Daric was one she was not going to make.

———

"Why do I have to take dance lessons, Archie?" Meredith whined as she got home after another rigorous training session with Madame Giselle. "I bet no one else had to take ballet or ballroom dancing," she grumbled as she collapsed on the couch. "I'd be better off sparring with Connor or learning to pick locks with Killian. Fucking hell, I'll spend time with Quinn, if it means I never have to wear toe shoes again!"

"Language!" Archie admonished. He let out a sigh as he walked into the living room and stood in front of her. "Tsk tsk, my dear Meredith, I told you. Your brothers are bigger and stronger than you. You'll never be built like them."

"And so?" Meredith retorted in that voice only fourteen-year-old girls seemed to be able to pull off. "That doesn't mean they're better than me."

"Exactly," Archie replied. "They're not better than you. Not if you use your assets to your advantage. Ballet and modern dance will help you strengthen your muscles, gain flexibility, and increase your stamina. Plus, you'll learn grace, style, and elegance."

She stuck her tongue out. "What the hell—I mean, heck do I need to know those things for? I thought you were going to teach me to become a master thief like you?"

Archie let out a deep sigh. "Go and take a shower, Meredith," he ordered in his serious voice, the 'do-not-fuck-with-me' tone he used whenever she and her brothers tried to question his teaching methods. "Put on that new dress and shoes I bought you and meet me outside when you're done."

"Fine," she mumbled and went upstairs, stamping her feet like a kid all the way to her room.

Twenty minutes later, she bounded down the steps and opened the front door. Archie was already waiting for her inside his Aston Martin and so she quickly slipped into the front passenger seat.

"Where are we going?"

Archie didn't answer her, but turned the key in the ignition and pulled out of the driveway, heading towards the city. They arrived 45 minutes later, and Archie pulled into the driveway of a famous old hotel downtown. He exited the car, opened Meredith's door and offered his arm. With a roll of her eyes, Meredith took it and let him lead her inside.

They took the elevator to the rooftop restaurant and then gave their jackets to the coat check girl. Meredith had never been anywhere so fancy, and she suddenly felt self-conscious. The decor was elegant, and there was a full band playing in the corner while tables had been set up around a crowded dance floor. Dozens of couples were dancing, swaying to the beat of the classic tunes.

She thought of asking Archie what they were doing here but thought better of it. Her mentor was more of a "show" than a "tell" kind of guy.

Archie led her to the middle of the dance floor and placed his hand on her hip and took her other hand in his. She followed his lead, and they began to dance.

"I'm sure you've absorbed some of Madame Giselle's lessons," he said.

"Yeah, well I'm not sure how they're going to help me," she pouted.

"My dear, everything can be a lesson, you must remember that," he said with a twinkle in his eye. "Grace," he began as he spun her. They brushed up against another couple, and Meredith's keen eyes saw Archie's hand dip into the man's breast pocket to retrieve his wallet. "Style," he continued, twirling her around and extending his hand so he could unclip another woman's diamond earring. "And finally..." He dipped her, bending down low so he could reach the pants pocket of the man behind her, pulling out a gold pocket watch. "Elegance."

Meredith watched in wonder as Archie used his magic hands to deftly relieve the various dancers on the floor of their possessions. When the song ended, he gave Meredith and elegant bow and then they walked off the dance floor.

"What are you doing?" she hissed when Archie dumped his loot into the trash bin outside the restaurant. "That's like, thousands of dollars worth of stuff!"

Archie huffed. "My dear, the point wasn't to steal. It was to learn. Now," he put on his coat and helped Meredith with hers. "Lesson's done for tonight. Tomorrow, we start again."

CHAPTER SEVEN

D aric tossed and turned in his new bed. His new lodgings were quite spartan, but the bed was a little bigger than the previous one in his cell. The mattress was adequate, though not luxurious. But it wasn't the reason why he couldn't sleep.

Why he offered his help to find Meredith's father's killer, he didn't know. Seeing the Lycan in pain made his gut clench. It was an uncomfortable feeling that grew and grew until he couldn't stand it anymore. Not knowing what to do, he approached Grant Anderson.

"Daric?" Grant frowned when he saw the warlock. "What are you doing here?"

"It seems my bodyguard forgot about me," he said and explained what happened.

"So, you saw everything?"

Daric nodded.

"Did you know this Archie Leacham?" Grant asked.

"The name sounds familiar," he lied. He'd never heard of the name nor did he know why Stefan would have contact with a human connected with the Lycans. While the Lycans may have thought that Daric knew a lot about Stefan's operations, they were wrong. Stefan trusted only one person: himself. He wove secrets upon secrets, and neither he nor Victoria Chatraine knew all of the master mage's plans and schemes. "I would like to offer my assistance. If he is an agent of the mages or a victim, then I'm the best person to help the Lone Wolves."

Grant paused. "You want to help Meredith and her brothers?"

"If their father had a connection to Stefan, then perhaps he knew something that could help us find out what he's up to next," Daric quickly explained.

"Hmmm...that wouldn't be a bad idea, but how can I trust you?"

"How can I earn your trust if you don't give me a chance?" Daric countered. "Besides, in my state, I'd be no match for four powerful Lycans."

"I'll check with the Lone Wolves," Grant relented. "But they should be receptive to help."

"Excellent, I'll be ready in the morning," Daric said.

After the Alpha had helped him return to the 16th floor, he walked straight toward his room. However, his eyes were immediately drawn to Meredith's door.

It was as if he could feel her sadness and pain, even with the wall between them. Unable to help himself, he went into her room to check on her. What possessed him to take her into his arms to comfort her, he couldn't say, only that he had to do it. The tears on her face didn't belong there, and he wanted to make sure she'd never cry like that again.

Daric clenched the sheets in his fists. The only way he'd achieve that was to stay away from her. But he couldn't forget the way her lush body molded perfectly to his, and how her lips brushed against his chest as she cried. He had to shift his hips away from her or she would have noticed the growing bulge of his cock. He was a bastard, thinking only of his own lust when she was in pain.

As he saw his first sunrise in a long time peek over the horizon, Daric gave up trying to sleep and got up, then headed into the shower. He stripped and walked into the glass enclosure, turning the water to the hottest setting he could stand. As he stood under the water, his thoughts kept drifting back to Meredith. And her soft and luscious curves. Her breasts pressed against him, her soft hair tickling his skin. He reached down and found himself fully hard and aching for her. As his fist wrapped around his cock, he wondered if her grip around him would be just as tight. She would probably be hot and wet as he slid into her, her long legs would wrap around him as he pumped his cock into her pussy. Or no, Meredith was wild and free. She'd probably want to be on top half the time. He could already imagine her sweet body over him, her tits bouncing as she rode him until her body shook with pleasure, her head thrown back and her lips parting, moaning his name.

Daric let out a groan, the orgasm coming faster than he'd anticipated. He slapped his palm against the wet tiles, bracing himself as his seed spurted out of his cock, spilling down onto the slick floor. After a few ragged breaths, he finished his shower and grabbed the towel hanging from the rack. It would be a long day, especially since he'd be in Meredith's company, but perhaps with the other Lycans around, he could stay focused on the task. Maybe this Archie Leacham *was* connected to Stefan in some way and then he could get closer to his goal of ending the master mage.

He lay on the bed, contemplating his moves for the next few hours. Finally, a knock came at his door.

"Let's go," Meredith said as she stood on the other side of the door, her arms crossed. Despite the pallor on her face and dark smudges under eyes, Meredith looked lovely this morning.

Her long, blonde locks were still slightly damp from her shower and hung down her shoulders in waves. She wore black boots, black leggings, a navy jacket and a tank top that said, "I wish I was a unicorn, so I could stab idiots with my head." He raised a brow at the shirt, but she shrugged. Meredith began walking to the elevators, but Daric stopped.

"Wait," he called.

"We need to get going."

"I have not eaten," he said. "And neither have you."

"I'm not hungry. I'll get you a muffin on the way to the police station."

"Isn't breakfast the most important meal of the day?" Daric asked. "We need our energy today."

Meredith let out a long, drawn out sigh. "Fiiiiiine. Let's go to the kitchen."

She pivoted and headed the other direction, stopping at one of the doors in the hallway and calling out "Breakfast in the kitchen!" before continuing.

The common kitchen in the security barracks was large and roomy, with various appliances for cooking in one corner and several tables on the other side. A large spread was already laid out on one of the buffet tables. It was early yet, and so there was no one in the kitchen except for the young man who was adding more food to the already-heaping buffet table. Lycans, it seemed, had healthy appetites.

They walked to the table and Meredith took a plate, got an apple and proceeded to walk to one of the tables.

"Come back," he said.

"What do you want now? Do you want me to get your food, too, warlock? Shall I get you some tea and crumpets, and some fine silverware?" she mocked.

With a sigh, he grabbed her arm and pulled her to the buffet table, ignoring the shock of electricity that tingled his skin as they touched. She tried to protest, but he sent her a warning look as he piled her plate with toast, bacon, eggs, and sausages.

"You'll need all of this today," he said, as he dragged her to one of the tables. "Sit."

Meredith mumbled something about bullies and sat down on the bench. Daric sat across from her, his own plate piled with food.

"Eat," he said.

She picked up a piece of bacon and took a bite. "Happy?"

"Only if you finish your plate," Daric replied, taking a spoonful of eggs.

"Ugh," she said, rolling her eyes and began to pick at her food.

They sat in silence and a few minutes later, Killian, Quinn, and Connor walked in. They headed to the buffet tables, piled their plates high and walked to Meredith and Daric.

"So," Killian said as he sat down next to Daric. "You must be the warlock. The Alpha told us all about you."

"Daric," he replied, giving the other man a nod.

"Hey, runt," Quinn said. He plopped down next to Meredith on her right and then gave her a gentle shove with his shoulder.

"Quit it!" she said with a pout.

He laughed and then began shoveling food into his mouth.

Connor, the quiet, tall one, said nothing as he sat on Meredith's left, but gave Daric a look that would have made any lesser man run in the other direction. Daric stared right back at him, their gazes locked in fierce combat, the tension around them growing thick.

"Stop," Killian commanded. He was obviously the leader of the trio, but Connor didn't move an inch. With a sigh, Killian put his fork down. "Okay, on three, you two will stop it. One, two, three."

Daric and Connor turned their gazes away at the same time, and the tension began to dissipate.

"So," Quinn began, then turned his bright blue eyes at Daric. "How are we sure you're not going to zap us or disappear into thin air?"

"I'm powerless," Daric said, raising his right wrist to show them the bracelet.

"Nice jewelry," Quinn replied. "But what does it do?"

"It stops him from using his magic," Meredith explained. "I don't know how exactly, but I know it works. My best friend, Jade, made it and she's a genius."

"You have a best friend?" Killian asked with a raised brow.

"Is she pretty?" Quinn asked with a wicked smile.

Meredith pointed her fork at her brother. "Yes, but, don't even go there. You do not want to poke the dragon."

"You mean, bear?" Quinn asked, and Meredith just shrugged.

Even Daric had to suppress a smile, thinking of how Creed would react to Meredith's handsome brother making advances on his pregnant mate. But then again, Quinn looked like the type of person who looked for trouble.

"So, without your powers, how can you help us?" Killian asked, his eyes narrowing at Daric.

"I have knowledge of most of Stefan's dealings," Daric explained. "If your father did have contact with Stefan or any of his closest lieutenants, then I would know."

"All right, but you better play it straight with us," Killian warned. "I don't fuck around, and if you try anything, you're gonna regret, you hear?"

"I have better things to do than lead you astray," Daric replied.

"And why are you helping us?" Quinn asked.

"Because your father's connection to the mages may help me get closer to finding Stefan and destroying him."

That seemed to satisfy the two Lycans, though Meredith shot him a suspicious look. Connor kept his attention on his food, slowly demolishing the two plates piled high in front of him.

The rest of the meal was continued in silence, though Quinn would occasionally tease Meredith, with Killian joining in on occasion. Daric supposed this is what siblings were like, but he wouldn't know. He did understand that the two were ribbing Meredith in good nature, and perhaps, to distract her from the sadness obviously looming in her eyes. The third Lone Wolf, Connor, continued to eye him suspiciously. Daric sensed there was something not quite right with that one, but he wasn't interested in knowing what, as long as the Lycan didn't get in his way.

———

As soon as they finished breakfast, Meredith led them to the garage in the parking level of the building, where Alex Westbrooke was waiting for them.

"Hey Meredith," the other Lycan greeted. He narrowed his eyes at Daric but didn't say anything else.

"Hey Alex, how's the baby?"

"Doing good, she's learning to turn on her tummy now," Alex replied.

Killian stiffened beside Meredith, and she gave him a strange look. The other Lycan said nothing, but instead introduced himself and the other men to Alex.

"Well, here's your ride," Alex said, as he handed Killian the keys and nodded to the large white SUV parked beside him.

"Take care of her." With a final wave, he left and headed towards the elevators.

They piled into the SUV, with Killian taking the wheel and Quinn slipping into the passenger seat beside him. Meredith climbed into the back, squished between Daric and Connor. She moved closer to Connor so she wouldn't have to touch Daric, which was nearly impossible considering the size of the two men. She tried not to stare at Daric, no matter how hot he looked, with his long hair pulled back into a ponytail and a bit of scruff on his face. His white t-shirt stretched across his chest, and his jeans molded perfectly to his ass.

Meredith groaned inwardly. Why did the Goddamn warlock have to be so fucking hot and look like all her wildest fantasies come true, and then some? His scent was driving her crazy, and it took all her power to control her traitorous whore body and the she-wolf inside her. Her brothers would definitely notice if she was aroused, which would be awkward and embarrassing.

Thankfully, it didn't take too long to get to the police station. Killian parked the car, and they all filed out, then walked into the NYPD's 7th Precinct on Pitt St.

Killian and Quinn walked to the desk sergeant, and after a few minutes, an older man with salt-and-pepper hair wearing a drab brown suit came out.

"Mr. Smith," the man greeted, shaking his hand. When he found them, Archie had gotten them all fake identities with the last name of Smith. "Thanks for coming back and agreeing to talk to us."

"Well, I was hoping you'd tell us more about our adoptive father's death, Detective Conrad," Killian replied. "By the way, this is our sister, Meredith."

Detective Conrad nodded to her. "I'm sorry for your loss, ma'am."

"Thank you," she replied quietly.

"I'll take your statements in one of our interrogation rooms," he said, jerking his thumb toward the bullpen behind him. They followed him, but, before they crossed the threshold that separated the reception area from the back room, he stopped suddenly. "Sorry, family only," he said, looking at Daric.

"I'm her husband," he declared, putting an arm around Meredith. "You can take our statement together, but I'm afraid I won't be much help. I've never met my father-in-law."

She stiffened for a moment and then relaxed against his embrace.

Conrad gave them a suspicious look. "Wait a minute, you're married, but you've never met her father? Didn't he come to the wedding?"

"I got knocked up by accident!" Meredith declared quickly, placing a hand on her belly. "It was a quickie wedding in Vegas. Last week." Inside, she was dying. *Oh, why the hell did I say that?* Being so close to Daric was probably frying her brain cells.

"But, a beautiful one, *min kjære*," Daric added, giving Meredith a sweet smile.

Conrad seemed satisfied by their answer and continued to lead them into the bullpen, and then down the hall to one of the interrogation rooms. It was already set up, with a table in the middle and several chairs. "Please, take your seats."

The detective sat across from them, and then took out a leather-bound notebook and a ballpoint pen from inside his suit jacket. "Okay, let's begin." He opened the notebook and uncapped his pen. "When was the last time you all saw your father?"

"Two weeks ago," Killian said. "Him, Quinn, Connor and me went to dinner. We go every week, but we missed last week's Sunday dinner because he said he was busy."

"And you, Ms. Smith?"

"Eight months ago," Meredith answered, trying to keep her voice even.

"That long?"

"We had a falling out," Meredith explained.

"Over what?"

Meredith went quiet, her shoulders slumping. *Archie*...She bit her lip, trying not to cry. "I...I..." she began, the lump in her throat growing. Hadn't she cried out all the tears yet? Would this pain she carried around ever leave? Could she stop missing him?

An arm around her shoulder made her jolt. Daric's presence and his hand rubbing up and down her arm soothed her.

"It's alright, *min kjære*," he cooed. "I'm sure the detective doesn't need all the details."

"It might help," Conrad prodded.

Meredith nodded and took a deep breath. "We had a difference of opinion. I mean, I found out a secret about my birth family that he kept, and I was angry at him." She paused. "And I left, and haven't seen him since."

"So, you're all from Portland," Conrad said, looking over his notes. "Why did he come to New York?" He looked at Meredith. "Your brothers said you lived here. Was he coming to see you? Did you know he was here?"

She shook her head. "No. I only heard about his death yesterday."

"Hmmm...well," he said, scratching his chin. "The coroner has ruled the death to be a suicide."

"What?" Meredith slammed her hands on the table. "No, Archie wouldn't do that! You don't know him! He wouldn't have—" She choked on her tears again and slumped down on the chair. When Daric tried to put an arm around her, she shrugged him off.

"There were no witnesses, and when we checked the

rooftop where he jumped from, there were no signs of a struggle or even another person up there with him. So," he continued. "It seemed Mr. Leacham hopped on a plane to New York, and decided to kill himself by jumping off a roof."

"Sounds suspicious to me," Quinn said, his boyishly handsome face drawn into a frown.

"Exactly. The coroner may have ruled it a suicide, but I'm still trying to figure out why he killed himself and it's not adding up."

Meredith's mind was reeling. As the detective and her brothers continued to talk, she tried to make sense of everything. A glance from Killian told her that this wasn't over. For one thing, none of her brothers knew the real reason she left. How could she tell them? How could she reveal to them that the man they considered their father and raised them, took care of them, had been hiding something big from her, from all of them?

The detective continued to prod and grill them, carefully though, but it was obvious he was trying to get more information. Finally, after two hours, he put his notebook away. "Well, I'm gonna try and keep working on this, but to be honest, my captain'll want my attention on other cases. With Mr. Leacham's death being officially ruled a suicide, my hands are tied." He stood up.

"Thank you for trying, Detective," Killian said, shaking the older man's hand. "Maybe we'll never find out what happened to him."

"In some of these cases, the deceased may have simply been depressed," he said, shaking his hand. "You all are young now, but, growing old, it takes a toll on you, ya know? By the way, I have his personal possessions. The things we found on him, plus the things he left in his room. If you can sign for it, we can give you the items on his person and ship his suitcase to you. The coroner will be contacting you when they're ready to release his remains. You can talk to their office about how you want to handle that."

"Much appreciated, Detective Conrad," Killian said with a nod.

Conrad left the room and came back with a plastic zip bag. "Here you go. Again, I'm so sorry for your loss."

Killian took the bag. They all thanked the detective and then followed Conrad as he led them out of the police station.

"Archie wouldn't have killed himself, you all know that," Meredith said as soon as they were alone.

"We know," Killian confirmed. "Something's not right, I can feel it."

"But who could have done it?" Quinn asked.

"With the police off our backs, we'll be able to find out," Killian said. "Meredith," he turned to his sister. "Is it true? What you said in there? Is that why you left?"

She hesitated. "I found out that he knew my birth family and kept it from me." She bit her lip. Meredith didn't want to lie to them, but now wasn't the time to tell them either. She didn't have all the information anyway. "I was so mad at him that I left."

Connor, normally silent, let out a low growl. "You should have come to us first. You shouldn't have just left."

"I know, Connor," she said sadly. "I'm sorry. I'm sorry I left without telling you guys."

"We missed you, Mer," Quinn said. "It wasn't the same without you."

Meredith felt the tears choke up again and she took a deep breath. "I missed you guys, too, even your ugly mug, Quinn," she said with a smile.

"Ha! You never change," Quinn replied, ruffling her hair. "What's with all the crying, runt? Is it the pregnancy hormones

—Ow!" he cried when Meredith hit him in the arm. "Oh my God, are you blushing?"

Meredith's cheeks were red. "I am not!" she protested and then ran towards the parked SUV. What was Daric thinking, introducing himself as her husband? Heck, what was *she* thinking, saying she was pregnant? It seemed like a good idea at the time. Otherwise, they would have had to leave Daric outside. And what the heck did he call her in front of everyone? The way Daric said it made her blush even more. His voice was like silk, an intimate caress as the words rolled off his tongue. Gah, the man was impossible.

They caught up with her and thankfully, she was done blushing. Killian unlocked the car and Meredith quickly jumped in, scooting to the middle of the backseat and she was once again trapped between Connor and Daric.

"What should we do now?" Meredith asked as Killian locked the doors.

The other Lycan took the plastic bag and opened it, taking the contents out and placing them on the console between the front seats.

Meredith held her breath, staring at Archie's well-worn leather wallet, his wedding ring, house keys, and various bits of paper. Was this really all that was left of her mentor? Another sob threatened to escape her, but a warm hand over hers made her freeze. She didn't want to look down at the seat, but she could imagine Daric's large fingers over hers. Swallowing a gulp, she looked back at the items.

"Hey, what's that?" she asked, her eyes drawn to a business card. It was plain white, made of a thick and expensive card stock. On the front was one word in a red script font. "Merlin's?" she read. "Does that sound familiar to any of you?"

Killian lifted the card and examined it.

Quinn shook his head. "I don't think that's in Portland," he said, taking his smartphone out of his pocket. After a few taps and swipes, he frowned. "No, not in Portland, not in New York. In fact, I can't find any trace of any business named Merlin's with that logo."

"May I?" Daric asked, withdrawing his hand from Meredith's and extending it towards the other Lycan.

Killian gave him the card, and the warlock took it, turning the card over. "You can't see it?" he asked.

Meredith looked at him. "See what?"

A smile spread across his face. "There is an address printed on the back. This card is infused with magic. Only the person it was intended for can see it."

"Then how come you can see it?" Killian questioned.

"Hmmm...the spell is quite crude, which is why I can see it or perhaps it was intended only for witches and warlocks," Daric explained. "Although I can't use my powers, magic is still part of me."

"What does it say?" Quinn asked.

"The address is 235 Princeton Street," Daric read, then handed it back to Killian.

Quinn quickly punched in the address into the built-in GPS unit. "Let's go."

The drive to Princeton Street wasn't very long, and it was only a couple of blocks from the police station. Princeton Street was a small alley in Soho, just off one of the more fashionable shopping streets.

As Killian cut the engine, he looked back at Daric. "Did you read that address right?"

"Yes," Daric confirmed.

"I don't see any sign. Can you see one?"

Daric peered out the window, in front of the warehouse with the numbers "235" above the door. "No, there is no sign. Perhaps we should investigate?"

They filed out of the vehicle and walked to the warehouse door. It looked just like any converted factory in lower Manhattan. The building was about four stories tall and made of solid brick. It looked well-kept, but the windows were darkly tinted. The main door was made of steel, and there was no signage or anything else to indicate what was inside.

"Should we try to pick the lock?" Quinn asked Killian.

"How about if we simply knock?" Daric asked. The four Lycans looked at him with strange looks on their face. The warlock shrugged, then rapped his knuckles on the door.

A few seconds later, the sound of metal scraping against metal screeched through the air, and the large door opened a crack. A short, balding man with sharp green eyes peered at them.

"Finally!" he said, opening the door wider. "You're here." His voice was high-pitched and nasal. "You're late, by the way, Mr. Merlin has been waiting for 20 minutes. He doesn't like to be kept waiting."

"Our apologies," Killian said smoothly. "We got lost. GPS isn't worth shit these days, you know."

The man rolled his eyes. "Fine, fine, just follow me. I'll take you to the dressing rooms, and you can begin."

Dressing room, Meredith mouthed to Killian, who shrugged. As they followed the man across the warehouse, she looked around, trying to piece together what this place was. Red seemed to be the dominant color, judging by the red velvet curtains, the tables and chairs scattered across the floor, and the various decorations on the wall. The decor was classy and sleek, and it looked like any high-end club or bar in Manhattan. The ceiling was high, and there was a second lofted level that wrapped around the walls, allowing patrons a clear view of the main stage.

They walked towards the stage, which for now, wasn't fully

set up. It wasn't too large and had a catwalk in the middle, while various props and set pieces were scattered around.

The balding man led them to the side, drawing a curtain apart to let them through. From there, they followed him down a narrow hallway, until they reached a door at the end.

"Dressing room's in there," he said, jerking his thumb towards the door. "You can change in there, but I suggest you don't take too long. The boss'll be down in five minutes, don't take longer than that to get on stage." With a final nod, he left them.

Meredith opened the door and walked in. Inside were rows of dressing tables, chairs, and mirrors. She suddenly realized what type of establishment they were in. "Merlin's is a strip club!" Her eyes swept across the room, looking at the various bits of sparkly, furry, and bejeweled costumes hanging all over the chairs and dressers.

"A magical strip club, apparently," Quinn said, his eyebrows wagging. "Hmmm...I've never been with a witch before. You think any of these girls will give a wolf a chance?"

"Ugh." Meredith smacked him on the arm.

"What the hell was Archie doing at a strip club?"

"Well, he was single—ow! Quit it, Meredith!"

"Oh, shut up, that didn't even hurt," she said. "Well, there's only one way we can find out what Archie was going here." She pivoted and began walking to the door.

"What are you doing?" Connor asked.

"What does it look like? I'm going to audition."

"No," four voices protested.

"What the fuck—"

"You can't—"

"No way are you—"

"I forbid it!" Daric's voice was tense and strained, his sea-colored eyes flashing with anger. "You will stay in here and keep your clothes on. I'm a warlock; I'll go and see what this Merlin knows about Archie."

"Ugh, stop!" She put her hand up. "Seriously? You think this guy will just tell us about Archie? Why? Out of the goodness of his own heart? If he had anything to do with Archie's death, then you know he's not going to say anything to us. Our best chance to find out what happened is for me to get in here, sneak into his office and search for any information that could lead us to Archie's killer."

The four men looked at each other. Finally, Killian let out a sigh. "Fine, but you need to be careful."

"What?" Daric asked incredulously. "You're going to let her get up on that stage and take her clothes off?" He looked at Connor. "Don't you have any honor?"

"I don't like it," Connor replied, crossing his arms over his massive chest. "But, she's right. If Merlin suspects what we're up to, I doubt we'll have another chance to get into this place."

Daric grabbed Meredith's arm. "There is another way."

"What?" she challenged.

"I don't know...but we will find another way."

She yanked her arm away from his grip. "Keep looking then. In the meantime, it's time to put those dance lessons to good use."

Meredith walked out, not waiting for Daric's protest. She was glad she at least had her brother's support. Frankly, though, she was nervous. She'd never taken her clothes off in front of an audience. Archie had sent her to modern, ballet, and ballroom dance classes, but she doubted stripping was what the master thief had in mind when he wanted her to learn this particular skill set.

When Meredith reached the main stage area, the props had already been cleared. The lights were also dimmed and a single spotlight was on stage. Assuming that's where she was supposed to go, she walked across the stage, into the spotlight. With a deep breath, she gripped the bottom of her shirt, and began to lift it up.

"Darling, what are you doing?" a voice said from the darkness.

"Uh...auditioning? Your guy said—"

"No, no, no!" came the exasperated voice. "House lights on!"

The lights in the club flickered on, and Meredith squinted, trying to see who else was in the room. At the foot of the stage was a tall man, dressed in all black. He climbed the steps and walked over to Meredith.

"Darling, I appreciate the effort. I like the hipster, look it's very in," he said, waving at her t-shirt and leggings. The man was handsome, tall, lean, and his black hair was slicked back. The most curious thing about him was his eyes. Meredith had never seen eyes that dark. They were like pools of ink. "However, you're not what I'm looking for."

"I'm not?" Meredith frowned.

"Did an agency send you?" he asked. "Those guys are always mixing up appointments; perhaps you were supposed to go to a different audition."

"Different audition? Isn't this Merlin's, the strip club?"

The man let out a long, drawn-out sigh. "Darling, this *is* Merlin's, but I'm afraid you're all wrong for us. We're not some some sleazy titty club. We only cater to the most discerning patrons here. Some very wealthy and very special witches."

Meredith laughed out loud. "Oh. My. God. This is a *male* strip club?"

"Of course," the man said. "I'm Lucien Merlin, owner and proprietor...and you..." He narrowed his eyes at her. "I've never had a Lycan performer here before. Hmmm...say," he scratched his chin. "Does your agency have any men performers?

Meredith bit her lip. "Don't move from that spot, Mr. Merlin—"

"Lucien, please. Or just Merlin. Mr. Merlin was my father."

"Right, Lucien. I've got just the guy for you," she said. "I mean, guys."

"All right, but I haven't got all day."

Meredith skipped off and ran offstage. She nearly collided into Killian, who was walking towards her with a scowl on his face.

"Meredith, we've changed our minds," Killian said. "We'll find the information another way. We can't let you strip in front of slimy businessmen and God-knows-who-else."

"I won't have to," she said with a smile.

"Good," Daric said. "Now let's get out of here."

"No, wait, we can still get some good intel here, come with me," she said.

The four men looked at each other and followed her to the stage. "How about these guys?" she said.

Merlin's eyes lit up. "Oh...hmmm..." He looked at the three Lycans appreciatively. "My oh my," he said, fanning himself. "You'll do. But I don't need all of you."

"What the fuck are you talking about?" Killian asked, stretching to his full height.

Undeterred, Merlin came closer. "Your friend here said she brought along some male Lycan strippers. You are looking for a job, right?"

"What the fuck?" Connor cursed and the air grew heavy.

"Oooh, boy, put those pheromones away." Merlin shook his head. "No, not you, definitely not. I want to thrill our clientele, not scare them. Though I may know one or two who would love a private booking with a guy like you if you don't mind a little rough role playing."

"Wait, this is a male strip club?" Killian asked.

Another long sigh escaped Merlin's lips. "Look, is this your first time to an audition? I'd really rather not waste my time here," he said. "Just get out if you're not interested."

"We are," Quinn said. "And hey, I'm your guy," he said, flashing Merlin a smile. "I'd love a chance to perform for your clients. They're witches, right?"

Merlin nodded. "Most of them, and a few warlocks, too. But, you know, most warlocks are so uptight, present company an exception," he said in a low voice. "Can't let the secret out, right? We put a glamour on our building and our marketing materials to make sure we only attract the right clientele. Some do bring their human friends, but only if they're in the know."

"Right," Killian said, flashing Meredith a pointed look.

"Ok, so blondie's got the job...what about..." he looked over to Daric. "Oh, my. Four Lycans and a warlock walk into a strip club...sounds like the beginning of a corny joke."

Meredith snorted.

"Hmm...women go crazy over the Viking look these days," Merlin said. "How about it? You two?"

"Yeah!" Quinn side, pumping his fist. Daric remained stoic but gave a curt nod.

"No!" Meredith protested. Eyes swung over to her. "I mean...no problem, right, guys?"

"Of course," Quinn said, giving Daric a friendly slap. "My boy Daric and I will be drowning in witch pus—" He stopped when Meredith gave him a dirty look. "I mean, yeah, we're professionals and everything."

Merlin's eyes narrowed but then turned to the others. "Well, lucky for you all, I'm always short staffed. That's kinda what happens with places that cater to the magical, you know? It's easy to lose employees, and confusion potions are a bitch to hand out. Do you all need jobs? I could use a bartender and a couple more bouncers."

"I've worked a bar before," Meredith said.

"And Connor and I will take care of the front door," Killian added.

"Excellent. Now, go and grab your tax forms from Ivar," he said, gesturing the to balding man who had let them in. "We're all legal here, you know, with all the authorities. You can start tomorrow night."

CHAPTER EIGHT

"A male strip club?" Killian groaned as they left Merlin's. "I know, right?" Meredith said. "Hmmm...I wonder why I've never heard of that one?"

"And what would you know about male strip clubs?" Connor asked.

"Um...purely research purposes," she answered quickly.

"Woohoo, I can't believe it! A job that finally calls for my good looks, instead of my stunning intellect," Quinn said, rubbing his hands together. "And all those horny witches stuffing dollar bills down my g-string."

"Uh, I don't think it's that kind of place, Quinn," Meredith deadpanned.

"You're right, Mer," Quinn replied. "Merlin's is too classy. They'll be stuffing at least twenties."

Meredith groaned. She did not want to think about those witches—with a b—shoving dirty bills down Daric's underwear. Whatever possessed the warlock to agree anyway? She glanced over at him and Quinn, who was still obviously psyched about the whole stripping thing.

"C'mon, dude," the Lycan said to the warlock. "Tell me

about these witches—what do they like? Do they prefer their men shaved clean down there or a little bit of hair? Because I can groom if necessary, though I already keep my pubes pretty trimmed."

"Ugh, Quinn, no one wants to hear about your pubes," Meredith groaned, sticking her fingers in her ear.

"You're just jealous of me and my man Daric here, cuz we're getting all the attention tonight."

"Jealous?" Meredith said defensively. "I'm not jealous!"

"Oh yeah, well why are you all red, huh?"

"Ugh, I don't want to talk to you."

———

The ride back to Fenrir took longer than it seemed, at least to Daric. As he sat in the backseat of the vehicle, he could feel the anger rolling off from Meredith. And it seemed to be directed at him.

Confusing woman. He offered to remove his clothes in front of an audience, so that she could find her father's killer. Why was she not more grateful? Of course, he was relieved that Meredith would not be the one stripping that he instantly agreed. The thought of her exposing her luscious body to an audience made something ugly rear up in him. When she left to go to the stage, he convinced her brothers not to let her go through with it, and they were easily swayed. He hoped it was not yet too late, and they were about to stop Meredith when she came back and told them what Merlin's really was. He wasn't judging Merlin. After all, men and women should equally be able to enjoy sex and express themselves.

The other warlock seemed none the wiser when he hired their group. However, Daric was suspicious that Merlin didn't even blink an eye at their little ragtag group. Was Merlin an opportunistic businessman who saw the Lycans as a way to line his pockets or did he suspect more? Daric supposed they were going to find out soon enough.

As Killian parked the car, Meredith reached over Connor's lap, unlocked the door, and quickly scrambled over the giant man to get out of the car. The Lycan gave him a menacing glare before he left the car. It was evident that despite his gruff exterior, Connor had a soft spot for his sister and was overly protective of her.

He followed the Lycans to the elevators. Meredith squeezed herself into the far corner, crossing her arms over her chest and refusing to look at him. Well, perhaps it was a good thing. He and Meredith were like oil and water. Or more like gas and fire. They were explosive whenever they were around each other, and would only leave hurt behind if they ever got together. Never mind that he couldn't escape her delicious scent nor could he take the vision of her stripping—only for him—out of his head. He bet she would be a tease, giving him glimpses of her naked skin, before taking it all off.

The motion of the elevator jolted him out of his reverie as the elevator stopped on the 16th floor.

"I'm going to the gym," Meredith said angrily as she stalked off.

"Jeeze, what's gotten her panties in a twist?" Quinn asked.

Killian sighed. "Who knows?"

Daric said nothing but walked down the hall to his room. He let out a sigh. Against his better judgment, instead of going inside, he pivoted and went in the direction of the gymnasium.

When he got there, Meredith was lying down on the bench, lifting the barbell. She had stripped down to her sports bra and leggings, her boots haphazardly discarded on the floor beside her. Above her, the blonde Lycan man who had been familiar with her during training stood and kept his hands hovering near the bar.

"That's it, Mer," he said, encouraging her. "Three more... two more...one more. Great!" He helped her put the weight set back on the support rack.

Daric stalked over to them, his eyes staring daggers at the other man.

"You're not supposed to be in here," the Lycan said, stepping in front of Meredith.

"The Beta said the training floor was the one place I'm not allowed to go to," he explained.

Meredith grabbed her towel from the rack and wiped her face and chest. "Thanks, Tate," she said gratefully, giving the other Lycan a smile. When her face turned to Daric, however, her smile turned into a frown. "What do you want?"

"It's clear that you are still upset over this morning's visit to the police station. I wanted to see if you were all right," Daric said, then looked over at Tate. "But I suppose you've decided to seek comfort elsewhere."

"Thanks for pretending to care, warlock," she spat. She stood up and took a swig from the water bottle she swiped from the floor. "I'm perfectly fine. I'll see you later, Tate," she said, walking away from the other Lycan.

Daric frowned and then followed Meredith out the door. "You did not seem fine," he countered. "You just left."

"Yeah? Well maybe I didn't want to hear about how you and my brother will be drowning in witch pussy, okay?" she said, gritting her teeth. "But I suppose that's your type, right? Classy, rich, went to college on daddy's dime? Probably thinks the sun shines out of her own ass. Tell me, how do witches and warlocks fuck? With the lights off, under the sheets?"

He felt his anger spike. What was wrong with her? Daric wanted to shake her. "And you prefer vulgar Alpha males who stare at your breasts instead of appreciating your beautiful face, and undress you with their gaze?" he countered. "Maybe you were truly disappointed you didn't get the chance to strip down in front of a room full of men."

"How dare you!" she screamed, lunging at him in anger. He was too quick for her, however, and he grabbed her wrists, then pinned them to the wall. He used his thighs and legs to stop her from kicking at him, but not before she landed a hit on his bruised rib.

"Goddamn it, woman, stop!" he groaned.

"I will if you let me go!"

"I'll let you go if you promise to stop trying to maim me!" He leaned in close, so close he could see the light smattering of freckles on the bridge of her nose and inhale the fragrance of the perfume that drove him wild.

She bit her lip, and as her perfect pearly white teeth sank into her plump lips, all he could think about was kissing her. He shouldn't. But she was so close. Her squirming body felt so good against his, and he could feel his cock responding to her.

"Get off her!" A large hand grabbed his shoulder and pulled her away.

"Christ!" he cursed, ducking away from Connor.

"You keep your hands and your eyes to yourself, warlock," Connor warned.

"Stop it!" Meredith cried. By this time, Killian, Quinn, and even Tate were in the hallway, staring at them.

"What was he doing?" Connor asked.

"None of your business!" Meredith exclaimed.

The giant Lycan turned back to Daric. "You had her pinned up against the wall. What were you doing? Are you trying to fuck her?"

Tate walked over to Meredith, slipping an arm around her shoulders, murmuring soft words into her ear. Jealousy and anger surged through Daric, and he wanted nothing more than to turn every bit of matter in the Lycan's body to dust. "I'd sooner sleep with a mutt." Daric instantly regretted his words, as Meredith's face crumbled and then slipped into a mask of coldness.

"I'm going to my room," she mumbled and then turned to leave.

"Meredith!" Tate called and then followed her, both of them heading back to the barracks.

Daric was so distracted, that he didn't see the massive fist as it connected with his jaw. Connor's fist was like solid rock. No, it was more like solid steel, and Daric reeled back, bracing himself against the wall to stop from falling from the floor. He rubbed his jaw, reveling in the pain. He deserved it and more, for what he said to her.

"You fucking asshole," Killian grabbed him by the collar and slammed his head back into the wall. The three other Lycans stood behind him, and he could feel the anger radiating from all of them.

"I apologize, my words were out of line," Daric said.

"Don't apologize to us," Quinn said, the usually cheerful man's voice edgy and tinged with danger. "Say sorry to her."

"I will," Daric stated in a determined voice. There it was again, that uncomfortable feeling in his gut that wouldn't go away. "But allow me to apologize to you as well, for the slur."

Killian let go of his collar and sighed. "Like I said, it's not us you should be apologizing to. But I doubt Meredith will forgive you easily for that one."

"Why the hell would you say that to her?" Connor said, his anger rising.

"Connor," Killian said, putting a hand up to the other Lycan. "He doesn't know."

"Know what?" Daric asked.

Killian let out a deep sigh. "It's not my place to say, but Meredith told us that when she first shifted into her wolf form in front of her adoptive parents...well, they called her a mutt. That's what they would call her to insult her."

"Fuck!" Daric cursed, running his hands through his hair. "She will never forgive me."

"Just try," Killian encouraged.

"And bring her lots of chocolate. And maybe some Disney Princess movies," Quinn added.

Connor said nothing, but let out a grunt before turning and walking away from them.

"And stop provoking Connor. Meredith is his favorite, and you'll be in for a world of pain if you mess with her," Killian added.

"I'm not provoking him," Daric countered.

"You are by looking at her like that," Killian warned. "Don't even try it, warlock. You hurt her, you answer to all of us."

Daric nodded in understanding but wondered if it was too late.

CHAPTER NINE

Meredith stared at the ceiling, her eyes fixed on a small spot where a bit of paint had chipped off. How long she'd been staring at the spot she wasn't sure, but it was already dark outside. At some point, she had discarded her workout clothes, showered, and slipped into a sleep shirt and shorts.

She felt numb. Daric's words had cut so deep. She knew he was a cruel bastard, but not like this. The pain that slashed through her was so unbearable that she had to shut down. Had to cut herself off from everything before the feelings and memories came back.

You mangy mutt!

Come back here, mutt! You'll do as I say or else!

You better not be sassing me back again, mutt!

Echoes from a long time ago came back to haunt her now and then. Daric's words brought them back to the surface, ringing clear as if she'd just heard them from Jedd and Marie's mouths seconds ago. Did he see her past, when he touched her? Heard the words and used them against her to hurt her? And to think she thought she kinda liked him, especially after he listened and comforted her. Was it all a joke to him? Or a way to get out of here?

Her stomach grumbled loudly. She realized she hadn't eaten since breakfast and a loud gurgling sound made her sit up. "Fine, fine, I'm gonna get something to eat," she said to no one in particular.

Glancing at the clock, she winced at how late it was. At least there probably wouldn't be anyone in the kitchen at this hour.

She got up, slipped on her flip flops, and then walked to the door. She yanked it open and when she tried to walk out, promptly collided with something solid.

Meredith's jaw grew slack when she saw who it was, and she tried to close the door. But, Daric's hand snaked between the door, blocking her so she couldn't shut it. He pushed it open and walked inside.

"Get. Out." She said, turning away from him and crossing her arms over her chest. "I don't want to see you right now. I'm going to talk to Grant tomorrow and tell him that you're not coming with us anymore."

"Meredith," he said with a long sigh. "I'm sorry. My words hurt you, and I apologize. It was uncalled for."

"You bet it was!" she shouted, turning back around to face him. "Did you see them calling me...that word when you touched me? Did you see my past?"

"What are you..." he paused and shook his head. "No, I didn't use your stepparents' words to hurt you. I'm afraid I did all that on my own," he said, his head lowering.

Meredith could hear the sincerity in his voice. Damn him. She didn't want to forgive him. She wanted to hate him so she could stay away from him. So she could stop wanting him.

"I know what I said was unforgivable," he said somberly. "But I hope you'll let me make amends."

"H-how?" she asked, in spite of herself. What she really should be doing was tossing the warlock out of her room.

"Wait," he said and walked back to the door. He picked up a large, brown paper bag he left on the floor. Walking back to Meredith, he handed her the bag.

"What's this?" She peered inside. Curiously, she took out a small, familiar package. "Oh, my God. How did you get all this chocolate? And *The Little Mermaid*?" Her eyes went wide at the green and white DVD box in her hands. "This is my all-time favorite Disney movie!"

"I know," he said with a small smile. "Dr. Cross was nice enough to help me procure these on short notice, even after she gave me a few choice words when I told her why I needed them." He gave a wince. "Do you happen to know why she would call me 'a tap-dancing son of a monkey'?"

Meredith snorted. "Don't worry, Sebastian's rubbing off on her. I'm sure she's going to learn better things to call you." She plopped back on her bed, turning the entire paper bag over, spilling all the contents on her bed. There was a huge pile of chocolate bars, a half dozen Disney DVDs, and two plastic-wrapped sandwiches.

"You didn't come out for dinner," Daric said.

She didn't say anything, but ripped open a candy bar, biting into it. "Thanks," she said, chewing through the nougat and chocolate. "Soooo good."

You know which treat you really want to bite into, her she-wolf said.

I'm so happy eating my chocolate right now that I'm not even mad at you. I'm just going to ignore you while I get my fill of sugar.

"Well, enjoy your evening," Daric said, as he turned away.

"Wait!" she called, waving the chocolate bar in the air. "I mean...have you eaten?"

He gave her a small smile. "Yes, I've had my meal in my room."

"How about dessert?" she said, gesturing to the pile of treats on her bed. She then winced inwardly as she saw a strange look pass over Daric's face. "I mean, chocolate. Obviously."

"I have to confess...I've never seen such a variety of chocolate," he grinned.

"Then come and try some."

Daric walked back and sat on the other edge of her bed, peering at her haul. He picked up one candy bar, opened it and took a bite. "Hmm...not bad."

"Not bad?" she asked in an exasperated voice. "Don't you like chocolate?"

"I'm afraid I don't have much of a sweet tooth," he confessed.

"Fine, more for me!" Meredith said gleefully as she opened another package. "Hmmm....caramel and nuts...my favorite."

As she bit into the bar, she saw him watching her, his gaze dipping down to her lips. Heat rushed through her body, and it was a wonder all the chocolate didn't melt right then and there. Jesus, he looked so sexy, sitting across from her, wearing jeans and a black tank top that showed off his arms.

Grreeeoowwwl. Yum.

Ugh, shut up. She shoved another piece of candy into her mouth, hoping it would quiet the she-wolf.

"Meredith," he began, placing his hands on his lap. "I really am sorry for what I said today. I hope you will forgive me someday."

She sighed. "I've said some bad things to you too, but never that personal."

"I know. Again, I'll apologize however many times you need me to."

"I don't know why...you know it didn't hurt me much when

they called me a...that word. I mean, after a while it was actually getting old," she let out a nervous laugh.

"No child should have to hear such an insult," he commented.

She bit her lip, trying to figure out Daric. He was confusing. One minute he was insulting her and the next he was coming to her, giving her chocolate. Did that saying about Greeks bearing gifts apply to heart-stoppingly handsome Vikings? As she lifted her head up, her eyes clashed with his. She was transfixed as she stared into them. They were like mesmerizing pools of seawater and reminded her of the Caribbean ocean. Blue-green and clear.

"Daric," she whispered softly.

He moved closer, pushing the pile of chocolate and DVDs aside. His fingers touched her jaw, and she closed her eyes, allowing his scent to permeate through her senses. Rich, heady, and a thousand times more delicious than the actual treat she had devoured minutes earlier.

"There is one line we cannot cross," he warned. "And we are getting dangerously close to it."

Her eyes flew open and she held her breath when she saw how close his face was to hers. "You're right," she said, staring at his mouth. "So...totally...right..."

Meredith gasped when his lips touched hers. His kiss was gentle and soft, not at all what she expected. She placed her hands on his hard chest, the skin radiating with heat even through his thin T-shirt. She moved closer to him, climbing onto his lap as she wrapped her arms around his neck, her mouth opening up to him. A moan escaped her mouth as she tasted his tongue, the slightest hint of chocolate there making her melt against him.

She wasn't sure when his kisses became urgent. But before she knew it, she was on her back, and Daric was pushing her knees apart as he settled between her thighs. She wrapped her legs around him, heels digging into his back and she groaned when she felt his rock hard erection dig into her hip. Her panties flooded with wetness, and she eagerly rubbed herself against the ridge of his cock straining through his jeans.

As Daric's warm mouth continued to assault hers, his hand slipped between them. Large fingers skimmed over the wet spot on her panties, rubbing over her pussy lips through the damp fabric. She squirmed against him, pushing her hips up, wanting more.

"Daric," she moaned when he ripped his lips away from hers to travel lower, dragging his stubbly jaw against the soft skin of her neck. She closed her eyes, waiting for him to slip his fingers inside her when suddenly she felt the heavy weight of his body lift off her.

She sat up quickly, breathing heavy as she watched him slink away from her.

"I...I'm sorry," he said quickly. "I shouldn't have done that."

"What?" she asked. "Why?"

"Why?" He looked at her, then stood up. "You know why. This...cannot be."

"It's just sex!" She shot to her feet. "Look, it doesn't have to be this big thing...I'm not looking for that, and I know you aren't either. But you want me, judging by the size of your boner," she pointed out, gesturing to his lap.

"That doesn't mean I'm going to act on it," he reasoned. "Meredith, I truly am sorry for what I said. For everything I said that hurt you, but you and I both know we can't do this."

"Fine," she said angrily. "Get out of my room."

"Meredith—"

"I said get out!" She pointed to the door.

"As you wish," he said with a curt nod before leaving.

Meredith wanted to slam something. Preferably a chair. Into Daric's handsome face. His rejection hurt, sending her she-wolf howling with pain. No, he was right, she told herself. Too many complications. There was an entire sea of complications if they went down that path. She had to focus on the task at hand and Daric would just be a distraction.

With a sigh, she picked up the discarded candy and DVDs, sweeping them back into the paper bag. She couldn't help but feel touched by the gesture, even if Daric was acting like a dickweed right now. God, she threw herself at him. Did she have no shame? She was gorgeous, had a killer body, funny, and had an amazing personality. She could sleep with any guy she wanted, given the chance; she didn't need the attentions of a certain warlock who would just mess up her head and her life.

She plopped back on her bed, considering taking a shower. She should at least change her underwear, as she had sacrificed another pair of panties to the sex gods, thanks to Daric. Rolling over and burying her face on her pillow, she groaned. His scent was sticking to her, and it wasn't just because she had chocolate all over her bed. She should really wash it off, but the scent felt too good on her skin and clothes. God, what was she going to do tomorrow and for the rest of the time she had to work with him?

———

"Meredith!" Archie's voice was strained as he called her attention. "Stop daydreaming and think."

"But I've tried everything!" She stood up and threw the tools on the ground. "This is stupid!" She kicked the heavy old safe, but only succeeded in hurting her toe. She let out a string of curses.

"Meredith needs to put like, twenty bucks in the swear jar!" Quinn laughed.

"Shut up!" She grabbed a wrench and threw it at Quinn, who ducked out of the way. He stuck his tongue out at her.

Killian shot him a warning glare. "You can do it, Mer. We all have to go through it."

Connor gave her a confident nod, and then hit Quinn on the head, which made the younger man cry out in protest.

The old man let out a sigh and walked towards her. "Meredith. You must learn patience. You're young, I understand that, but you must try."

"Why do I gotta learn how to open this stupid old safe! No one uses these anymore!"

"My dear, I'm trying to equip you with all the tools you need to survive. Lock picking, pickpocketing, safe cracking, self defense, your gymnastics training and dance lessons - all of these are tools you may need some day," the old man explained. "What kind of mentor would I be if I let out you into the world without proper training and guidance?"

"But this safe—"

"Is an exercise," he interrupted. "Patience and critical thinking. You can't rush into jobs without a plan and you certainly need to be prepared when things go sideways. Now, go."

Meredith let out a groan. "Fine." She kneeled down in front of the old safe and began to work on the old safe again.

Sweat poured down her face as she tried to remember everything Archie had taught her. She knew the type of safe it was and the model, and based on that, she knew how many numbers there were in the combination. Placing the stethoscope in her ears, she took a deep breath and carefully turned the dial, listening for the soft click that indicated the right number.

Twenty minutes later as the last number clicked into place, the heavy metal door opened.

"I did it!" Meredith said, raising her fists in the air.

"I knew you could do it!" Killian said, rushing over to her. "And you did it faster than Quinn or Connor did."

"Really?" she asked, her face breaking into a wide smile. "But not faster than you?"

"No one is faster than me," Killian teased. "Except Archie."

Archie strode over to them and clapped Meredith on the back. "I'm proud of you, Meredith," he said. "For not giving up. Never give up. There's always a way out of any situation."

CHAPTER TEN

The next day was spent preparing for their operation at Merlin's. Meredith stayed as far away from Daric as possible, barely acknowledging his presence. Not that it was hard because the warlock seemed just as determined to avoid her. If the three Lone Wolves noticed anything, they didn't say.

They came up with the best possible plan on short notice. Connor and Killian were going to stay by the doors to do their job, but at some point, Killian would slip away and try to break into Merlin's office. Connor could take care of the door by himself—after all, how much trouble could a bunch of women be? Meredith would be working the bar, which would give her an excellent view of the entire area. Meanwhile, Daric and Quinn would work the backstage and try to get information from the other dancers.

They arrived at Merlin's late in the afternoon, since the club didn't open until after 9 pm. Merlin explained that since he technically hadn't auditioned Quinn and Daric, they weren't going to go on stage tonight, but instead, would be working a private party in one of the VIP rooms. Meredith didn't know if she was relieved, disappointed, or mad. Although Daric wouldn't be performing in the main room, he would be up close and personal with a couple of witches at some bachelorette party. Based on her (somewhat limited) experience, she knew that would mean more close (but not overly sexual) contact. It was one thing for some little whore witch to stuff bills down Daric's g-string, but another for him to be in close contact in an intimate setting.

As she stood behind the bar, Meredith seethed, thinking of the possibilities and she nearly broke a glass with her grip. She had to stop thinking about Daric; had to swallow the jealousy threatening to show its ugly head. The she-wolf was growling and clawing at her insides, wanting to get out and scratch some witchy eyes out.

"Hey, new girl," the head bartender, Jon, called out. "Don't break the goods, yeah? Anything broken is coming out of your tips."

"Yeah, yeah," she shot back.

They broke for dinner, just before the doors opened. Meredith took two bites of her sandwich and a swig of her soda, but that was all she could manage. Despite her cool and collected exterior, she'd always been nervous before a job, and she didn't want to risk puking all over the bar tonight.

Soon, the doors opened. Killian and Connor stood by the door, checking IDs and purses as they went in. Meredith rolled her eyes as she spied some of the women giving both men appreciative glances (though most looked wary of Connor's size, his scar, and near-permanent scowl.) She could only imagine what Quinn would be like tonight. And then there was Daric. Would he take advantage of his proximity to the women? They were witches, and therefore, not forbidden to him. He obviously wasn't a virgin, and he'd been locked up for weeks without any company. Hot rage and jealousy surged through her again, and she forced it deep down, focusing on the drink orders that were now coming in from the tables and the people standing at the bar.

It had been a while since she'd slung drinks, but it came back to her, the rhythm of taking orders, mixing drinks, and ringing them up. The work was soothing, as it required all her concentration, which meant she didn't have the time to think about Daric. She did, however, keep an eye on the main floor. Merlin and Ivar seemed to never leave, with the warlock stopping from table to table, talking to patrons and laughing with them. He also sent Ivar scrambling around, getting drinks or whatnot for the guests.

Finally, the lights dimmed, and the first performer was up. "Oh boy," Meredith said, her eyes zeroing in on the stage. The fireman bit seemed overdone, but this was New York City, after all. The stripper pulled out all the stops, dressed in a fireman's outfit with a hat, and dragging a hose onstage with him. Of course, he played with the hose, moving it between his legs and the women went wild. Meredith was about to turn away when he started stripping, and then her mouth went dry. The man slipped off his jacket and threw it offstage, revealing a wide chest that was completely hairless but had a well-defined set of pecs and abs. She briefly wondered if she could somehow coax Sebastian into proposing to Jade so that she could have her bachelorette party here. Of course, she'd probably have to bribe or blackmail Sebastian to make him agree.

"Watch out for that one," Jon said as he came up behind her. "James is a big man whore. And he loves hitting on the new girls."

"I'll keep that in mind," she replied, as she began clearing the used glasses on the bar.

The performances continued, and by the time the fourth

guy was on stage, Killian gave her the signal from across the room. *Right, the job.*

She scanned the room and saw Merlin seated at one of the tables, while Ivar stood in the corner, waiting for his boss' next command. She nodded, letting Killian know that the two men were in her sights. Killian said something to Connor and then slipped away. Merlin's office was located in the back room, opposite of the stage. When they went there to sign some papers, they saw that the door had a standard keypad lock, but Quinn was able to hack into the system using his phone and cracked the code. Hopefully, Merlin didn't think to change it before tonight.

They really should have used the in-ear comm units Fenrir used for their ops, but with all the lights, sounds, and electronic systems in the club, it was too much of risk. In any case, Archie had taught his pupils how to communicate without any electronics, since he was so old-school. She was glad they listened to him now.

A few minutes later, Killian came back. He shook his head at her as he came closer. Her brother was probably the best thief in the world right now, but he wasn't that good that it would have only taken eight minutes for him to break in and search the office. That only meant one thing.

"What's wrong?" she asked quietly as he approached the bar. She handed him a glass of water with a slice of lemon. "Did the code not work?"

"The code worked," he said, taking a swig of the water. "But I couldn't get in. There was some sort of invisible barrier." He shook his head. "I've never had to break into a place protected by magic before."

"Damn," she muttered under her breath. Fuck. Magic. They were idiots. Of course, Merlin would use magical protection on his door. They didn't even think of that. Maybe they could ask Lara Chatraine for advice on how to break in. Or Daric would know, right? That's right, he would know. She looked over to Jon.

"Hey, Jon, I'm gonna take my smoke break, okay?"

"Alright, but make it quick," the other man said. "There are two more sets, then there's going to be an intermission. We'll be in the weeds if you're not back by then."

Meredith took off her apron. "Will do!"

"Where are you going?" Killian asked.

"Who else would know about magical barriers?" she asked.

Killian gritted his teeth. "I'll go talk to him."

"No, you've been gone long enough, someone might notice," she reasoned. Meredith pointed with her chin towards the door. "Besides...I think Connor might be needing your help."

"My help?" Killian swung his head over to the door. A group of women had surrounded the Lycan and their ring leader, a curvy brunette, had her hands on her hips and staring him down, despite the fact that she was more than a foot shorter than him. "Christ, I swear, when women get drunk, they're trouble. Fine," he relented. "Talk to the warlock. See if he knows what we can do about the office." He stalked off, heading toward Connor.

Meredith slipped away from the bar, moving discreetly against the wall as she made her way backstage. She followed the same path they took yesterday, down the small hallway in the back, all the way to the dressing room.

She opened the door, but unlike yesterday, the dressing room was not empty. In fact, it was filled, wall-to-wall with hard bodies. Hard, half-naked bodies—nope, wait, a guy in the corner just bent over and stripped his g-string off. Meredith was wearing a short skirt and a tube top that had half her tits spilling out, but she suddenly felt very overdressed.

Meredith squared her shoulders, then slapped a palm over

her eyes as she made her way across the room, hoping no one would notice her as she tried to look for Daric or Quinn.

"Are you lost, babe?"

She stopped in her tracks and slowly turned around. "Uhm, I was looking for someone." She looked up. Aw shit. It was the fireman from earlier. James. He was cute, and had closely-cropped blonde hair and blue eyes, which were staring down at her, eyeing her cleavage. Even if he was hot and had a bangin' body, Meredith felt her skin crawl at the way he looked at her.

"Oh yeah? What are you looking for, babe?"

"Not what, who," she said. "My...er, Quinn and Daric. The new guys."

"Oh," James said in a disappointed tone. "They're still out back in the VIP room. I heard the girls shrieking. Must be having a good time," he said. "But, why don't I take you back there? You can wait for them to come out. Though I'm not sure what time they'll be done. The boss'll want to make sure the women are satisfied."

"Right," Meredith answered. "Lead the way." He gave her a nod and a smile, and then led her out of the dressing room. He turned left, walking down a hallway on the right side of the stage.

Anger, jealousy, and rage must have clouded her judgment because she suddenly had a very bad feeling in the pit of her stomach. "Are you sure we're going the right way?" They were halfway down the hallway, and it didn't seem like it was leading to any of the VIP rooms.

"Oh, I'm pretty sure we're in the right place, babe," James said with a smile that didn't quite reach his eyes. He moved closer to her and trapped her by placing his hands on either side of her head. "You don't need those two. Not when you got me."

"Oh brother," she said aloud and crossed her arms over her chest. "Seriously?"

"Ooooh, you like to play hard to get, babe?" He suddenly grabbed her wrists and pinned them over her head.

Meredith looked almost bored as she contemplated whether to knee him in the nads (effective, but too easy) or if she could squeeze the air from his body by wrapping her thighs around his neck (slow and challenging, but more satisfying to watch as his dumb face went blue).

"Well?"

"I don't play hard to get," she said, an edge to her voice. "But, I suggest you let go of me and show me the VIP room. Now."

James leaned down and whispered in her ear, his hot, disgusting breath on her skin making her scream on the inside. "And why would I do that? Do you want me to tell the boss that you snuck away from the bar to come back here and play hanky panky with the dancers?"

She sighed. If she hurt James, it might blow their cover. "Look, I'm not interested. I was looking for Quinn and Daric."

"They're not done yet, so why don't you just spend a few minutes here with me—Fuck!" James suddenly howled as his head jerked back and his body staggered away from her, releasing her pinned wrists.

"What the hell are you doing?" Daric asked, his large hand wrapped around James' neck.

"She...she wanted it—" He stopped short as the warlock's fist slammed into his jaw, and he fell on the floor, his eyes rolling back.

"What did you do?" she shrieked. "You're going to ruin things for us!"

Daric's eyes flashed in anger, and she could feel the rage rolling off him. She had never seen him so angry, and if he were a Lycan, she was pretty sure her she-wolf would be cowering in fear right now.

"I'm sorry to ruin your fun," he said sarcastically.

"Fun? What do you mean—what are you—" Meredith squealed as Daric bent down and suddenly her world was upside down. "Put me down, you shit head!" The warlock had slung her over his shoulder, her ass up in the air. When she tried to wiggle down and push away from him, he gave her butt cheeks a slap, which shocked her into silence, and if she was honest, aroused her.

Meredith heard the sound of a door opening and then suddenly everything was plunged into darkness. Her feet touched the ground, and she was pushed against the wall. As her enhanced vision adjusted, she realized they were in a storage closet somewhere, based on the various boxes, props, and set pieces piled around them.

"What the fuck is wrong with you?" She tried to move towards the door, but Daric's hands wrapped around her arms and held her in place against the wall.

"If I had known that James' advances were not unwanted, I might have left you alone," he said in a raspy voice.

"You believe that asshole? I didn't want him to touch me! He said he was taking me to the VIP room to see you!" she huffed. "So, did you get your fill of witch poontang? What, a dozen or so screaming girls pawing at you not enough and you were looking for more?"

"Are you jealous?" he asked.

"What? You're an asshole, Daric!" she said, shoving at him again. He caught her wrists and pinned them against the wall on either side of her head. *Oh, God.* When James did that all she could feel was disgust, but when Daric did it...well, there goes another pair of panties sacrificed to the sex gods.

"I think I like seeing you jealous, *min kjære*," he whispered in her ear. "And as for getting my fill..."

Before she knew it, Daric was kneeling in front of her,

pushing her black skirt up to her waist. He yanked her panties aside before touching his wet, hot tongue on her slick pussy lips.

Meredith bit her lip to keep from screaming out. A small cry ripped from her throat, and she realized she kept her hands pinned to the wall, despite the fact that Daric had let go seconds ago. She shoved her fingers into his hair, scraping her short fingernails against his scalp.

Daric let out a small moan against her cunt as his tongue lashed at her. His lips found her hard clit, and he sucked on the bud, making Meredith buck against his face. His large hands encircled her hips and fingers dug into her buttocks as he pushed forward, his tongue doing delicious things to her.

"God...Daric...please...more..."

A ripping sound made her gasp, and she knew he had torn her panties. His left hand moved down her leg, wrapping around her ankle and hoisting it over his shoulder. "Daric!" she cried softly, as he opened her up even more and his tongue teased at her entrance. "I—uh!" She gripped his hair so tight she was scared she'd rip it off his scalp. It was too good. His tongue fucked into her, lapping at her, and tasting her wetness. He nibbled at her lips, then ran his tongue along her slit before plunging back inside her. His other free hand splayed over her lower abdomen and his thumb found its way to her clit, massaging the small bundle of nerves.

It was too much, and she lifted her left leg, hooking it over his shoulder so she could ride his face. Her thighs gripped his head, and she braced herself against the wall for leverage.

"Daric...I..." She closed her eyes and threw her head back as pure whiteness burst from behind her eyelids. She'd never cum harder or faster, and the waves of pleasure continued to wash over her as her orgasm came on. Daric wasn't satisfied, however, as he continued to eat her out, his lips and tongue sending more shockwaves through her body and she gripped him tighter.

Meredith took a deep breath as she finally remembered to breathe. She touched the ground (literally and metaphorically), but she kept her back braced against the wall. Daric stood, pressed his body against hers and captured her mouth in a soft kiss. Holy fucking crackerjacks, she could taste herself on him. It was wild, dirty, and only turned her on more.

She reached down between them, her hand slipping under his jeans and wrapping around his cock. He was hard—and fucking hell—huge. A brief feeling of panic washed through her, one she hadn't felt since before she lost her virginity. Motherfucker, she was glad she was so aroused right now, so they might not need any lube. Her other hand deftly popped his jeans open and took his length out from his briefs.

"Meredith," he whispered her name against her lips. She snapped her teeth at him, giving his lower lips a playful nip, which only made him buck against her hand.

God, she was so ready for this. The tip of his cock brushed against her stomach. He only had to bend down and angle his hips so he could slip into her. Or he could lift her up and fuck her against the wall.

He groaned and dug his fingers into her hips, pulling her closer. His hands wrapped around hers, guiding his cock lower.

She held her breath. So close and—

Meredith froze. Her keen hearing picked something up from the outside. Shouts, screams, tables and chairs turning over. And Killian's voice, calling for her.

"Goddamnit!" she hissed, pulling away from Daric and pushing her skirt down over her hips. "We gotta go. Shit's going down outside." She quickly sidestepped around him and yanked the door open.

He lagged behind her, but she couldn't stop and wait for him. She didn't have the strength to say no if he dragged her back into the storage closet. She picked up her pace when she heard him lumbering behind her.

There was commotion outside in the main room. A couple of the tables had been overturned, and a few of the patrons had scrambled to the side.

"Come with me," Ivar said as he walked over to them. "Your friends are waiting for you."

"What have you done to them?" Meredith asked, her hands grabbing Ivar's jacket collar. "I swear, if you've hurt them..."

"Relax, she-wolf," Ivar said, wrenching away from her. "They're fine. Just a little confused."

They followed Ivar to the back, all the way to Merlin's office. He punched in the code and walked inside, the magical barrier obviously lifted.

The three Lone Wolves were sprawled all over the office. Killian was sitting in one of the armchairs, his hands rubbing his head. Quinn was occupying most of the couch in one corner, while Connor was on the floor, his large body spread out. Merlin sat in his chair behind the desk, a scowl on his handsome face.

"What have you done to them?" Meredith growled as she stalked over the warlock.

Merlin stood up, and Meredith suddenly felt the power emanating from him. She stopped short and looked back at Daric. He must have felt it, too, because his brows were drawn together in confusion.

"Tsk tsk, she-wolf. They'll be fine, just a bit of confounding potion to stop them from tearing my club apart," Merlin drawled. "What kind of place do you think this is, anyway? You Lycans are such brutes, I swear. Ivar," he called to his assistant. "I should have listened to you. They've brought me nothing but trouble."

"I told you, boss," Ivar admonished.

"I suppose my curiosity got the best of me," Merlin sighed. "Take a seat, she-wolf," he said, gesturing to the chair opposite Killian.

"What did you do to them?"

"What did I do to them?" Merlin exclaimed. "That one," he pointed to Quinn, "chased down one of my best dancers! Do you know how much money Sven rakes in? I told you the Viking look was hot! He was human, too, which meant he didn't cause a lot of trouble." The warlock shook his head. "Anyway, in the middle of intermission, I see Sven tearing out from the backstage and that oaf—in full wolf form—hot on his heels. Then those two," he gestured to Connor and Killian, "grab Sven and tried to take him down. I got there just in time to throw the confounding potion on them to knock them out. And now poor Sven's gone."

"You chased him down? Why?" Meredith asked Quinn, but the other Lycan didn't answer, except to let out a pained moan.

"While your friends are recovering, perhaps you'd care to tell me what four Lone Wolves are doing in New York, traveling with a warlock? Does the Alpha know you're in his territory?"

"You know the Alpha?" Meredith asked.

Merlin laughed. "Of course. I may not be bound by your society's ridiculous territorial rules, but I'm smart enough to know that it's better to keep Grant Anderson as a friend instead of foe. Well, not friends, strictly speaking," he clarified. "But, he's well informed of my activities and knows I'm just a humble businessman, trying to eke out a living."

Meredith snorted at his words. "Right. So, why did you hire us?"

"Really, I'm explaining myself to you first?"

Meredith shrugged. "If you want to know why we're here."

"Fine," Merlin huffed. "Like I said, curiosity. And, it seems witches and Lycans are slowly getting along, I thought I'd expand my clientele. Thought it would be good for business. Now, tell me what you're doing at my club? And I know you weren't looking to make some cash. That one," he motioned to Killian, "tried to break in here."

"We just wanted some information." Meredith explained to Merlin what had happened to Archie and how they found the card.

"That was it? Why didn't you ask me?"

A groan came from Quinn. "Ask you? That was all we had to do?"

"Well, if you were just regular Joes off the street, of course, I wouldn't tell you anything. But, if you are working for Grant Anderson, all you needed to do was ask. Nothing would make me happier than having the Alpha of New York owing me a favor."

"Well, can you give us the information now?" Meredith asked. "I'll let Grant know, of course."

Merlin paused. "Fine. Give me the card and Archie's photo."

Killian, who managed to sit upright, handed Merlin his phone and the card they got with Archie's things.

"Hmm..." Merlin examined the card. "This is just our standard calling card. Only witches and warlocks can see it, but it was also enchanted with a spell so a particular person could read the address." He looked over at Daric. "I suppose that's why you have the warlock. He was the one that led you here."

"Can you tell if it was enchanted for Archie?"

The warlock shook his head. "I'm afraid not. There are traces of the spell, but only the witch or warlock who cast it would know who it was intended for. However," he continued, looking at the photo on Killian's phone. "Ivar," he called. "Take a look at this. Is this the man from last Wednesday night?"

The other man walked to Merlin's desk and stared at the photo. "Yeah, that's him."

"So, he was here? You saw him?" Meredith stood up and slammed her palms on the desk. "Tell me, who did he meet? What did they say? Did they leave together?"

"Calm down, she-wolf," Merlin ordered. "Ivar and I noticed him immediately. Wednesdays are our biggest weeknight. Witchy Wednesdays, we call it, and this place is packed with witches since we offer some great deals on drinks and private shows. So, when an older human gentleman shows up, he stuck out like a sore thumb. But, you know, we don't judge here, whatever floats your boat," Merlin shrugged.

"Did he talk to anyone?"

Merlin and Ivar looked at each other. "Yes, he did. He met with another individual. They sat down to talk in one of the corner booths."

"Who?" Meredith asked.

"See...that's the other thing that made your father's presence memorable. This person that he met with stayed in the shadows and as far as we could tell, heavily glamoured."

"Glamoured?" Meredith echoed.

"He means the person was using a glamour spell to take on the appearance of another," Daric supplied. Meredith jumped in surprise, not realizing that he was standing behind her.

"That's right," Merlin confirmed. So, even if we did have a photo or video of him, you'd be seeing a totally different face. He could look like Ryan Reynolds or Penelope Cruz or Colonel Sanders."

Quinn let out a groan and stood up, though he was still disoriented as he swayed from side to side. He sank back down on the couch and covered his eyes with his arm. "The guy," he began. "Sven..."

"Why did you chase him down?" Killian asked.

"I asked him about Archie. The same questions we'd been asking everyone. Then he starts getting antsy, and I could smell the sweat and nervousness coming off him. Before I knew it, he pushed me aside and ran. And so, I shifted and chased after him."

"Do you think he killed Archie?" Killian asked.

"Maybe."

Merlin shook his head. "This Archie...you said he was killed that same night? Do you know what time?"

"The Detective put his death around midnight," Killian supplied.

"Sven was sweet," Merlin said. "A little naive, I would say. I can't imagine him killing anyone."

"Then why did he run?" Killian challenged.

Merlin shrugged. "Look, I'm sorry about your father. I'll do what I can to help if you put in a good word with the Alpha for me."

"Done," Meredith agreed with a nod.

"Excellent. We'll go and track down Sven, he's probably at home, the poor thing. The way he tore out of here, looked like you spooked him good," Merlin said. "Sven only started...what... a month ago?" Ivar nodded. "I don't think he has a lot of friends. He was kind of quiet and kept to himself. I think he said his aunt was a witch back in Canada or something, which is why he knew about us. Give your contact details to Ivar, and we'll call you, but not until after we talk to him. I want to reassure him that you're not trying to hurt him."

"Thank you," Killian said. "Any chance you got something to take this headache away?"

Merlin laughed. "Just be glad you're Lycans, and you have enhanced metabolisms. If you were human, you'd all be in the hospital by now."

CHAPTER ELEVEN

"Meredith, this is the reason you asked me to come in early today?" Jade said, placing her hands on her hips.

"It's important," the other Lycan retorted. It was the day after the strip club incident, and Meredith was sitting on one of the tables in Jade's office, her legs swinging back and forth.

The Lycan had found a way to send Jade a message from the computer in the common room (she was still banned from having her own personal electronics) and asked that the scientist come in early before she had to bring Daric in. She sent the email on high priority, with subject EMERGENCY and programmed it to send three times every fifteen minutes. When Meredith got a reply from Jade at three in the morning telling her that yes, she'd meet her at the lab at 8 a.m. if she would please stop bombing her inbox, she turned the computer off and went to bed.

As soon as Jade (grumpily) walked into the lab, Meredith shoved a giant cup of coffee in her hands and proceeded to tell the Lycan scientist what happened the night before. In full, descriptive detail. With reenactments.

"You like coming in early, anyway!"

"Not to hear about your sex life!" Jade said in an exasperated voice.

"We did not have sex," Meredith pouted. "I told you, he only licked my—"

Jade stuck her fingers in her ears. "I don't want to hear it again, please. Once was enough to scar me for life."

"Fine." Meredith rolled her eyes. "We didn't..." She held up one hand and formed the fingers into a circle, then pushed her index finger into the hole in and out several times. "He only..." She then made a V with her pointer and middle fingers and stuck her tongue between them.

"Eww, please don't do that again," Jade gagged.

"How am I supposed to tell you about what we did, then?" Meredith asked in an exasperated voice. "Shadow puppets? Sky writing?"

"How about you don't give me any more details? Stick to general information," Jade groaned. "Oh, and by the way, *supposed* best friend of mine. You neglected to tell me about the death of your father *and* the fact that you have three brothers. How are you taking this?"

"I'm fine!" Meredith assured her. She hadn't seen Jade since her brothers arrived in New York. Grant said he'd be the one to tell Jade that she and Daric wouldn't be in the lab for a few days. "Not like you thought to ask about me anyway," she grumbled.

Jade hopped on the desk next to her and put an arm around Meredith's shoulders. "I'm sorry, Meredith. I got caught up with work and Sebastian and the baby. We're going to have the loft renovated and have a couple rooms put in. Actually..." she smiled at the other Lycan. "I was hoping maybe you could have your own room in there with us. You'll have a little apartment, actually, on a separate floor. Maybe someday, the Alpha will let you move out of here, and you can have a little home away from Fenrir."

"Really?" Meredith's eyes widened.

"Of course! Besides, I know Aunty Meredith's going to be the best babysitter ever!"

"Just as long as little Meredith doesn't decide to set my hair on fire when I tell her she can't have that cookie!"

Jade laughed. "Well, according to Dr. Faulkner, there's little chance the baby will be a dragon shifter. Although Sebastian has a dragon inside him, his fundamental DNA hasn't changed. We're going to run tests and map out—"

Meredith placed a hand over the other Lycan's mouth. "Blah blah, science word vomit. Let's get back to my problem!"

"And what is the problem exactly?"

"That Daric is confusing, stubborn, sexy, and sending me mixed signals!"

"Don't forget the part about him being a warlock who was, until recently, an ally to our greatest enemy who had me kidnapped, tried to get my True Mate under his control, threatened my unborn child, attempted to kill our other best friend's husband, had the Alpha kidnapped—"

"I get it, I get it," Meredith groaned as she hopped off the table. "I can't resist bad boys, what can I say?"

"This isn't some romance novel where you're the girl next door who gets mixed up with the leader of a motorcycle club!"

"I know—what are you saying? You sound like you know what you're talking about with the romance novels," Meredith said with a raised brow.

"Ugh! You're not listening to me," Jade said. "Or rather, you only hear what you want to hear. Really, Meredith? Out of all the hot men around here, he's the one you want?"

Her inner she-wolf was bobbing its head up and down, tail wagging. *Yes, please*, the she-wolf growled happily. Ugh, it was bad enough her inner wolf was batshit crazy over Daric; she just wished her little hussy of a body (i.e. her vajayjay) didn't want him so bad.

"You really are mental," Jade said.

"Oh my God, you're the one sleeping with a fire hazard, and I'm mental?"

"But Sebastian's not evil," Jade protested.

"But Daric's not evil, either," Meredith retorted. "I mean, he's on our side now...right? Kind of?"

The scientist shook her head. "I still can't believe you want to sleep with him."

"I didn't say I was going to go through with it." The she-wolf growled in protest. "I mean, c'mon. Just look at him? Wouldn't you want to climb him like a tree?"

"I would not," Jade exclaimed. "And I already have Sebastian."

"What if he was dead?"

Jade's eyes suddenly began to glow, and the air became thick.

"For crying out loud, Jade," Meredith said. "I didn't say I was going to kill your mate."

"But you said—"

"Fiiiinnnnnnnne," the blonde Lycan said in defeat. "What if Sebastian were...turned into a llama?"

"A llama?"

"Yeah. If Sebastian turned into a llama, and he couldn't, you know, perform. Because it would be weird."

Jade sighed. "Fine. Sebastian's a llama and then?"

"Well, if you had Daric or someone like him come up to you, wouldn't you want to sleep with them?"

"No."

Meredith threw her hands up in frustration. "I swear, I can't talk to you about these things. When does Lara come back?"

"Maybe we need to come up with an Operation: PTC for you," Jade sighed, referring to Operation: Pop That Cherry, Meredith's original plan to help her get rid of her virginity.

"Pshaw, it's been a long time since I punched my V-card." Meredith frowned. "Say, you're a doctor, right? Medically speaking, if I haven't had sex in like, years, does it come back?"

Jade rolled her eyes. "No, it does not. But let's get back to the task at hand."

"You mean, Operation: Get Meredith Laid?"

"I mean, Operation: Get Meredith Laid But Not To A Possibly Evil Warlock Who Could Betray Us," Jade retorted.

"Operation: GMLBNTAPEWWCBU? Doesn't quite have the same ring to it." Meredith supposed Jade was right. Maybe all she needed was a good fuck, from any man. The she-wolf, of course, howled in anger. The little bitch just wouldn't let up. Satan's tits, it was the wolf's fault she was in trouble.

The sound of a knock on the door interrupted them.

"Come in!" Jade called.

"Dr. Cross?" Daric called as he opened the door. "I'm here for our session." The warlock suddenly froze when his eyes landed on Meredith. "I didn't know you were already here. Alynna told me that someone else would be bringing me here, I thought you were unwell."

"Did you have a late night?" Jade snickered.

"We did not come home until midnight and..." he drifted off and narrowed his eyes at Meredith. "You told her about last night, woman?"

"Duh, she's my best friend. Of course, I told her about..." Meredith did the gesture with her fingers and her tongue.

"Trust me, I didn't need to hear it," Jade said, slapping her hand over her forehead. "Or watch the reenactments."

"How could you give her such intimate details?" Daric roared, stepping closer to them.

"Well, what was I supposed to do? Just forget everything?" Meredith challenged, crossing her arms over her chest. "Little chance of that happening, buddy. Not when I have the beard burns on my thighs to prove it."

"Lalalala...I'm getting out of here..." Jade sing-songed, sticking her fingers in her ears and walking out of the lab, the door slamming behind her.

———

"You just had to make things awkward, didn't you?" Meredith's amber color eyes stared up at him brazenly, her bizarre statement ringing in Daric's ears, but not making any sense.

The damn Lycan was infuriating. And wildly inappropriate. And beautiful. And Daric could still taste her in his mouth and remember how the sweet honey flowed from her delicious, greedy little cunt and onto his tongue.

"Well?" she asked, her gaze never leaving him.

He had surely gone insane. Whatever possessed him to take Meredith into the closet and go down on her? It was that other dancer, James, of course. He and Quinn had just finished "entertaining" the ladies in the VIP room. It was mostly serving them drinks, and doing small talk, though Quinn was eager to show off his dance moves. He was glad the Lycan was more than happy to do most of the job. Perhaps many of the witches were fascinated at being in such close contact with a Lycan, since the two groups rarely mixed. Daric, on the other hand, mostly stood on the sidelines.

As they walked into the dressing room, he heard the other men talk about how James was "going to score with that hot new Lycan bartender." He saw red, and rage filled his veins. There was only one place James could have taken her—the hallway that led to the alley outside where all the dancers would take their smoke breaks. He hoped he wasn't too late, for what, Daric wasn't sure, but all he knew was he needed to see Meredith.

Seeing her pinned up against the wall by that vain idiot, however, was not what he had in mind and instantly, he wished he could take James to the far reaches of Antarctica and leave him there. He satisfied himself with taking the man down, especially when he implied Meredith had wanted him. Daric knew that wasn't true, but he wanted to make sure anyway, by finding out if Meredith wanted him as much as he wanted her. They came so close to having sex in that closet, and even now his cock was beginning to respond, not just to the memories, but also to Meredith in front of him, her breasts heaving against her black tank top that showed off her creamy skin.

He let out a sigh. "I'm not the one who made things awkward with Dr. Cross. Why would you discuss such intimacies with her? Would you like it if I told your brothers?"

"Eww, gross! And that's different," she reasoned. "And Connor would pound your face in. In his mind, I'm still his virginal little sister."

"Obviously, I'm not well-versed in female relationships," he said. "But, you need to stop discussing such things with other people."

"I'm not taking out an ad in the New York Times," she said in an exasperated voice. "Did you want to forget last night happened? Is that it?"

Before he could answer, thundering footsteps going up the staircase to the inner lab caught their attention. Daric sighed inwardly in relief, not quite ready to answer her question. For both their sakes, they should forget what happened last night. But his cock had other ideas, and he shifted uncomfortably.

"Meredith, are you in here?" Quinn's face popped in through the door.

"Quinn? How did you get here?" Meredith asked, frowning.

"We got that Alynna chick to take us here. By the way, your scientist best friend is hot!" Quinn said with a grin. "I'm digging the naughty librarian look. She just needs the glasses."

"And I'll be digging the way you'll look burned to a crisp," Meredith retorted, rolling her eyes. "So, what's up?"

"We just got a call from Merlin," her brother said in a sober voice. "They found Sven. He's in the hospital."

Daric felt a strange sensation, like his gut instinct telling him something important was about to happen. "We should go see him now."

CHAPTER TWELVE

The New York Downtown Hospital was unusually busy for a weekday morning. The three Lone Wolves, Meredith, and Daric walked right in without anyone stopping them. They made their way to the elevator and Killian pressed the button for the eleventh floor. "Merlin said he's in 113A."

As soon as they reached the floor, they filed out, following the directions posted on the walls to the right room. Quietly, Meredith opened the door, walking in first into the near-empty semi-private room. Two of the sections had their curtains drawn, and after peeking behind the first one and seeing an older woman sleeping, she signaled to the rest that Sven was in the other bed.

They approached the bed at the end, carefully slipping between the drawn curtains. A blonde man, probably in his late twenties, was lying very still on the bed. His face was covered in bruises, and a tube was stuck down his throat.

"Looks like he was nearly beaten to death," Quinn said as he looked over the chart at the foot of the bed.

"What else do we know?" Meredith asked.

"Not much," Killian said. "Apparently, Sven had no other relatives or friends in New York. They called Merlin's because he had the phone number written down on a piece of paper in his wallet."

Daric's eyes narrowed at the young man. Something about him seemed familiar, but he couldn't say where he had met or seen the man before. He surely would have remembered, though with his face in his current state, who knows what Sven really looked like?

"Daric?" Meredith asked, a concerned look on his face. "Are you all right?"

"Something about him..." he trailed off but moved closer to the man. "I need to know."

"Know what?" Killian asked.

He paid the Lycan no mind, but instead, took a deep breath and placed his hands on Sven's arm. Instantly, a jolt of energy rushed through him, and the visions filled his head. Tall cliffs. Greenery. Clear water. Wildflowers on a hill. Suddenly the vision changed. An older man in a hat, falling fast. Another man, dark haired, pushing him off the side of a building. And then blood everywhere.

Daric let go of Sven, staggering back.

"Daric!" Meredith cried as she grabbed onto his shirt. Connor gripped his shoulders to steady him.

"What did you see in your vision?" Meredith asked. "Was it Archie?"

He grew quiet but nodded. The first vision was strangely familiar, like a place he had been to before, but it was from a different perspective. That vision felt like it was all Sven's, rather a memory. The second one, however, was different. That was not the man's memory. It was one that was shared or sent to him, and the feel and colors of that particular vision were not only familiar but also known to Daric. "Let's go back to Fenrir," he declared. "We have much to discuss with the Alpha."

"Hold on, you can see the future?" Killian asked. "Did you see who killed Archie?"

"Not quite," he said and explained to the three Lone Wolves about his seer powers.

"The man in the hat," Quinn frowned.

"That was Archie," Connor supplied.

"Possibly," Daric said. "I didn't see the dark-haired man's face, but I know someone who might."

"Who?"

"My mother. It was her vision, which somehow ended up in this man's head."

———

As they drove back to Fenrir, Killian called Grant and explained what happened. After getting clearance from Jared, Grant's admin, they were able to take the private elevators to the penthouse executive level of the Fenrir Corp headquarters. Once there, they headed straight to the Alpha's office, where Grant, Nick, Alynna, and Alex were already waiting for them.

"So, this Sven," Grant said after they arrived. "He's somehow connected to Archie's killer, and to your mother, Daric?"

The warlock shrugged. "It seems like a coincidence."

"I don't believe in coincidences," Alynna interjected.

"Neither do I," Daric agreed. "Which is why I need to talk to Signe, she's the only one who can shed light on the situation."

"I've spoken with Vivianne Chatraine, the leader of the New York Coven. Unfortunately, she won't allow three Lone Wolves, especially ones unfamiliar to her, into their compound."

"Will Signe come here?" Killian asked.

Grant shook his head. "She refuses to leave and wants Daric to come to her."

"Then how are we supposed to see her?" Meredith asked.

"Daric should go to the compound," Alynna said.

"Meredith can drive him there," Alex suggested.

"What?" The blonde Lycan looked from Alex to Alynna to Daric.

"It makes sense," Grant said. "You're friends with Vivianne's daughter, and she already knows you. I'm sure she'd be willing to give you permission to come along. Daric, does that sound good?"

"If I can see my mother, of course, Alpha," Daric agreed.

"Wait, you're just going to let us go on a road trip?" Meredith looked at the four Lycans suspiciously.

"I think you've proven yourself trustworthy and you'd still be in New York Territory," Nick said, making Meredith's jaw drop in shock. "Besides, you know you can't really get away from us," the Beta remarked, eyeing the ever-present tracker on her ankle.

"It's only three hours one way," Alynna added. "If you leave early in the morning, you can be back by midnight. You'll even have time for a leisurely lunch and maybe a quick dinner stop."

"It's settled, then," Grant said. "Take one of the cars and drive up to the coven compound. Talk to your mother and find out about the visions. If Archie's death is connected to Stefan, then this is our best chance of finding out how."

CHAPTER THIRTEEN

"Did you manage to get him, Victoria?" Stefan asked. "I told you this was an important job."

"He will not be able to talk, Master," Victoria assured him. "Our men made sure of that."

"But he's still alive?"

"I—I'm afraid so." Victoria bowed her head. "They said that the police came and they were spooked. But don't worry, I'll personally see that he will not live to see another day. Who is he, anyway?"

Stefan rubbed his chin, and his eyes narrowed into thin slits. "I'm not sure, but our ally said that we had to get rid of him. The man was following him and had witnessed something important."

"Did he say what?"

"I can only guess," Stefan pondered. "Wait. Is there more?"

"The place where he worked, it was a place where witches frequented. Merlin's. And apparently, a couple of Lycans had paid a visit as well."

"What?" Stefan asked. "Were they after the man, too?"

"We don't know," Victoria confessed. "We will keep an eye on him. If the Lycans show up again, we'll know."

CHAPTER FOURTEEN

Meredith supposed that she was lucky this was only a day trip. It wasn't like this was a big vacation or road trip. This was a job, the last job she would be doing for Archie and the most important one.

It felt weird, being in the car with just Daric. Thank God for music streaming services, and she could at least listen to the radio at full blast as they sped down the highway. Whether Daric was disturbed that her road trip playlist included songs like *Highway to Hell*, *Airbag*, and *Killer Crash*, she didn't know. The warlock hadn't said more than a few words since they left Manhattan over three hours ago. Instead, he stared out the window, his face a neutral mask.

"I think we're almost there," Meredith declared as they entered the town of Little Water, New York. After driving through the town, they followed the back country road for another 15 miles. They almost missed the turnoff that would lead them to the compound if Daric had not pointed it out.

By the time they entered, two figures were waiting for them. One was an older, redheaded woman and the other was a tall, burly man wearing a plaid shirt.

"Welcome, Meredith, Daric," Vivianne Chatraine, leader of the New York coven, greeted as they exited the SUV. "How was the trip?"

"Long," Meredith said with a sigh.

"Well, you'll be happy to know, we have lunch ready," the older woman said with a grin. "Hello, Daric."

The warlock stopped short, his eyes flickering in surprise. Intense blue-green eyes scrutinized Vivianne, and then he shook his head. "Forgive me for being rude," he said with an apologetic bow.

Vivianne shook her head. "Don't worry about it, Daric. I'm sure it's shocking to see me, especially since Victoria and I are twins."

"But they're nothing alike," the large man beside her said in a gruff voice.

"Oh, I'm sorry for being rude," Vivianne laughed. "This is my husband, Graham Chatraine."

Graham eyed Daric suspiciously but gave the other warlock a nod.

"Wow, this is Mr. C?" Meredith exclaimed. "But you..." she looked at Vivianne and back again at Graham. The witch had always seemed so classy and worldly. Meredith often joked with Lara that she wanted to be Vivianne when she grew up. And Graham? Well, with his white beard, he looked like Santa Clause, if Santa hit the gym every day the rest of the year when he wasn't delivering presents. He was over 6 feet tall and had wide shoulders with thickly muscled arms straining under his shirt.

The witch chuckled. "I know, I know. But trust me," she said, giving Meredith a wink. "It works." She turned back to Daric. "I'm sure you're eager to see your mother. She's been anxious and has been waiting for you. She's back at the house."

"Thank you again, for helping her," Daric said. "For that I owe you."

"We always help those in need," Vivianne said. "You know that, Daric. You're a warlock after all. Now, let's go to our house."

Although Vivianne was chatting with Meredith, she only half-listened as she tried to sneak glances at the warlock. Daric remained quiet as they walked to the house at the end of the compound. What was he feeling right now? Anxious? Nervous? It had been years since he'd seen his mother, so she could only imagine.

They entered Vivianne and Graham's house and went straight into the kitchen. Next to the stove was a tall, but slight woman, stirring a steaming pot of what smelled like seafood soup. She had delicate, elfin features, and her closely-cropped blonde hair only made her look more pixie-like. As she turned to the newcomers, her blue-green eyes widened and filled with tears, and Meredith knew this was Signe.

Signe dropped the spoon on the floor and then rushed over to Daric, embracing him in a tight hug. The warlock wrapped his arms around her, soothing her back as her frail body wracked with sobs.

"Oh, forgive me, I'm sorry," Signe hiccuped as she disentangled herself from Daric. "I'm just overcome with emotion."

"Yeah, someone's been cutting onions around here," Meredith said as she discreetly tried to wipe the tears from the corner of her eyes.

Signe's gaze landed on the Lycan, her eyes scrutinizing Meredith. "Daric, who is your...friend?"

"Mother, this is Meredith," Daric introduced. "She drove me here."

Meredith bit her lip and balled her hands into fists to stop herself from smacking his stupid face. "Right. I'm the driver," she said with only a hint of sarcasm in her voice. "Nice to meet you, ma'am." She held out her hand, but Signe embraced her instead. Meredith was taken aback by the gesture, and she stood in the older woman's arms awkwardly but sank into the hug after a few seconds.

"Thank God you're finally here," Signe gasped, then shook her head. "I mean, thank you for bringing him here. For," she looked at Daric, "driving my son here."

"No problem," she murmured. "Just doing my job, ma'am."

"Call me Signe," she said. She walked back to the stove and picked up the dropped spoon. "I'm so clumsy; please forgive me. I wanted to make some *fiskesuppe* for Daric. It was his favorite when he was a child."

"I remember," Daric commented.

"Graham was kind enough to go fishing this morning, so it's quite fresh."

"I've also been making a pot roast and other fixings," Graham added. "We can eat in five minutes."

"Will you help me set the table, Meredith?" Vivianne asked, and the Lycan nodded.

After everything had been set up, they all sat around the large kitchen table for lunch. Meredith had a bit of Signe's fish soup, which frankly wasn't her kind of thing, but she politely finished her small bowl. She was more of a meat-and-potatoes kind of gal, so she was glad Graham had made pot roast, mashed potatoes, and green beans. Yummy...Vivianne Chatraine was a lucky woman because the food Graham made was better than sex.

"Uh, thank you?" Graham answered in a puzzled voice.

"And yes," Vivianne said, flashing her husband a naughty smile. "I am lucky."

"Oh fuck-nuts, I said that out loud, didn't I?" Meredith slapped her palm over her mouth. "Sorry."

Daric gave her a disapproving look.

Oh God, Meredith thought. *I'm such an idiot. And Signe must think I'm a trashy, foul-mouthed ho.* She wasn't sure why she needed the witch's approval, but Signe having a good opinion of her felt important.

"So, Daric," Vivianne said, quickly changing the subject. "You really can't stay overnight? I assure you you're very welcome as long as Signe is here. She's staying in one of the empty cottages, so there's plenty of room for you and Meredith."

The warlock shook his head. "Thank you for your offer, but the Alpha wanted us back in New York right away."

"It does seem unusual, you two traveling alone." Vivianne looked to Meredith. "I hope you understand about me not allowing your brothers to come here. I have to protect my coven, too."

"No worries. I'm just glad I can drive Daric here," she said sweetly while giving the warlock the side-eye.

"Thank you again. I'm so happy he's found you," Signe said, then quickly cleared her throat. "I mean, I'm so happy he's found someone to bring him here."

"Uh, you're welcome." At least Signe was grateful. Maybe the witch didn't hate her.

"Now," Graham began as he stood up. "I have dessert. Chocolate cake and coffee?"

"Yes, please," Meredith said eagerly. "I love chocolate."

"That she does," Daric replied, which earned him a dirty look from the Lycan.

"I'm fine, thank you, Graham," Signe said. "If you really must leave, then perhaps we should spend some time together? We can take a walk in the woods out back. You probably will want to leave for New York before it gets too dark."

"Yes, excellent idea." Daric stood up. "Vivianne, Graham, thank you for your hospitality and the meal. We will be back in a few hours." He helped his mother out of her chair and led her out of the house through the back door.

Meredith remained seated, unaware she had a scowl on her face until Graham placed a plate with a large slice of chocolate cake in front of her. "This should help," he said gruffly.

"Uh, thanks..." She took bite. "Oh. My. God. This is the best chocolate cake I've had. If you weren't married already..."

Vivianne laughed. "Sorry dear," she said, patting the younger woman's hand. "You're gonna have to find one of your own."

"Ew, no," Meredith grumbled through another mouthful of cake. She swallowed and took a gulp of water. "I'm never getting married."

The witch sighed. "That's what they all say."

"What do you mean?"

"Oh, nothing. Would you like another slice?"

———

Daric followed Signe as she led them down a path to the woods behind the Chatraine home. The leaves on the trees were already beginning to turn, and there was that crisp and cool feeling in the air that signaled the beginning of autumn.

They didn't speak at first, merely enjoying each other's company. Daric had so many questions in his mind he wanted to ask her but feared bringing up the memories of her captivity.

Finally, Signe spoke. "I'm fine, Daric, you can talk," she said as if reading his mind. "Being here, surrounded by other witches, has been good for me. You can relax."

"I can't, Mother," he said, gritting his teeth. "Not while he is still out there. He must pay for what he's done to you. You were his prisoner for eighteen years."

"And so were you," she said, linking her arm with his. "Don't forget, you were also a captive. Not locked up behind bars or with chains, but still a prisoner."

"Yet I did unspeakable things," he said with a frown. "If you only knew—"

"Shhhh," she protested. "You are now working towards redeeming yourself, and I know you will. I have seen it."

"What else have you seen, Mother?"

Signe looked at him cryptically. "I cannot tell you, but there are other things we should talk about. Like, why you are here."

"Yes," he nodded. "The Alpha has told you?"

"He explained it somewhat. But, it's best if you show me what you saw."

Daric stopped and turned to his mother, taking her hand. He closed his eyes, feeling the link between them. He searched his memories, finding the vision from Sven, sending it to her through their connection.

Signe gasped, and her eyes flew open. "These were all the visions from the boy? Sven, you said? Is he hurt?"

He nodded. "Yes. He's alive, thank God, and recovering in the hospital. Do you recognize anything?"

The older witch grew pale, and she nodded. "The first one, it reminded me of our village. But, from a different perspective. One I'd never seen before. It's like watching a familiar place through someone else's eyes."

"Exactly," Daric agreed. "And the second? It is your vision, right?"

"Yes," she confirmed. "It was indeed my vision. I had it just before I was released. Daric," she said, her voice trembling. "That vision was for you. I mean...I can't go into detail, but it was important for you to see it." She took his hands in hers. "I couldn't use our link, knowing that Stefan would see it, too, so I thought I'd cast a wider net."

"What do you mean?"

"I thought, if you and I were the only seers in the world, if I sent out the vision, then you would eventually pick it up. I kept trying and trying until Stefan came to bring me to you."

Daric frowned, and then he realized what his mother was saying. "I didn't, but I suppose this Sven did. How? He is human."

Signe shrugged. "I don't know, Daric. Perhaps he was meant to see it. Maybe he is connected to us in some way."

"We have lost all other connection with the larger world," Daric pointed out. "We have only each other now, Mother."

The witch smiled sadly. "Yes. Our village is long gone, I've seen it in my mind. I guess not many young people want to fish or hunt these days."

Daric laughed. "Yes. They prefer the convenience of the modern world."

"So," Signe continued. "The man in the hat, you know him?"

"Not personally, but he was Meredith's adoptive father, and I'm helping her and her brothers find who killed him. It's starting to look like Stefan may have had something to do with his death as well."

Signe looped her arms through her son's and then tugged at him. "Let's continue our walk since it's such a lovely day."

They went deeper into the woods, where it grew even more still and quiet. This place was special. Daric could feel the magic surrounding them. It was a subtle presence that hung in the air. The feeling was refreshing, something he hadn't felt since he was a child.

"Now," Signe began. "Tell me about Meredith."

"She and her Lycan brothers were raised by the man in your vision. His name was Archie Leacham. The police suspected—"

"No, no," his mother interrupted, shaking her head. "Tell me about *Meredith*."

"What about her?" he asked.

"What is she like?"

"She is brash, crude, loud-mouthed, stubborn, headstrong." He let out a sigh. "Beautiful. Loyal. Kind hearted. And she hides her vulnerability behind that brassy exterior."

"And you can't stop thinking about her," Signe finished. "Don't lie to me, Daric, I'm your mother. And you need to be careful what you send me through our link."

"I didn't realize..." Daric felt embarrassed and turned his head away. "I hope you didn't see anything inappropriate."

"I didn't. But I could feel her at the edges of your thoughts and feelings," she explained. "So, tell me, why are you avoiding Meredith and denying what you feel for her?"

"You don't understand," he said, unlinking their arms.

"Then tell me so I can."

"I don't know where to begin, Mother," he shrugged. "She was my enemy, and she's also bonded to the New York clan against her will. I don't know where her loyalties lie."

"Ah, so you can't trust her? Do you think she trusts you?"

"I don't...I mean, that's not the point. Also," he took a deep breath. "When I touch her, I see nothing, Mother."

"Nothing?"

Daric shook his head. "Yes. For the first time, I've encountered someone whose past and future are unknown to me. What does it mean? Does she have no future?" A cold fear gripped him. "Will she die, Mother?"

She shook her head. "I don't know, Daric, but just because you can't see what lies ahead for her, doesn't mean it's bad. Maybe you just weren't meant to see it. But maybe, just maybe, you should follow your heart." Signe placed a hand on his chest. "It's a good one. Like your father's heart."

Daric's face became stone-like. "I cannot, Mother. Not while Stefan is alive."

"Your need for vengeance is clouding what's real. The truth." She sighed and laid her head on his chest. "My son, don't let the hate overcome you. Stefan must pay for his crimes, but don't get any more blood on your hands. Or have hers tainted."

"What do you mean—"

Signe pulled away. "Come, we should head back.

CHAPTER FIFTEEN

Meredith stayed behind at the house as Daric and Signe went for their walk. She helped Vivianne with the dishes, as Graham went off to do some work on the house. They chatted, and Meredith was glad to have had some time alone with the witch. Having never known her mother or been around females much growing up, she secretly enjoyed the attention from Vivianne. She felt a pang of envy that Lara grew up with such a lovely and supportive mother (though, according to her friend, sometimes *too* supportive), but then again, Meredith couldn't—and wouldn't—change her past.

"Are you all right, dear?" Vivianne said as she handed Meredith a clean dish to put away.

"What?" Meredith shook herself out of her thoughts.

"I'm just wondering. You seemed distracted, that was all," the older woman said slyly.

"Uh, just tired from the drive," she sighed. She wished they didn't have to go back to Manhattan. The coven compound reminded her of Archie's place outside Portland. His mansion was built on an acreage and surrounded by trees and greenery.

This time of the year, the leaves would be turning, and soon the entire landscape would have been bursting with golds and reds.

"Are you sure you can't stay?"

She shook her head. "Grant's orders were explicit. Get in and get out."

"I'm sorry about your father, dear," Vivianne said quietly.

Her automatic denial of Archie being her father didn't come out this time. "Thank you," she said gratefully. "Please, let me," she said, taking a tray of clean dishes from Vivianne's hand. "I can put these back."

As she opened the cupboard and began to place the dishes on the shelf, she looked out of the window, wondering how far Daric and Signe had gone. She frowned. That butt hole. Calling her his driver. None of his other insults had stung as much as that one did. She drove me here. *Really, asshole?* That's how he introduces her to his mother?

"Uh, Meredith, dear," Vivianne said, taking a glass from her. "Maybe I should put away the dishes...before you break them with your bare hands."

"What? Oh. I'm so sorry Vivianne," she said, shaking her head. "I don't know what's gotten into me."

"Not Daric, I'm guessing?" the witch asked wryly.

Meredith's head jerked toward Vivianne so fast, she thought she'd get whiplash. "What...uh, never mind." Maybe she should be glad she didn't have a mother to embarrass her or have the awkward sex talk with.

"Oh, you two," Vivianne sighed. "I don't know if you were going to stab each other with your forks or have at it on the kitchen table." She shook her head. "The sexual tension between you is practically electric."

"And that's all it is, just tension," Meredith pouted.

"Dear, you're a woman," Vivianne said. "You're young, gorgeous, and sexy. Just take what you want."

"You don't think I'm insane?"

"Why? For getting horny? For wanting that hot piece of ass?"

Meredith was shocked at Vivianne's words.

I like her, the she-wolf said, seemingly popping up out of nowhere. *You should listen to her, instead of your stupid friends.*

"You young people today," the witch tsked. "I swear, I don't know how you all can be such prudes, with your sexting and hookup apps. You're worse than Lara."

"Are you suggesting I try to bang Daric?"

"Why, yes," Vivianne encouraged. "You should do just that."

Do it! Do it! Do it!

Oh shut it, horny bitch.

The wolf laughed and tossed its head.

Meredith groaned. "I think...I'll get some rest before the drive back. Great pep talk, thanks," she said before she scampered out of the kitchen.

Try to seduce Daric? Daric had been the one coming to her. Maybe she should be the one to come to him this time.

———

"Thank you again," Daric said to Graham and Vivianne, as they walked him and Meredith to their car. "For your hospitality and taking care of my mother."

"Please, come and visit anytime," Vivianne said.

Signe embraced her son one more time. "Think about what I said."

"I..." Daric hesitated. "I will think about all of it. Thank you."

The witch turned to Meredith. "It was lovely to meet you,"

she said with a bright smile on her face. "Please, take care of my son."

"Uh, yeah, sure," she said, frowning. What did the witch mean?

After their final goodbyes, Meredith and Daric got into the SUV, and soon, they were driving back to New York City. Much like their trip upstate, the warlock remained quiet, but he seemed different this time. Even more withdrawn. They were already halfway into their drive, and neither had said a word.

"Did you find out anything from your mother?" Meredith finally said, when she couldn't take his silence and the distance between them.

"Yes," he said, his voice cold and eyes turning hard.

"Well? Are you gonna tell me or what?" she asked impatiently. Maybe she shouldn't listen to Vivianne. It was obvious something had happened while Daric and Signe talked. Did the witch tell her son to stay away from her? Possibly. And that thought slashed at her gut.

"Perhaps it would be best to wait until we talk to your brothers, that way I don't have to waste my time explaining things twice."

"Right." Because it was a waste of his time talking to her. "Well, we should—"

Meredith let out a shriek as the vehicle suddenly lurched forward and began to sputter. She swerved to the side of the highway, getting out of the way.

"What's wrong?" Daric asked.

She shrugged and tried to start the car. The engine gave one last heave and then nothing. "Motherfucker!" she cursed, slapping her palm on the wheel. "Goddammit! This stupid piece of shit!"

"Do you know what's wrong?" he asked.

Meredith shook her head. "I know zilch about cars." With a

sigh, she reached over to the dash and got the cell phone Alynna had given her for emergencies. It was locked down, and she couldn't use the data to access the Internet, but she could call and send text messages. She supposed this counted as an emergency.

CHAPTER SIXTEEN

"So, you're not sure what's wrong with it?"

"Nope."

"And you don't know when you can repair it?"

"Nope."

"And you don't have a rental or know if there's a rental car place nearby?"

"Nope. Nearest one's at least an hour drive away," the old mechanic, Joe, said, rubbing his greasy hands on a rag. "Sorry, missy. Nothing I can do for you. Except maybe give you two a ride to the nearest motel? Maybe your people can come pick you up in the morning?"

Meredith kicked the tire of the car in frustration, then let out a string of curses.

Daric looked apologetically at the older man. "Sorry about that. My companion and I really needed to get home. Thank you, we will take you up on your offer."

"Gimme five," the man said and walked toward his office.

"Are you done?" Daric asked Meredith.

She gave a long sigh. "Yeah. Well, nothing we can do about it." Looking outside, she saw that it was already dark. "Looks like we're stuck here. I'll call Alynna." She walked out of the garage, pulling the phone out of her pocket and dialed the single number programmed into the device.

As soon as the SUV stalled, Daric and Meredith called Alynna and explained what happened. Unfortunately, there was no one around to help them or drive two hours to come pick them up, so she said she'd search for the nearest mechanic to give them a tow. About two hours later, an older man in an ancient tow truck pulled up next to the SUV and introduced himself as Joe. He towed the car back to his garage, which was actually in a small town another hour away, in the opposite direction of Manhattan. As they waited for him to fix the vehicle, they walked to the diner across the street and had some dinner before going back to Joe's garage.

When they got back, they found the old man staring at the SUV, a confused look on his face. Joe said he wasn't sure what was wrong, but he said it might be a computer issue, something he couldn't fix. And now, here they were, stuck in this tiny town.

Meredith came back after a few minutes. "Alynna said she'd have Alex pick us up tomorrow at noon. He'll be bringing a mechanic, too. She said just to go and get a couple of rooms and stay the night."

Joe came out of his office and led them back to his truck, opening the door for Meredith in the back and gesturing for Daric to ride up front with him. He hitched their car back onto the tow truck, and soon they were on their way. Fifteen minutes later, they arrived at the motel complex.

The Cozy Inn Motel looked like any standard old motel, single story and the structure built in a U-shape, with the reception in the middle and the rooms on either side. Across the street was a bar, the words "Dirty Bird" emblazoned on the side in hot neon lights.

Joe dropped them off and pulled the SUV into one of the empty slots at the end of the building. Daric thanked him for his help and followed Meredith into the motel.

The two of them walked into the reception, where an older, dour-faced woman was waiting behind a desk, reading a trashy romance novel.

"Good evening," Daric said. "We would like two rooms, please."

The woman let out a long sigh and took out a large, leather bound book from underneath the desk. She opened it up and peered down at the pages. "No," she said.

"No?" Meredith asked. "No, you don't have any rooms or no, you don't want to give us any?"

"No, I don't got two rooms," she replied gruffly. "I got one room."

"What?" Meredith exclaimed. "That can't be right! You must have at least two rooms! Who the heck would come stay in this Godawful—mmmph!"

"We'll take it," Daric said as his hands wrapped over Meredith's mouth. The Lycan wrenched herself away from him, her face growing red with anger.

The woman shrugged. "Fine. Cash only. And I'm gonna need a deposit."

Meredith grumbled as she took out a wad of cash from her purse, slapping it on the desk. The woman handed her a key, sat back down and returned to her book.

"Let's go," Meredith said as they walked towards the room, which was the nearest one to the reception area. She slipped the key into the lock and opened it.

The room wasn't luxurious, but Daric supposed it would have to do. The only problem was that there was only one king-sized bed in the middle of the cramped room. He strode over to the bed and grabbed a pillow.

"I'll sleep on the floor. Perhaps I can ask for a blanket," Daric said, trying to find a spot that would look comfortable or at least fit his frame.

"Don't be ridiculous," Meredith said as she sat on the bed. "The bed is big enough, and if it weren't, then I should be the one on the floor. You're humongous."

The thought of sharing the bed with Meredith made his body react instantly, and he imagined her sweet, lush body wrapped around him. "No, I will sleep on the floor."

"For God's sake!" She grabbed the pillow from him and threw it back on the bed. "Grow up, Daric. It's just one night. I'm sure it's an inconvenience sharing a bed with me, but you'll live."

"It's not that." How could he explain it to her? Knowing that she'd be so close to him, he wouldn't be able to resist the temptation. He'd already gone too far; he was not going down this road.

"What, you think I'm going to attack you in your sleep? That I won't be able to resist your charms and throw myself at you?" she mocked. "Last I checked, you were the one who brought me into that closet! Or was I imagining someone else's tongue on my pussy?"

"Dammit, woman!" He grabbed her arm. "Don't you ever think before you speak?"

"Fuck you, Daric!" She pulled away from his grasp. "You know what? No, I'm not fucking you. Ever." She stormed to the door.

"Where are you going?" he shouted.

"To find someone who does want to fuck me!" she screamed, slamming the door behind her.

Daric sat on the bed and ran his hands through his hair. "Goddamn woman."

As Meredith stomped across the parking lot to the Dirty Bird, she slowly counted her steps, hoping that it would calm her down enough to stop her from doing something stupid. Her inner wolf, however, was going crazy, scratching at her and begging her to go back to Daric.

"Shut. The. Fuck. Up. Bitch!" she growled. "I'm done with you for tonight."

The she-wolf let out a whine but quieted down. *Good.*

Walking into the Dirty Bird, Meredith pushed her way inside the crowded room and walked straight to the bar. "Whiskey," she grumbled at the man behind the bar.

"A shot?" the bartender asked.

"A fifth," she replied, slapping a couple of bills on the counter.

The man shrugged, grabbed a bottle from behind the bar and placed it in front of her, along with a glass. "Pace yourself, little lady."

She grabbed the bottle, unscrewed the top and drank straight up, taking three large gulps before slamming it back down. "I'm not a lady," she declared.

"Yeah, well, I'm gonna cut you off the moment you start acting crazy," the bartender warned.

"Fine," she said. The burn down her throat felt good, and she was already starting to feel the wonderful numbing effects of the alcohol. Exactly what she needed, so she could stop feeling that awful pain from Daric's rejection, for the nth time in a row. *God, I'm an idiot*, she thought as she took another swig. Wanting a man who didn't want her. Who was, apparently, repulsed at the thought of even sleeping next to her. Scratch that; she was the queen of idiots. Meredith, Empress of the Idiots, First of her name.

The alcohol was burning off way too fast, thanks to her Lycan metabolism. She took two long drags from the bottle, her eyes watering as the alcohol burn came too quickly. At least the numbness came back, and she steadied herself as her body began to sway. What was the plan anyway? Get drunk off her ass and then what? She checked her pockets—ah, the car keys were there. Maybe she could sleep in the car tonight.

"Hey there, sexy mama," a voice from behind her called. She turned and saw a man staring at her. Or staring at her boobs maybe.

"Fuck off," she said, not really in the mood. "This is a solo party."

"Oh yeah? You sure I can't convince you to make it a party of two?" He flashed her a set of pearly white teeth. The man was about her height, with wavy brown hair and brown eyes. Meredith supposed he was handsome, but, ugh. No way. She was horny, but not that horny.

She stood up and faced the stranger. "I said fuck off." She wanted nothing more than to break the bottle over his head, but not only was that a waste of good liquor, but she didn't have any more money on her to buy more.

"Hmm...I bet you'd be a little hellcat in bed," he said and brought his hand behind her to cup her ass.

Meredith instantly reacted, grabbing the man's hand and then twisting it around. He let out a yelp of pain as she slammed his face down on the bar.

"Crazy bitch!" he screamed. "I think you broke my arm!"

"Just be glad that's the only thing I broke, asshole," she said, releasing him. "God, I am so done with men today!" she declared and then grabbed the bottle of whiskey, then walked to the door, pushing it open with all her might. Unfortunately, someone on the other side pushed the door in at the same time, sending her flying back and falling flat on her ass.

"Goddammit!" she cursed as she got up. When she saw who was standing over her, she got even more enraged. "What are you doing here?"

"Looking for you," Daric replied, raising an eyebrow at her. "Can you not go five minutes without causing trouble, woman?"

She pushed him with all her might. "Get out of my way!" When he wouldn't budge, she sidestepped around him and ran out the door.

Meredith let the cool air into her lungs, not that it helped calm her down. She stalked towards the car, ignoring the heavy footsteps behind her. Fishing the key fob out of her pocket, she unlocked the door.

"Meredith! Meredith, for God's sake, stop." He grabbed her before she could get inside.

"Why the hell did you follow me?" she asked, looking up at him. "Why can't you leave me alone?"

"Because I can't stand the thought of you with anyone else!" he roared, pushing her up against the side of the car. "And I can't bear to think of you hurting because you think I don't want you." He gripped her arms, his fingers digging gently into her flesh. "Not when I've never wanted anyone as I want you." He pressed his hips against her, his erection evident.

"Daric," she gasped, and let out a soft moan as his lips came down on hers in a savage kiss. Unlike their other kisses, this one was not gentle. It was passionate and wild, with Daric driving his tongue into her mouth like he couldn't get enough of her. Oh God, his scent was that of full-blown arousal, and it was driving her crazy. She wanted to get as close to him as possible, practically crawling out of her skin with need.

"Meredith," he whispered, and she whimpered when he pulled away.

"Why, Daric?" she asked, gazing up at him, trying to find

answers in his sea-colored eyes. "Why don't you want to have sex with me?"

"Because, *min kjære*," he sighed, brushing a lock of hair from her face. "It wouldn't just be about sex."

Before she could react, he moved down again for a kiss, and she moaned into his mouth. His hands cupped her ass, lifting her up against him.

"I can't wait," she groaned.

Needing no more encouragement, Daric opened the rear door of the vehicle and pushed her inside. He climbed in and closed the door behind him, then crawled over her.

Meredith spread her knees, inviting him to come between her legs. He came down on top of her, and took her mouth again, pouring every bit of himself into their kiss. She cried his name as he dragged his lips down lower. He lifted her shirt, yanking down the cups of her bra and freeing her breasts.

"Yes," she moaned when he took a nipple into his hot mouth, sucking and gently biting it. "God, you're a tease."

He looked up and smiled at her, nipple still in his mouth. A hand snaked between them, slipping under her leggings and panties. "I've only just begun."

A finger slipped inside her, making her hips buck up. Another joined in, and soon, Daric was dragging his fingers in and out her, while his thumb found her clit.

"Fuck!" Meredith moved her hips against his hand, seeking her orgasm.

"Cum for me," he urged. "I want to feel your sweet cunt grip my fingers."

Fuck, Daric talking dirty was hot, and it wasn't long before her orgasm came, crashing over her like a strong wave. Her hips surged up and then crashed down, her ass hitting the leather seat.

"Beautiful," he declared, leaning down to kiss her.

"I need you, Daric," she said. "Please."

"I've waited so long, *min kjære*." He took his shirt off and then tugged down her leggings and panties in one movement, tossing them away. He lifted his hips, unbuttoned his jeans and shoved them down his thighs.

"Now, Daric," she demanded. "I need you inside me now."

He guided his cock to her entrance, and she could feel the swollen head pushing at her. Slowly, he filled her, stretching her, as if making sure she felt every inch of him. She held her breath and bit her lip, waiting for the slight discomfort to leave her body.

"Meredith," he gasped as his cock bottomed out. Taking a deep breath, he began to move his hips. She wrapped her legs around his waist, trying to push him deeper with every inward thrust.

Fuck, it was so good, much better than she'd imagined. Daric's cock, fucking in and out of her, dragging along the inside of her pussy. Dear God, she wanted to weep from pleasure. She dug her fingers into his back, scraping her fingernails down his skin as he continued to thrust into her.

He eased in and out, ramming his big cock into her. Taking her. Consuming her. Owning her. He growled in pain as her nails left marks down his back, and he grabbed her hand and thrust it between them, making her touch her clit as he fucked into her.

Daric pumped into her faster, hips fucking furiously as he drove her to the edge. The first pulse of her orgasm burst through her quickly, the scream rising in her throat. She bit down on his shoulder to stop herself, not enough to draw blood but certainly leaving teeth marks. Large hands slipped under her ass, pressing her up closer to him, filling her deeper and another pulse of pleasure zinged through her.

"Daric," she cried as his body tensed and his thrusts became more erratic and volatile. She felt his cock swell, and then shoot his warmth inside her, filling her up. He continued to thrust into her, and she reveled in the feeling of his sticky cum pushing and flowing out of her, running down her ass.

He grunted and gave one last thrust before collapsing on top of her. Planting a quick kiss on her lips, he settled his head between her breasts, his ragged breathing slowly becoming even.

When Meredith finally opened her eyes, she wasn't sure if five minutes or five hours had passed. Looking up, she saw the windows of SUV had fogged up. Her skin was slick with sweat, and the whole car smelled like Daric and sex. She groaned when he shifted his hips, and his cock slipped out of her.

"We should get to the room," Daric said, lifting his weight off her. He backed up, opened the car door, and slipped out.

"Jesus," Meredith muttered, her eyes watching as Daric tucked his cock back into his jeans, and stretched his hands over his head to put his shirt back on. His muscles rippled under his skin, and her gaze was drawn to the perfect line between his pecs, lower still to his flat stomach and defined abs and the delicious V of his hips. A small cry of disappointment left her lips as the fabric of his shirt covered his torso.

"You look beautiful," he said, grinning at her as she realized that he had caught her staring. Meredith looked down at her body—her lower half bared, her shirt over her chest and tits popped out of her bra. The heated look in his eyes made her blush all over, particularly since he stared at her thighs, sticky with his seed.

With a sigh, Meredith hoisted herself up and grabbed her discarded clothing. She turned away from him and wiggled into her leggings. She heard a groan from behind her, and she turned her head.

"Your ass is perfect," he growled.

"Thank you," she said saucily, shaking her ass at him. "I work—" She let out a yelp as his arm wrapped around her waist and hauled her out of the car. Daric hoisted her over his shoulder, like some maiden about to be ravished (maybe he really was descended from Vikings) and began to walk back to their room.

"Daric put me down. I can walk, you know," she chuckled.

He landed a playful slap on her butt. "Still? I have to do something about that, then."

She laughed harder, her shrieks of delight ringing across the parking lot.

CHAPTER SEVENTEEN

The first rays of the sun were peeking from behind the curtain by the time Daric collapsed on the bed and gathered Meredith into his arms. Her soft, plush body molded against his perfectly, and if he weren't exhausted from having sex with her twice more after they got back from the car, the press of her ass against his cock would have stirred him again.

The wicked little she-wolf was voracious, and he found himself matching her sexual appetite. As soon as they got into the room, she demanded he strip so she could admire his body. She pushed him on the bed, and ran her hands over his body, declaring him to be the "hottest fucking thing she'd ever seen." God, her dirty mouth was a turn-on, but it was better when it was on him. Sucking and licking and teasing at him. He also enjoyed it when she climbed on top of him, taking his cock all the way inside her and riding him like her life depended on it, and falling apart when she came around him.

He woke again, not much later and Meredith had somehow pushed him to the edge of the king-sized bed. Her body was splayed diagonally across the surface, taking up the middle part. Her slim arm was slung over his chest, her messy blonde hair spilling over her shoulders and face, and her head was laying on his chest. There was a small streak of dried drool down the side of her mouth, which was open as she snored softly.

A smile spread across his face. Meredith had never looked more adorable to him than in this moment. His she-wolf. Gently, he nudged her, trying to get more space on the bed, but she let out a protesting moan and wrapped her legs around his torso, her grip like steel.

"Come on, I need some space, too," he whispered, brushing her soft hair aside.

"No, my bed," she said. Her eyes remained closed, but the slight smile tugging at her lips indicated she was awake.

"I'm going to fall off the side," he retorted. "Move over, or I will spank you, my she-wolf."

One eye cracked open. "Is that a promise? Because you know I enjoyed it last night."

He laughed and then rolled her over, pinning her body with his. "Yes, I know you did. I'll have to find some other ways to punish you when you disobey me." He rubbed his stubble along the sensitive skin of her neck, making her shriek. "Looks like I found it."

"No...noooo..." she gasped in between cries. "Daric!"

He captured a nipple into his mouth, sucking on the bud. Her breasts were perfect, just the right size for his hands and the large, pink nipples were very responsive. His mouth moved to the other breast, his tongue lashing across the bud, making her moan and push her hips up at his already hard cock. When he finally released her nipples, he moved his hand between her legs and found her already dripping wet.

"Daric," she moaned. "Again."

Daric sat back on his heels and then grabbed her right ankle.

Instead of hoisting it over his shoulder, however, he flipped her, so she was on her stomach.

Meredith gasped and then lifted that perfectly-shaped ass up at him. "Take me," she begged. "Now."

Not needing further encouragement, he grabbed his cock and teased her entrance, spreading the precum on the tip across her wet slit. She let out a grunt of disappointment at his teasing and moved back, pushing herself onto him. Daric suppressed a laugh. His she-wolf was relentless.

He thrust his hips forward, burying himself to the hilt so quickly it made her yelp in surprise. She was slick, tight, and so hot. Her pussy gripped him, pulsing around his cock. Meredith's body was responsive and sensitive, and he couldn't think of anything but her and that delicious wildflower scent when he was inside her. Grabbing her hips, he pulled her back, driving as deep as he could with each thrust.

Meredith let out a growl, a real one, and it drove him wild. He bent down over her, pushing her on the bed, fucking into her so hard the headboard slammed against the wall with each thrust. She mewled, squeezing around him so tight as her body wracked with her orgasm.

"Fuck...fuck...Daric...fuck me...your cock is so good...give me..."

That dirty mouth pushed him over the edge again, and his cock twitched as he pumped her full of his cum. She milked every last drop, the naughty little thing, until he was so spent he fell on top of her.

"Woman, you'll kill me before lunchtime," he growled as he rolled onto his back.

She let out a throaty laugh. "Lunchtime? That means I have a few hours still."

"Minx," he teased, grabbing her by the waist and pulling her against him.

She opened her mouth to say something, but her stomach gurgled loudly. "Whoops...I guess it's been a few hours since dinner."

"Well, I suppose we have to eat sometime," he said, sitting up. "Come, I believe they advertised a free hot breakfast in the dining room. I'm sure we'll find something to your liking."

They got dressed and left the room, then headed straight to the small breakfast room in the lobby. Meredith immediately ran to the buffet table and piled her plate high with food.

"What?" she asked as she shoveled some scrambled eggs into her mouth. "I'm hungry."

He shook his head. "Just don't choke on your food, *min kjære*."

"What does that mean, min kyareee?"

"*Min kjære*?" he corrected. "It means—"

A ringing from Meredith's purse interrupted him, and she grabbed the bag, taking out the small cell phone inside. "Hello? Oh hey, Alex. Yeah, we're good," she said, nodding her head. "Some clothes? Yeah, that would be great, I'm starting to smell funky. Sure, no prob. See you soon!"

"Is Alex Westbrooke on the way?"

"Yeah, he just left Manhattan. He should be here with the mechanic in two hours he said, depending on the traffic." She finished her bagel in two bites and then dumped a couple of donuts into her purse. "Are you done?" she asked, eyeing his bowl of oatmeal. "Two hours isn't much time."

He chuckled and pushed the bowl away. "We will make do."

They were laughing and giggling all the way back to the room, but as soon as the door closed behind them, Daric pushed her against the wall of the door, then picked her up to bring her to the shower, where they had another rigorous round of sex.

Meredith was picking up their clothes on the floor, and she

took a sniff of his shirt. "Holy satan's balls, this smells like me. And sex. The SUV!" she suddenly remembered. "Fucking hell, that backseat is going to smell like us fucking."

Daric exited the bathroom, wearing only a towel around his waist. "Perhaps we could open the windows before Alex gets here."

"Good idea," Meredith said. She was about to open the door when she heard a knock coming from the other side.

"Meredith? Are you in there?" Alex Westbrooke's voice called. "I have your clothes."

"Holy crap, we gonna have some 'splainin' to do, Luuuuuuuucy."

"Who is Lucy?"

"I'll tell you later."

———

Meredith quickly opened the door, thanked Alex and grabbed the bag of clothes he had in his hand before slamming the door in his face. She and Daric changed into the fresh clothes and left the room before Alex could get a whiff of the inside.

It seemed leaving their sex scent in the car was the least of Meredith and Daric's worries. In their rush to go back to the room last night, they left the door of the SUV open, and a gang of raccoons had gotten inside. The plush leather seats were now torn, and stuffing was scattered all over the interior. There was also droppings and trash inside, making the smell unbearable, especially to the Lycans and their enhanced senses. God, Meredith had never been so happy those trash pandas existed.

"Jesus, Nick's going to have kittens," Alex moaned, pinching his nose. "How the heck did this happen?"

"The short in the computer system must have turned off the

alarm," Ben, the mechanic who came with Alex, said as he shut the hood.

"But how did they get in?" Alex asked. "Do raccoons know how to open doors?"

"Yes," Meredith and Daric said at the same time.

Alex eyed them suspiciously, then turned to Ben. "You got this, Ben?"

"Yeah Alex, no worries. I'll drive her back to Fenrir, okay?"

"Great, thank you. I owe you one." Alex fished the keys of his Jeep out of his pocket. "Let's head back."

"Shotgun!" Meredith said as she raced to the front passenger seat. She climbed in, declaring her victory with a fist pump in the air.

The drive back was pleasant, and Meredith liked Alex. The other Lycan always treated her nicely, plus he totally rocked that hot dad image, especially when his eyes lit up when he talked about his daughter. Not that she'd ever try anything (unless she wanted Alynna to kill her). Besides, it wasn't like she didn't already have someone to rock her world. She took a sly glance at Daric, who flashed her a smile from the back seat. Heat crept up her neck because, with that one look, she knew what he was thinking.

She turned away and took the phone from her pocket. Hopefully, no one would notice if she kept this particular device. Even though it was an older model, it still might be useful. For one thing, she had sent Jade a message this morning, asking her for a tiny little favor. Without another thought, she slipped the phone into her bra.

———

Two hours later, they arrived at Fenrir. Meredith thanked Alex and let him know that they would be joining them for their meeting in the Alpha's office, but they had to stop by Jade's lab first.

"Why do we need to go to Dr. Cross' laboratory?" Daric asked when they were alone in the elevator.

"It's a surprise," she said to him cheekily. They entered the lab and Meredith told him to wait.

"Jaaaaade!" she called as she entered the other Lycan's office. "Do you have it?"

"We really need to talk about your constant need for danger," the Lycan scientist said. "I suppose sex with your enemy is one of the biggest adrenaline rushes."

"Blah blah blah, possibly evil warlock, yadda yadda, bad idea," Meredith said nonchalantly. "There, I saved you the lecture by giving it to myself. So, did you get what I asked?"

Jade sighed and took out a white box from under her desk. "Here you go. And you owe me. And I mean money. Do you know how much La Perla lingerie costs?"

"Please, your baby-daddy's a bazillionaire, and you've got that fat trust fund. Consider this my payment for saving your life a couple of times." Meredith squealed when she opened the box. "Jade, you're the best friend a girl can have."

"How about you never send me NSFS texts again, with details about your sex life, and we'll call it even?"

"You mean NSFW?"

"No, I mean Not Safe For Sebastian. I had to erase all your texts, in case he was looking over my shoulder."

Meredith ignored her as she took the lacy bra out of the box. It was purple, with delicate lace flower detailing. There was also a pair of matching panties, garter belt, and stockings. "Jade, you have great taste! Did you pick some out for yourself, too?"

"Of course I did," the Lycan smiled. "I'm wearing it now. I can't wait to surprise Sebastian tonight."

"High five!" Meredith exclaimed, lifting her palm up, which

Jade heartily slapped. "God, Jade, I can just imagine Daric's face when he sees me in this. Maybe I can inspire some more dirty words from his mouth."

"Ew, TMI," Jade said, wrinkling her nose. "I can't imagine Daric talking dirty. He's so...so formal in his speech."

"Think obscene Shakespeare in the Park. I swear it's like poetry that will make your panties burn."

"So, 'shall I kiss thy breasts and tickle thy womanly mound'?" Jade asked, giggling uncontrollably.

Meredith laughed. "Yeah. Or 'dost thou want to be taken in the cunt or up the b—"

"Meredith!" Jade admonished.

A knock on the door broke off their banter. "Come in," Jade called.

Daric peered in. "Is everything all right?" he asked, his face drawn into a frown.

"It's all good," Jade said, trying to hide her smile. A sound from the outside lab chimed. "Ah, that's one of my experiments. I have to check on my data." The scientist scurried off, leaving Daric and Meredith alone.

"Hey," Meredith said, pushing the box behind her, hoping he didn't see. Maybe she should have slipped it on like Jade did.

"Hello," he greeted back as he strode to her, crossing the distance between them in a few steps. He trapped her between the desk, placing his hands on either side of her. "Did you get what you needed from Dr. Cross?"

"Uh-huh," she nodded.

"And what is it?"

"I told you, it's a surprise."

He looked behind her and saw the box. "Is it your birthday?" he asked, a deep frown marring his face. "You should have told me."

She chuckled and put a hand on his chest. "It's not. But it

might be yours." He narrowed his eyes at her, and she only laughed harder. "Oh, come here, you." She grabbed his shirt and pulled him down for a kiss. Daric was surprised at first, but quickly recovered and returned her kiss with the same enthusiasm. He picked her up and placed her on the desk, careful not to crush the box. She moaned into his mouth, wrapping her legs around him.

Suddenly, a loud crash and shouting from the outer lab made them quickly pull apart.

"Meredith! Daric!" Jade's shout rang in Meredith's enhanced ears.

"Jade, you taco blocker!" Meredith hissed as she hopped off the desk.

"A what?" Daric asked, adjusting the front of his jeans.

"You know," Meredith said in an exasperated voice. "Muffin muzzle? Twat swatter? Clam jammer?" Daric continued to look at her strangely. "Never mind. Let's go see what kind of trouble Jade is in again."

Meredith quickly walked out of the office, peering down into the lab. "What the hell is—Quinn!" *Oh, fuck a duck.*

Jade was standing between Sebastian and Quinn, and the former's stance looked like he was ready to bash her brother's face in, while the latter was standing defensively, his hands in the air.

"Quinn!" she called again, taking the steps two at a time. "Do you have a death wish or something?"

"Who is this asshole?" Sebastian growled, his rage barely contained.

"Hey, sorry man, I didn't know she was yours," Quinn said.

"I told you she wasn't available," Meredith scolded.

"You said not to 'go there,' not that she was already with someone," Quinn retorted.

"What the hell did you do anyway?"

"I was just talking to her—"

"You were sniffing her hair when I walked in," Sebastian shouted.

"It's how we Lycans greet each other!" Quinn lied.

"Sebastian," Jade pleaded, putting her hands on his chest. "Calm down, nothing happened. He didn't even touch me!"

"He better have not!" Sebastian's eyes glowed gold and the air around them grew heavy.

Jade sighed and wrapped her arm around his waist. "Let's go home, okay?" she soothed and then whispered something in his ear. Whatever it was seemed to calm Sebastian. With a nod to Meredith and Daric (and one last warning look to Quinn), he put an arm protectively around Jade, and the two left the lab.

"Jesus Christ!" Quinn staggered back once they were gone. "What the fuck is he?"

"A dragon," Meredith deadpanned.

"No, really, what is he?"

She shrugged. "I told you not to go there, and you went there anyway!"

"Hey, you know I can't resist pretty faces! But you should have told me she was knocked up. I don't do attached women."

"How the heck did you get in here, anyway?" Meredith asked in an annoyed tone.

"I hacked the elevator system, duh," Quinn replied matter-of-factly.

"Well, what did you want?"

Quinn's voice turned serious. "We need to go back to the hospital. Sven is awake."

CHAPTER EIGHTEEN

Killian and Connor were already in the SUV by the time Daric, Meredith, and Quinn arrived at the garage. As they drove through Manhattan, Daric pondered on his conversation with his mother about the visions. Although he had been occupied by the events of the last 24 hours, the bigger picture never strayed from his thoughts: find out how Archie was connected to Stefan and of course, kill the master mage. His need for vengeance hadn't tempered, but, looking over at Meredith, the stakes were much higher now. Aside from the distraction, there was one thing he realized just now: Stefan could use Meredith against him like he did with Signe. Cold fear gripped his heart, knowing how cruel the master mage was and there was no line he wouldn't cross to get what he wanted. For now, he had to compartmentalize what he was feeling and block out Stefan from his thoughts and visions. The link between them was growing weaker every day, but Daric would never take the walls down, not while Stefan was still alive.

Meredith looked up at him with her amber eyes, looking soulful and worried. He gave her a reassuring smile, wishing he could put his arms around her or even just touch her soft skin. It was nice to forget the world outside while they were alone in the motel room in the middle of nowhere. But that was only temporary, and now they had to go back to the real world.

They reached the parking garage of The New York Downtown Hospital and made their way to the 11th floor. When they got to Sven's room, they saw that Merlin was already there, sitting by the bed.

"Here they are, Sven," Merlin said to the younger man. "Don't be afraid. They just want to help you."

Sven's face was still swollen, his lip split and he sported a black eye, but at least now he sat upright and didn't need the breathing tube. He warily eyed the newcomers, examining each one until his gaze clashed with Daric.

"I...I know you...I think?" Sven frowned. "I'm sorry...I can't remember much."

"Where are you from, Sven?" Daric asked. He was sure he had never met him, but there was something eerily familiar about the other man.

"I came to New York to be an actor, but I'm from Canada," he replied. "But I moved to Toronto with my mother when I was six or seven. We used to live in Norway."

The young man's words jolted something in Daric, and he moved forward and touched Sven's hands. He closed his eyes, seeing the same vision he had seen before, but now there was more. It was slow, at first, like someone slowing down a roll of film, then speeding it up. The wildflowers, the cliffs, and the clear water beneath it. Then the inside of a house—small, but cozy. A tall blonde man and woman were embracing in the corner. The door opened, and the vision rushed forward to show more of the outside. Small huts, built with stone and wood. The structures were simple and rustic, set against the majestic backdrop of a fjord.

Daric's eyes flew open. "Our village," he said at the young man.

"Y-y-you know my old village back in Norway?" Sven asked, his clear blue eyes widening. "I can't even remember the name."

"Its name is lost, I'm afraid," Daric replied somberly. "But I remember what it looked like, just as you do. And I remember you. One time your mother asked me to watch you while she put the laundry up on the line to dry."

He shook his head. "I'm sorry, I don't remember."

"You are Ulric's son." The day Stefan came to his village, he killed three blessed witches and warlocks to take their powers. One of them was his father, Jonas, and the other was Ulric, the healer.

"How did you know—so you really lived in the village?"

"Yes. That day your father died, mine perished along with him."

Sven gasped. "I don't remember much. Mama made sure I didn't see. But after that, we fled and ended up in Canada with my uncles. Mama is human, like me."

"So, wait a minute," Killian interrupted. "You two grew up in the same village? But how does he know Archie?"

"He doesn't, but I can explain what happened," Daric said. He told the others what his mother said about sending her vision out. "I think because of our connection to Sven, and his father's abilities as a blessed warlock, he may have inadvertently received the vision."

"Like an antenna, tuned only to get visions of the future," Quinn deduced.

Daric nodded. "Exactly. She cast her net wide enough, and Sven here was able to get it."

"Wait...you saw the dreams I've been having?" Sven asked. "About the man in the hat?"

"Yes," Daric said. "Now, why don't you tell us what happened?"

Sven took a deep breath. "It was...a couple of weeks ago that I started having these dreams. I thought, well, they're just dreams right? But I kept having them over and over again, and they were so real." He shook his head. "Well, one night at Merlin's, while I was on stage, I saw him. The man in the hat."

"Did you see who he was meeting?" Killian interrupted.

"No, not while I was up there," Sven answered. "I was up first that night," he explained. "And I saw the man enter, but he was exactly as I saw in my dream. Same suit and hat. I...I..." he looked down.

"It's okay, Sven," Merlin encouraged. "Tell them what you said to me."

"I had this bad feeling, you know? So, I watched them from the wings. I followed them when they got up to leave. I wanted to stop the man from dying, but I was too late. I was walking outside the building where it happened. It was so fast, and I saw him fall. I'm sorry," he whispered, his voice strained. "I tried...I tried..."

Daric shook his head and placed a hand on Sven's shoulder. "It was not your fault. If you didn't save him, then it wasn't meant to be."

Sven looked at Quinn. "When you asked me about Archie... well, I panicked. I thought you were going to kill me, too, because I witnessed his death."

"So, when you ran out of the club that night we were there, what happened?" Quinn asked.

"That's the thing. I don't remember," the younger man said. "I remember rushing out and running for a couple of blocks. But then I realized there was a group of guys following me. They beat me up, but my memory's clouded."

"Could it have been a potion?" Killian asked.

"Very possibly," Merlin replied. "It's too late to find traces of it, but if he can't remember, the attackers may have used a potion. I spoke with the police this morning," the warlock continued. "It seems that Sven got lucky. A couple of cops were having a late supper at this diner next to the alleyway where the attackers cornered Sven. They heard the commotion and scared them away just in time."

"You got very lucky," Daric told Sven.

"I have a few more questions if you don't mind," Killian said.

"Make it quick," Merlin replied. "He just woke up a few hours ago, and he's still recovering."

As Killian asked Sven for a few more details, Daric quietly slipped out of the room, hoping the Lone Wolves would not notice. He walked out into the hallway and leaned back against the door, closing his eyes as he tried to make sense of it all. His mind was reeling from the revelation. Sven. Ulric's son. His father's death. He thought he had buried the pain of what happened that day so deep that he would never feel it again. But seeing Sven and their village had conjured up feelings he thought were long gone.

"Daric."

He opened his eyes and saw Meredith, staring up at him, concern marring her face. She slipped her arms around his waist and laid her head on his chest. "Are you all right?"

"Your brothers might see us," he said, his voice tight.

"I don't care," she said. "I know what happened in there is messing with your head. What he said...It's a lot to process, so talk to me."

"There is nothing to talk about," he said, unwinding her arms from his middle. "I'm fine." Thoughts of Stefan killing Ulric flooded his mind. Him standing over his father, driving his sword into Jonas. Then it changed. It wasn't Jonas on the other end of Stefan's sword. It was Meredith.

"No, you're not," she pouted, crossing her arms over her chest. "Don't keep it all inside, Daric."

"And you would rather have me spew out my thoughts and feelings without a filter, the way you do?" he said bitterly. Shock and hurt registered on Meredith's face, and Daric instantly regretted his words.

"Fine," Meredith replied, lifting her chin. "Go ahead and bottle up *all* your feelings." She walked away, heading toward the elevator.

Daric watched her leave, the uncomfortable pit in his stomach growing. As she disappeared into the elevator, he told himself that it was better this way. What they had last night could never happen again. He couldn't let his emotions run wild. No, he didn't have that luxury. And it was for her own good. Pursuing anything more with Meredith was like painting a target on her back.

"Hey, where's Meredith?" Quinn asked as he and his brothers came out into the hallway.

"I think she said she'd be downstairs," Daric shrugged. "Did you glean any more information from Sven?"

"A couple of details here and there," Killian replied. "But nothing more that could lead us to Archie's killer. He says that he didn't see the face of whoever did it."

"What should we do now?" Connor asked.

"Let's go back and regroup," Killian said. "We need to update Grant on what's happening anyway."

———

Meredith was tempted to walk out of the hospital right then and there. *Stupid ass, stubborn warlock!* She kicked the SUV's tire. It made her feel marginally better. But not a lot.

She knew Daric was hurting, probably remembering what had happened to his father. Maybe she was presumptuous, but he didn't need to push her away like that. But he was right—she was crude, mouthy, and maybe she didn't think before she spoke. But he made it sound like a bad thing. He said it to hurt her. Why, she didn't know. Meredith wasn't the only one hurt. Her inner she-wolf cowered and whined in pain.

Why doesn't he like us anymore?

I don't know, she answered. Maybe Daric decided their affair was over. He had gotten what he wanted, and he didn't need her anymore. The thought made her gut ache.

"Hey, stop daydreaming, runt, and get in the car," Quinn yelled.

She was jolted out of her thoughts, so engrossed in them she didn't hear her brothers and Daric approach or the door unlock. Normally she would have given Quinn a snappy comeback, but instead, she climbed into the back seat, squeezing herself into the end, hoping to get as far away from Daric as possible. Thankfully, Connor went in next, taking up the middle seat and the warlock sat at the other end.

"We'll head straight to the Alpha's office for a debrief," Killian said. "Then we can figure out our next move."

The traffic was light, so the drive back was quick, thankfully. The longer she was in Daric's presence, the harder it was for Meredith to control what she was feeling inside. All she wanted to do was scream at the warlock and smack him upside the head.

After parking the SUV in the garage, they proceeded to Grant's office, where the Alpha and Beta were already waiting for them. As they sat down to talk, Daric first recounted what his mother said and Killian filled them in on their trip to visit Sven.

"So," Grant began. "We know how Sven and Archie are connected. But, who killed Archie and why?"

"Perhaps we should think about why he came to New York in the first place," Nick said. "Did he have business here? Did he come to New York regularly?"

The three Lone Wolves looked at each other, and the silence in the room was deafening. Meredith recognized that look. It was the look her brothers had when they were hiding something. From her.

"Why was Archie here?" Meredith asked, standing up from her chair.

"It's not important," Killian said.

"You're lying," she accused. "You know why. And if you don't tell us now, I swear, I'm going to make you!"

"Meredith," Quinn warned. "Listen to us. All we need to do is find out who killed Archie."

"Why won't you tell me why he came to New York?" She walked towards Killian, placing her hands on either side of him. "What did he do? Was someone after him?"

"You don't need to know," Killian shot back as he remained seated. He turned away from Meredith, unwilling to look her in the eyes.

"What the fuck is wrong with you? All of you?" She looked at her brothers, one by one, until her gaze landed on Connor. "What are you hiding? Please, just tell me."

More silence.

Finally, Connor spoke. "He came to see you."

Meredith felt her stomach drop, and her knees shook. If she weren't braced against Killian's chair, she would have collapsed. All this time...

"No," she shook her head and pushed herself upright. "No,

no, no."

Killian stood over her and placed a hand on her shoulder. "Like I said, it's not important why he came—"

"Yes it is!" she shouted. "He came because he knew I was stuck here. He came to help me, didn't he?" When her brothers said nothing, she knew it was true.

"It doesn't matter," Quinn huffed.

"Yes it does," she countered. "Archie died because of me."

"Stop saying that!" Connor growled. He stood and walked towards Meredith. "We'll find the bastard who killed Archie and get our revenge."

"He shouldn't have died in the first place," she said, her eyes filling with tears. "And you should have told me when you got here! Why did you lie to me, you especially," she said accusingly at Connor. "You said I could always trust you."

"I'm sorry," was all the Lone Wolf said.

"I can't..." Meredith shook her head and turned to the door. She ignored her brother's calls, walking away swiftly and then breaking into a full-on run as soon as she was out the door. The edges of her vision were going black, and she couldn't breathe. She wanted to get out. Wanted to destroy something. Or hit something. Or just do anything to make the hurt go away.

———

Meredith ran to her room as soon as the elevator hit the 16th floor. She threw the door open and slammed it shut behind her. Rage, sorrow, anger, all kinds of emotions coursed through her. She thought she was getting over it. But now it all came back, stronger than ever, with a new addition—guilt. It was her fault. Archie was dead because of her. The she-wolf howled, and she begged to be let out. God, she wished she could. Just let the wolf take over so she could disappear into her furry body and escape the world, even just for a little bit.

She grabbed the chair and threw it across the room. It hit the wall, and one of the legs broke off. Next came the lamp, which she tossed on the floor, the base breaking into a million pieces. She ripped the covers and pillows from her bed, then climbed up on top of it and tore the poster on the wall. Letting out a rage-filled cry, she sank down on the mattress, wrapping her hands around her legs as she curled on her side and let the tears flow.

Archie. Oh, Archie. I wish you could hear me now. I'm so sorry for the things I said. For the way that I left.

She felt the bed dip and a large hand gently stroking her head, pushing her hair away from her face. At first, she thought it was Connor, but the chocolate scent tickling her nose told her otherwise. She quickly scrambled to the other end of the bed, squeezing up against the window. "What are you doing here?"

Daric's face was inscrutable, and he placed his hand on his lap. "I wanted to see how you were doing."

"I'm fine," she said, throwing his words back in his face. "As you can see," she nodded to her wrecked room. "I've just been spewing my feelings out."

He let out a sigh, his shoulders sinking. "It seems that even though I said I'd make amends, I cannot stop hurting you. I should be the one who thinks before he speaks."

She huffed in agreement but said nothing.

"I'm sorry. And I know you don't want to hear this or want to believe it, but you did not cause Archie's death," Daric said somberly.

"I don't want to talk about Archie."

"Then we won't," he moved closer, sliding over to her. "We can talk about me. And why I acted like an ass this afternoon at the hospital."

"You won't get an argument from me," she grumbled.

He gave her a faint smile. "I know better than to expect one." Daric let out a sigh. "The conversation with Sven and his visions brought back a lot of unpleasant memories. You know which ones, you were there when I told everyone about how Stefan came to our village and killed my father to take his power."

"I remember," she said quietly.

"It was like I was experiencing it again. Not only the moment Stefan killed my father, but also destroying my life. Taking away everything and everyone I cared for." He paused. "And then I thought that there was something else he could take away that would destroy me."

She sighed and moved closer, touching his shoulder. "Daric, Signe is safe. He'll never take her away from you."

"I'm not talking about my mother," he said in a soft tone, bending his head so he could rub his cheek on her hand.

Meredith froze. He couldn't mean...

"I would protect you until my last breath," he said. "And if Stefan found out, he will use you to get to me. He will stop at nothing to get what he wants."

"Daric..." She crawled closer to him, wrapping her arms around his waist and pressing her cheek to his back. She understood now. He was afraid, that's why he pushed her away. That's what he always did, it seemed. But, would he do it again? "What do you want to do now?"

The warlock turned around, slipped his arms around her waist, and pulled her to his lap. "I think I would like to spend the rest of the night showing you how sorry I am."

CHAPTER NINETEEN

"You know we should not meet like this."

Stefan laughed. "Are you afraid of me?"

"What? Never."

"Soon, it will not matter, anyway," the mage said. "Do you have the next part of the plan in place?"

"Yes. The New York clan seems to think they are untouchable. But soon, they will learn exactly what we can do to them."

"And you're certain you can move on your part of the plan soon?"

"Within the week, at least. There has been one or two voices of dissent on the Council, but soon they will see things my way."

"Good," Stefan said. "And once you detain the dragon and the warlock, our army can come in. How many of your forces have you gathered so far?"

"About fifteen or so, but I'm going to recall the rest."

"Not bad, I suppose," Stefan cackled. "For two decades' worth of work. This army will be unstoppable, and best of all, they will be under my command."

"Our command, you mean."

"Of course. Our command."

"Just remember that, mage. This is my life's work, too. If this doesn't work, then I'm as good as dead."

CHAPTER TWENTY

eredith felt lightheaded and her vision blurred as she looked at the paper in her hand. "No," she shook her head. This wasn't true. Archie wouldn't hide this from her! The bile was rising in her throat, and she slammed her fist on the desk.

"Meredith? What are you doing in here?" Archie's voice was angry. "You know this is my private space!"

She spun around, the piece of paper in her hand. Archie's face went pale as his eyes trained on the damning evidence she had between her fingers. "Meredith." The anger was gone from his voice. "I can explain. Please—"

"Really Archie?" She walked to him, waving the paper. "You can explain? How long have you had this?"

"I...I...since before I found you."

"You knew about my real parents!" It was her birth certificate. She found in the hidden bottom of his top desk drawer, among other things - keys, more papers, a tablet PC, and four envelopes, each with their names on it. Killian. Quinn. Connor. Meredith. She couldn't help herself, of course, and opened hers. The first thing that dropped out was the picture of a toddler with brown eyes and blonde hair. Then a birth certificate, where the last name she had lost was written down, as well as the names of her parents. Philip and Lila. "What else do you have on us?"

The old man sighed. "I did it to protect you. To help your kind."

"How? Did you...did you do this on purpose? Did you find us and collect us? Like toys? Or to train us from a young age to be your army of thieves?"

"No!" he protested. "That wasn't my intent. I wanted to help you and protect you!"

"From what?" she asked. "It sounds like we needed protecting from you." She threw the birth certificate and the envelope to the ground.

"Meredith, don't, please!"

"Don't touch me, old man!" She tugged her arm away from him. "I thought...I thought you..." A sob ripped from her throat, followed by a growl.

"Meredith! Control yourself!" He commanded. "Remember what I taught you! Don't let the wolf take over!"

But she couldn't hear him. The she-wolf inside her was howling, wanting to be let out. She was doing it to protect her, taking all the pain and shielding her. She shifted, right there in his study and ran out into the woods.

The last time she shifted uncontrollably was that night when Jedd has raised a hand to her and slapped her so hard she fell on the floor. Her wolf was not as big as it was today; a pup, really. She ripped from Meredith's skin and landed on all fours, snarling and growling at Jedd, who backed up into the corner of their trailer as the wolf stalked him. The she-wolf wanted to kill the man for hurting Meredith, but unfortunately, Marie was right behind her. Meredith's foster mother had taken the shotgun from the wall and pointed it at the pup. When she cocked the gun, the she-wolf knew that she was thwarted and ran off into the night.

The she-wolf ran for hours and hours, away from that place. She would take care of Meredith from now on, refusing to give back the body they shared until she was healed. Months went by, and they traveled further West. She would only let Meredith shift back when she was exhausted, but always making sure she had shelter for a few days, sneaking them into abandoned building and vehicles. She did her best to provide for Meredith, stealing clothes and food if she could. Months and months passed until they reached the coast. To a city called Portland where a hungry and exhausted Meredith saw the old man in the hat.

As the fully-grown she-wolf raced through the woods behind her home, she comforted Meredith.

Where do you want to go?

Anywhere. Anywhere but here.

And so, for the second time, she took Meredith away again.

She let out a soft cry, her body trembling as her hands scratched at the sheets. Her mind was cloudy at the unfamiliar surroundings and the past mudding up the present. Strong arms wound around her waist and pulled her to a hard chest. Lips pressed against the back of her neck and when she realized where she was, she relaxed against Daric.

"Meredith," he murmured sleepily. "It was just a dream."

"Yeah," she replied softly. "Just a dream."

——————

It seemed it didn't matter to Meredith if they were in a king-sized bed or the double mattress in Daric's room; she just always had to sleep in the middle of the bed, diagonally, and across his chest. Daric found himself squeezed against the wall, with the Lycan's octopus-like arms and legs wrapped around his torso. He gently untangled Meredith's limbs and moved her over so he would have some room to breathe. He pushed her to her side, curling up around her as she sighed and mewled sleepily.

His little she-wolf. Wild and free and so insatiable. Seeing as Meredith had trashed her room, she and Daric decided to move to his quarters for the evening, but not before she snuck back to the lab to retrieve her "gift," while he went to the kitchen to find some food for them. He thought to surprise her, laying out a makeshift picnic for them on the floor of his room and some blankets. However, it was she who surprised him, slipping into some sexy lingerie—a sheer lacy purple bra, matching thong panties, and a garter belt and stockings. He thought he was hungry, but it turned out it wasn't for food. Their meal was momentarily forgotten, as he tossed her onto the bed. Of course, when they were done, Meredith declared a food break, devouring every bit of food he brought.

He stroked her soft hair, brushing it aside and pressed his nose to the pulse behind her ear. Hmmm...he thought it was her perfume but the wildflower scent was all Meredith. She stirred and pushed her plush ass back at him, making his cock stir again. Daric thought he was spent and satisfied, but his body had other ideas. He couldn't get enough of her. Slipping his hand between her thighs, he parted them, and all he had to do was angle his hips—

"Open this fucking door!" An angry voice called from the outside, followed by what sounded like a fist rapping on the wood.

Who the hell was that? Daric rose from his bed, moving Meredith (who seemingly could sleep through anything) aside, and walked to the door. He yanked the door open.

Connor stood on the other side, his face drawn into a scowl. "Where is—" He looked down at Daric's naked state and then peered around him. "You asshole! I knew you were trying to fuck her!"

This time, Daric was prepared for the punch. He should have known better, however. Connor was a skilled fighter and didn't use the same tricks twice. His meaty hands wrapped around Daric's neck and squeezed.

Immediately, Daric tried to wrestle the other man's arms away from his neck. As his fingers touched Connor's forearms, he was assaulted with a vision. A young boy, no more than fourteen or fifteen. Hands wrapped in filthy bandages. A caged fighting ring. The vicious, bloodthirsty cheer of the crowd. And red everywhere.

As the air rushed back into his lungs, Daric's eyes flew open, and he was staring up at the ceiling in his room back in Fenrir.

"Daric! Are you okay?" Meredith's worried voice rang in his ear. She sat next to him on the floor, shaking his shoulder. "Connor, you dick hole! What the fuck did you do?"

"He touched you! I told him not to touch you!" Connor railed.

"For fuck's sake, I'm twenty-five, not fifteen!" She stood up and faced him, planting her hands on her hips, which looked ridiculous considering she was wearing only the bed sheet and was half the other man's size. "And FYI, I was doing plenty of touching, too!"

Connor's eyes bulged. "Stop talking like that, I don't wanna hear that shit!"

Daric got to his feet, swaying as he got up. Meredith rushed to his side to help him, but he waved her away. "I'm fine." He looked at Connor. "I'm sorry."

"For fucking my sister?"

"For what happened to you when you were younger. The cage."

Connor's eyes widened, and his expression turned hard. "How the fuck—" He lunged at Daric again, but Meredith stood between them.

"What's going on—oh, for crying out loud!" Killian groaned as he entered the room. Daric was still naked, Meredith was naked under the sheet, and Connor had murder in his eyes. "I can only guess what's happening here, but I trust you're all adults and can sort this out."

"Killian," Connor began. "Tell this asshole to stay away from her and outta my head!"

"Killian, tell Connor I'm not a child!" Meredith retorted.

"Then stop acting like one!" Connor shot back.

Killian rubbed his palm down his face. "Everyone calm down. Connor, go cool off. Meredith, Daric, for God's sake, put some clothes on and meet us in our room. Quinn broke his tablet PC, and he'll be back soon, so we can—"

"What did you say?" Meredith interrupted.

"I said put some clothes—"

"No, no," she shook her head. "About Quinn."

"He went out to buy a new tablet PC?"

"That's it!" Meredith's face broke into a smile. "I think I figured it out."

"Figured what out?" Killian asked.

"I'm not sure yet, but I'll wait until we're all together. We'll meet you in your room in five," Meredith said. "And try and calm down Connor, will ya?"

"I'll do my best," he said, glancing at Daric. "Can I trust you not to provoke my brother?"

Daric sighed. "I suspect I provoke him merely by existing, but I'll not needle him."

Killian nodded and left, closing the door behind him.

Meredith turned to Daric. "You saw something, didn't you?"

He nodded. "Has Connor told you anything about his past?"

"Just bits and pieces. Things he lets slip sometimes, others I could guess." She frowned. "Why? What did you see?"

"I'm sorry, *min kjære*." He shook his head. "It's best if I not tell you. Those are his secrets to tell. Now," he continued. "What did you discover?"

"I don't know yet, but I'd rather we wait until we get everyone together. I'll meet you at my brothers' room, okay? I need a quick shower and some fresh clothes." She gave him a kiss on the cheek and left the room.

Daric thought it would be prudent to shower as well, seeing as the Lycans' keen senses would probably pick up the scent of sex around him and Meredith, and he didn't want to risk Connor's wrath again. The visions from the Lycan's past disturbed him. It not only looked violent, but felt it, too, and he could now understand and sympathize with the Lycan. After all, he himself had gone through traumatic experiences, being trained by Stefan, though the master mage didn't send him out to do his bidding until he was at least an adult. But in many ways, he and Connor (and perhaps, he suspected, the rest of the Lone Wolves) were more similar than he'd thought.

He walked out of his room and down the hallway. As he was about to knock on the door, it opened.

"Come in," Meredith said. "We're all here."

The room where the brothers were staying was much larger, with a simple living room and small kitchen area and two connected bedrooms. Killian and Quinn were sitting on the couch, while Connor was leaning against the breakfast bar, still scowling at Daric. There was some tension in the air, but it probably wasn't just from this morning. Meredith was still obviously upset at her brothers, and they seemed wary of her.

Daric sat down on the loveseat opposite the couch and Meredith plopped herself beside him, brazenly linking her arm through his. Connor growled, but a warning look from Killian made him back down.

"Meredith," Killian began. "I want to say sorry, for not telling you why Archie came here. I hope you understand why."

"We don't blame you," Quinn added. "None of us do. We just didn't want you to think that it was your fault. We were protecting you."

Meredith sighed. "It's going to be hard for me to get over that, because no matter which way you look at it if he wasn't in New York, he'd still be alive." Daric slipped his hand into hers and squeezed, a gesture she returned. "But you're right. We need to focus and find out who killed him."

"You said you figured something out. What is it?"

She took a deep breath. "I know I got mad at you guys for keeping something from me, but I guess I'm a hypocrite because I kept something from you, too. Last night I was dreaming—no, I was remembering the last time I saw Archie. He had been acting weird for a couple of weeks, and I knew he was hiding something. So, I broke into his office." She relayed the rest of the story, about what she found in the hidden compartment in his drawer. When she got to the part where she said she found files with all their names on it, the tension in the room increased. Killian was the calmest and in control, but his hands tightened into fists. Quinn quickly stood up and began to pace angrily. Connor, on the other hand, remained eerily still, but his eyes turned dark.

"Did you read the other files?" Killian asked, his brows knitting together.

She shook her head. "No, I didn't." The three brothers seemed relieved by her confession.

Quinn sat down again. "Why did he have those files on us? Was he tracking us down? How did he know about us?"

Meredith shrugged. "I don't know. But, somehow, he'd gotten hold of all my records. It wasn't just my birth certificate and my picture, but also some newspaper clippings about my dad's death. He'd been murdered," she said, her voice trembling. "I didn't even know that. I was told he died in an accident." She straightened her back. "Look, whatever Archie's reasons were, he still saved me from a worse fate. And maybe he did the same with all of you. So, we need to dig deeper and find out how this is all connected."

"So, what did you figure out?"

"Well, when I was looking through his stuff, I was pretty sure I saw a tablet PC in that hidden compartment of his."

Quinn frowned. "A tablet PC? Archie barely knew how to email. He still used an old analog phone and texted in all caps."

"Don't you see?" Meredith said. "What was he doing with that tablet PC? He did everything on paper, and he hated using technology himself. Why keep it hidden, along with our files?"

"We need to find that tablet."

"And our files," Connor interjected.

"That too," Killian agreed. "We need to go back to Portland. If we leave today, we can come back by tomorrow if we find everything."

CHAPTER TWENTY-ONE

W ith her three brothers away for the next day or so, Meredith didn't have anything else to do. So, they decided to visit Jade so Daric could do more work with her. While Jade and Daric continued their research, Meredith sat in her corner of the lab, watching them as Daric tried to explain to her the nature of his powers. Jade seemed pretty engrossed at whatever the warlock was saying as she took down notes and asked questions. Too engrossed it seemed, to notice that her mate had arrived.

Sebastian frowned as he sat down next to Meredith, his eyes trained with laser-focus on Jade and Daric.

"Can the testosterone, will ya?" she said. "You know she only has eyes for you."

"Yeah, well, normally she'd be all over me. She barely noticed I'm here," he said, pouting.

"Please, she used to be worse. Lara said she would forget to shower when she went on her science benders."

"At least I know I don't have to worry about him, either," Sebastian said, eyeing her meaningfully.

"What do you mean—wait, never mind, she told you."

Meredith's face soured. "Are you going to give me a lecture, too? About how he's a warlock and our enemy and can't be trusted?"

"What, me, give a lecture to someone?" he laughed. "What is it with you Lycans and warlocks and witches? Anyway, I don't care about that shit. Seems to me, Daric is trying to make up for past sins. Plus, he didn't want to do any of those things that asshole Stefan made him do."

"You have a point, I guess," she said glumly. "But still, no one's gonna be happy."

"Fucking hell, Meredith, you gonna let other people dictate how you feel for anyone?"

Meredith swallowed a gulp. What did she feel for Daric? His confession had been intense, but he didn't say anything directly about his feelings.

"Of course, I'd be careful about letting Vrost know. You know he's going to shit a brick when he finds out."

"Hmm?" she asked, cocking her head at him. Nick did seem to have a particular hatred for Daric. Why, she didn't know. Hoping to put Sebastian out of his misery, she cleared her throat to get her friend's attention.

"Sebastian," Jade said in a surprised voice when her gaze landed on him. "I didn't hear you come in. You should have said something."

"You were busy."

"Hmmm...cranky-pants dragon," she giggled as she wrapped her arms around his middle and laid her head on his chest.

Sebastian drew her into his embrace and kissed the top of her head. "Ready to go soon, darlin'? I thought I'd take you out to dinner tonight. Somewhere so fancy and snooty we'll have to stop by somewhere else to get more food to take home."

Jade looked over to Daric, who gave them a nod. "Of course, let me grab my things." She disappeared into her office and came back to the main lab with her coat and purse. "I'll see you in the morning, maybe?"

"Sure," Meredith said. "Have fun you two. We'll close up here."

With one last wave and a nod from Sebastian, the couple left the lab. Meredith let out a sigh. Jade and Sebastian had fought hard for each other, and their journey was long but the reward well-deserved. She was glad they had each other.

"If I could use my powers," Daric began. "I could take you anywhere for a meal. We could have the finest meal in Paris, London, or Shanghai. Anywhere your heart desired."

"I don't care about that, Daric," she said, placing a hand on his arm.

He frowned. "Still, you deserve that and more."

"Well, how about I take you to the finest employee cafeteria in New York?" She offered him her arm.

With a smile, he took her arm. "Lead the way."

Meredith locked up the lab, and they took the elevator down to the employee cafeteria, which actually was quite excellent. There was a wide variety of food (all free), and if there was something you wanted, most of the chefs were happy to whip it up if they had the ingredients. After picking up their food, they walked over to the group of tables in the corner.

Meredith put her tray heaping with food on the table in front of her as she sat down, sliding into the bench, while Daric sat opposite to her.

"So," he began. "Is this our first date?"

She laughed. "I guess so. But we've already gotten over the awkward stage by having sex, so this is probably 90% better than most of the other dates I've been on." She took a spoonful of fried rice and swallowed. "Not that I've been on many." She reached over and took his hand.

He looked around them. At this time, the cafeteria was

mostly empty, but there were still a couple of employees lingering. "Are you sure this is wise? You know many Lycans here still despise me."

"I'm not exactly winning any popularity contests," she replied. "Although you know Nick Vrost'll probably blow a gasket." Daric winced, a gesture she didn't miss. "Care to tell me what that beef is about?"

The warlock sighed. "I'll understand if you feel differently after this, but it's better you hear it from me and not anyone else. Before Stefan revealed himself to the Lycans, he had Cady framed for crimes against the New York clan and then had her kidnapped. I mean, Victoria and I kidnapped her." He paused. "His plan was to have Cady and I...produce the next generation of witches and warlocks who could be turned into mages. That plan didn't work out, obviously, but you can see why Nick Vrost would hate me."

"Would you have done...anything?" she asked.

He looked away. "I would not have forced myself on her if that's what you're asking," he said, his voice raising slightly. "But I would have done anything to protect my mother and prevent Stefan from killing or hurting Cady in other ways."

Meredith grew silent, and when she didn't say anything, Daric withdrew his hand from hers. "Hey," she called softly, catching his hand back. "I'm not judging your past and what Stefan made you do."

"Are you angry?"

"Angry?" she asked. "I'm fucking furious. Furious at Stefan. He really will do anything to defeat the Lycans."

"His hatred knows no bounds," Daric commented.

"Look, nothing happened, right? With you and Cady, I mean."

"No," he replied. "But there are other things that I've done that I'll never be able to atone for."

Meredith looked at him. "Listen to me. I've done some things I'm not proud of—no, no, don't even think of telling me they're not the same as yours. It's not a contest of who did worse. But what I'm trying to say is that we can't dwell on the past, but move on forward. Do what we can to make up for past fuck ups."

"Sounds like good advice," he said, raising a brow at her.

She knew what he meant by that look of course. Could she ever forgive herself for causing Archie's death? "Yeah, maybe I should take it."

Daric stood up and then sat down next to her, nudging her over to make room for himself. "You are very smart, *min kjære*. I will do my best if you promise to do the same."

"I will," she replied.

"Good," he drew her close and kissed her cheek. "Now, let us finish our meal so we can go back upstairs."

———

Meredith's brothers arrived late in the afternoon the next day. When she and Daric walked into their suite, she immediately saw the tablet PC on the coffee table. "That's it," she said. "I mean, I can't be sure it's the same one, but it's similar."

"We found it exactly where you said it would be," Killian said. "Along with our files." He handed Meredith a brown envelope.

"Thank you," she said, taking it from him, staring at her name handwritten in ink on the flap.

"We all looked at our files," Quinn informed her. "And though we didn't share details, we didn't find anything solid that could lead us to Archie's killer."

"What about the tablet?"

"It has a lock on it. A simple 4-digit combination." Quinn

picked up the tablet. "I'm gonna run a couple of programs on it to try and figure out the code. We should have it in a few hours."

"1213," Meredith blurted out.

"What?"

"December 13. That was her birthday. Jenny, his wife," Meredith explained. "Try it."

Quinn shrugged and tapped the combination on the screen. "Sonofabitch," he cried as the display came to life.

"He didn't like tech, but he loved her," Killian said. "Is there anything interesting on there?"

"Hmmm..." Quinn's eyes narrowed at the screen. "There's nothing on here. No apps, no documents. Except this." He turned the screen to them. There was a single video file.

"Go on. Open it," Killian urged.

Quinn tapped the icon, which expanded and filled the screen with black. A few seconds later, Archie's face appeared on the screen.

"Play it," Meredith said quietly.

Quinn propped the tablet against a stack of magazines on the table, and they gathered around it. With a deep breath, he tapped on the play button.

On the screen, Archie sat in his study, facing the tablet's camera. "Killian...Quinn...Connor...Meredith," he began. "Whichever one of you found this, or maybe all of you did...but anyway, if you're watching this, then I'm probably dead."

Meredith gasped, and Daric put an arm around her.

"I'm so sorry," Archie continued. "Meredith ran away a couple of months ago, and it was all my fault. She saw the files, maybe you all have seen yours, too. She thought I had been 'collecting' you. And she was right."

The three Lone Wolves looked at each other, and the tension in the air grew thick.

"You see, it all began twenty-two years ago," he said. "My

Jenny and I were never blessed with children, and we were desperate to adopt. She was a Lycan, like you, as you know. We heard of a young Lycan boy whose entire clan had been wiped out in a mysterious attack. All dead, except this innocent boy. We wanted to raise him and petitioned our Alpha and the High Council, but they denied us. Jenny was distraught. She asked around, and no one could tell us who took him in or why our request was denied when this boy obviously needed a home. As far as we knew, he had disappeared into thin air. She was heartbroken, convinced that something was wrong. She died before she found out and I vowed I would find him. And so, I did. I found him. I found Killian."

Meredith's head snapped to Killian. "What was—"

"Shhh. Let's keep watching."

"And you all know, I don't have to explain. How I found all of you. Even Meredith. I kept my ears open for Lycan children disappearing or clans leaving pups behind with no one to care for them. I don't know what it meant, but I kept digging. I...I have my suspicions, but I can't be sure. I've kept my ears to ground and I've heard rumblings about mages and witches and such. Things are not as they seem. I'm headed to New York. I told you I'm going there because of Meredith. I may try to see her, but I have a feeling she's safe where she is. But that's not the real reason." He let out a long breath. "I'm going to meet with a contact of mine, someone connected to the Council. But, I have a bad feeling about this. I can't explain it. But if you're watching this and something has happened to me, I hope, first and foremost, you forgive me for keeping this from all of you. I was only trying to protect you. Don't try and find out what happened to me, but if you want to help me, find out what happened to you and what could have happened to all the Lycan children. The population of Lone Wolves has increased in the past two decades, and no one else has noticed. I think...

well," he shrugged. "But, I'm probably just some paranoid old man. I can't believe I'm recording this." He reached over to the front of the screen, and it turned black.

Meredith felt the tears roll down her cheeks and she buried her face in Daric's chest. Killian rose from the couch, running his hands through his hair in frustration as Quinn stared at the screen, his face in shock. Connor, on the other hand, slammed his fist into the wall, leaving a dent.

Killian finally spoke "The fucking Council."

"They did this to Archie."

"They did this to *us*," Meredith said bitterly. "They did something to our families and clans so we would..."

"We don't know that yet," Killian said. "But we need to find out."

"What are we going to do?" Quinn asked. "We should get out of here now."

"I agree," Connor said. "We don't know if we can trust anyone now." He eyed Daric suspiciously.

"No! We can trust the New York clan," Meredith said. "We can trust Grant Anderson."

"How the hell would you know that, Meredith?' Connor asked. "They locked you up in here, making you work for them and risk your life, and you want us to trust them?"

"Look, I made my bed, and now I gotta lie in it," she protested, standing up and crossing her arms. "But, I have this feeling...I think Grant'll help us. If there is something fishy going on with the High Council, he'll want to know and put a stop to them."

"Fucking Christ, listen to yourself Meredith!' Connor growled. As he approached her, Daric quickly stepped in front of him.

"Don't," the warlock warned him in a deadly voice.

"I'm not gonna hurt her, asshole," Connor bit back. "Now you, on the other hand—"

"Daric! Connor! Stop it!" Meredith cried. "Killian," she pleaded to the other Lycan. "We can't take on the Council alone. You know that."

The dark-haired Lycan sighed. "Fine, we'll go to Grant."

CHAPTER TWENTY-TWO

G rant's face became ashen after he watched the video. Beside him, Alynna and Alex looked distraught. While Nick's face was its usual cold mask, the burning anger in his eyes was unmistakeable.

The Alpha took a few seconds to compose himself before he turned to Killian. "Thank you for trusting me with this. I swear to you, on my father's grave and the life of my unborn child, that I had no idea that this was happening."

"I believe you, Alpha," Killian said. "Do you know why the Council would do something like this? I thought they were tasked to protect us?"

"It couldn't be the whole High Council, could it Grant?" Nick asked, his face grave. "Could it be just one or some of the members? Or an insider? If Archie met with someone from the Council, that means they came to New York without your authorization."

"That would be easy enough for any Lycan," Grant admitted. "You know we can't monitor all Lycan activities in the city. Permission is merely a formality, but the reality is any

Lycan can come to New York as they pleased, and wouldn't get in trouble as long as he or she didn't run into one of us."

"What does it all mean?" Alynna asked.

"We need to know more," Killian replied. "Whoever killed Archie must have done this because he knew too much about the Lycan children."

"There's something else you need to know about the Council." Grant massaged his temple with his fingers and relayed to everyone what happened when he met with the Council and about their concerns with Daric and the True Mate pairings.

"Looks like New York's getting some heat from the Council," Killian remarked.

Alynna frowned. "Could they really dissolve your territory?"

Grant nodded. "I'm afraid so. If they deemed us a threat."

"That's ridiculous. And our kids would never be a threat. We're ensuring the survival of our species!" Alynna said, throwing her hands in the air. Alex frowned at her and wrapped an arm protectively around his wife's middle.

"We must find out what the Council is up to," Nick said.

"Or if it is the Council doing this," Alynna interjected. "Hmmm...I always thought that Lljuffa wasn't trustworthy! She's also kinda creepy."

"They all weren't happy with the recent events," Grant said. "It could be any of them or all of them. This won't be easy, and we need to tread carefully," Grant pronounced. "If we make one mistake, then we not only risk getting our territory dissolved, but also have the rest of the Lycans after us."

"Wait," Meredith chimed in. "There's a way for us to get the information we need without risking New York, Grant."

The Alpha frowned. "How?"

"We could get it. As Lone Wolves, we're not pledged to

New York," she said. "If we were caught, you could deny everything."

"Absolutely not," Grant replied in a serious tone. "I don't want you risking your lives or freedom."

"It makes perfect sense, Alpha," Killian said. "Besides, the main mission here is to find out what happened to Archie and those children the Council may or may not have deliberately ripped from their clans."

"Fine," Grant relented. "What do you propose?"

"A little trip to Switzerland," Killian said.

———

The Lycan High Council headquarters was located in Switzerland, in the pretty city of Lausanne, located right on the shores of Lake Geneva. They were housed in a modern building not far from the center and looked like any office in the area. The Council headquarters was disguised as a think tank (cheekily named *Le Loup Institute*) and anyone who passed by it simply thought it to be an ordinary office building. However, it had a security system as tight as any Swiss Bank, and if this didn't scare would-be thieves, then the heavily armed Lycan security guards outside probably would.

Of course, the Lone Wolves weren't just ordinary criminals trying to break in. All four of them were trained by one of the world's best thieves. The plan was to distract the guards, hack into their security system and install a backdoor into their server room so Quinn could get into their files. Simple enough, but they all couldn't agree on how to move with the first part of their plan.

"You know, I could just try and seduce the guards," Meredith said.

"No," came the resounding disapproval from Connor and Daric.

"Yeah, what makes you think they'd be interested in you?" came Quinn's reply which earned him a slap on the head from Meredith. "Oww! I meant, what if they played for the other team? They're European, right?"

"You're-a-peein'," Meredith snapped back.

So, they had to devise a plan to distract the guards. Daric was the obvious choice, as he would appear like any normal human to the Lycans, but he couldn't do it himself. So, thanks to some glamour potions from the New York coven and a heavy blast of French perfume, Meredith came along to help him.

Daric put his arm around Meredith, and they casually strolled in front of the Council headquarters. The warlock whispered some French in her ear, because, of course, Daric spoke the language. Trying not to get distracted by the heat pooling between her legs, Meredith searched her brain for the little French she did know.

Once they were in front of the guard house, Meredith let loose. "*Va te faire foutre!*" she screamed at him. "*Fils de pute!*" She hoped that was convincing because "go fuck yourself" and "son of a bitch" were the only French phrases she could recall right now.

Daric answered back in rapid-fire French, begging and trying to touch her, but she kept batting him away. From the corner of her eye, she could see the two guards in the booth looking at each other, wondering if they should intervene in the lovers' quarrel.

"Grab me and slap me around a little," Meredith hissed.

"What?" Daric whispered. "I cannot do that."

She rolled her eyes. Making sure her back was turned to the guards, she gave herself a loud smack on the cheek. *Ow, that stung.* She let out a shriek and cry, forcing the tears from her eyes. Turning around, she ran to the guardhouse and started shrieking, hoping she was unintelligible enough so no one would notice she didn't speak a lick of French.

The two Lycan guards seemed distraught as if they didn't know what to do. Daric chased her into the guardhouse, shouting his apologies. One of the guards ran toward him, trying to stop him and he struggled as he begged and pleaded for Meredith's forgiveness.

With the guards properly distracted, Killian snuck into the building. Quinn had already hacked into the cameras some time ago and had been playing a loop of the footage showing no signs of activity.

Meredith and Daric continued their lover's quarrel, and each time the guards tried to make them leave, she would put on the waterworks and cower behind one of the guards, as Daric played the part of threatening/repentant boyfriend. This lasted another ten minutes, and it was a good thing that Connor flashed the all-clear signal from across the street (a mirror he had hidden in his pocket), indicating that Killian had made it out of the building.

The guards were threatening to call the police (a word Meredith recognized), so when Daric got on his knees, begging her for forgiveness, she quickly embraced him, made out with him with lots of tongue, and they reconciled.

"You didn't have to squeeze my ass in front of those men," Daric said glumly when they were out of earshot. "Or shoved your tongue down my throat."

"I know," she said cheekily.

He frowned when he saw the palm print on her cheek. "You shouldn't have done that, either" he said, touching the redness.

"It'll be gone in a few minutes, but that doesn't matter anyway. We have what we came for. Or we will."

They rounded the corner and met up with Killian. A black

car pulled in front of them, driven by Connor and they all hopped inside.

"Are we in?" Killian asked Quinn.

Quinn stared at the screen, his frown turning into a smile. "Yes! We're good to go."

"Great," Killian said. "Let's head to the airport."

CHAPTER TWENTY-THREE

The flight back to New York would take at least nine hours, even in the sleek private jet that Grant had chartered through one of his shell companies. Quinn had copied half of the data while they were on the ground so he could work on the encrypted files and scan them for any important data while they were on the flight. The rest he could easily access once they were in New York, thanks to the backdoor device Killian had managed to install on the High Council's main servers.

Meredith sat in the plush leather chair, trying to read her book with just her right hand. It was a little tricky, seeing as Daric had the fingers on her left hand threaded through his. He, apparently, mastered the art of flipping the pages with one hand as he was engrossed in his own book. With a sigh, she ended up putting the book on her lap. Across from her, Connor scowled. He was not happy when he saw the palm print on her face, but she quickly explained that she did it to herself. Her brother was overprotective, but this crap was getting old. When she whispered a joke to Daric about joining the mile high club, he growled, and she forgot that he had enhanced senses. So, she tried to keep the PDA to a minimum, but he couldn't begrudge her *holding hands* with her boyfriend, right?

Oh God, was Daric her boyfriend? That seemed like a weird term for what they had going on.

Her inner-she wolf yipped in happiness. *No, he's our mate. Ours.*

Hmm...mate didn't sound bad. It was less trite than boyfriend and more succinct than just lover.

"I can hear the wheels in your brain turning," Daric whispered in her ear as he leaned over to her. "Care to share what you're thinking?"

She laughed. "I don't think Connor wants to hear what I'm thinking right now."

"It can't be worse than what I'm thinking," he teased, his breath hot on her skin.

She sighed. "How many more hours until I can get you alone?"

"About eight more hours," he replied.

Meredith frowned. "Stupid brothers." They hadn't had sex since they left for New York and she was getting antsy. Obviously, since the airplane had no bedrooms, they couldn't do it there. Their hotel room in Lausanne had paper thin walls, and as soon as they started to get hot and heavy, Quinn pounded on the wall and told them he was going to sic Connor on them if they didn't keep it down. Needless to say, they spent a very frustrating night not getting any action.

"We could wait until everyone is asleep. I think I could probably hold you up against the wall in the lavatory," Daric teased.

She groaned, the image of them fucking upright in the bathroom made her clit throb and sent her nipples puckering. Hmmm, maybe she could wrap her legs around his waist while he thrust into her. God, she could almost taste his skin. She shook her head. "You're way too tall, you'd hit your head on the ceiling."

"It would be worth it."

"Knock it off, you two," Killian warned. When Meredith opened her mouth to protest, he shut her down. "Don't even think about it. Keep it in your pants for another couple of hours, okay?"

"Fine," she grumbled, sinking back into her seat.

Daric lifted the armrest between them. "Come, *min kjære*," he said, pulling her to his side. "Take a nap. You'll feel better in a few hours."

She settled against him, breathing in his scent, which always brought some comfort to her. Closing her eyes, she let sleep take over.

Raised voices woke her up and she jolted upright. She wasn't resting on Daric's chest anymore, but rather, she was laying on the reclined chair. "What's going on?" she asked sleepily. Her brothers and Daric were all surrounding Quinn.

Killian's face was drawn into a grave expression. "Quinn found something."

"What is it?"

"A directive from the Council," Killian replied. "They're sending people to New York to take Daric and someone named Sebastian Creed."

"Fuck!" Meredith sat up. She looked at Daric. "Shit. When?"

"Today. They should be getting there the same time we are."

"Great, just great," she moaned. "They might discover our little trip if they get there and Daric's not in his cell. What are we going to do?"

"We could probably beat them back to Fenrir," Killian said. "I've already called Grant from the satellite phone. He'll delay them as long as he can. That's not our biggest concern now, unfortunately."

Meredith frowned. "Wait, there's more?"

Quinn frowned. "Possibly. I didn't download the entire database, just bits and pieces. But, there's definitely something fishy going on in there." He typed on the keyboard.

"What is it?" Daric asked.

"Lone Wolves are pretty much independent. We don't have clans or Alphas, but we're still under the Council's authority."

"Yeah, I know," Meredith groaned. That was the reason she was serving her time, after all. Despite being independent, she still had to obey the Council. She hated having to register as a Lone Wolf, but she had no choice. Following rules helped keep order and prevented the humans from finding out about Lycans. After all, if the world were to find out about werewolf shifters, many of them, especially Lone Wolves like her without the protection of a clan, would end up in zoos or in labs.

"Well, I don't know what's going on exactly," Quinn said as he stared at the screen. "But someone in the Council has been accessing the files of Lone Wolves over and over again in the past weeks. Not just reading, but making copies and searching through confidential files."

"Is it a hacker?"

Her brother shook his head. "No, the Mac addresses are definitely coming from inside the Council. One machine."

"Whose?" Killian asked.

"I can't tell yet. I have to download that information when we get on the ground. I've just been doing a general search for anything in the databases with keywords related to Lone Wolves and came up with fragments of disturbing messages. Whoever did this tried to delete their tracks by trashing them, but they're still there. Once we get on the ground and I have a better connection we can figure out who it is and it'll make it easier for me to search."

"Fuck," cursed Killian. "Alright. Well, we still got a couple of hours before we land. And as soon as we do, we're hitting the ground running. Get some rest."

———

Killian wasn't kidding when he said they'd hit the ground running. Alex Westbrooke was already waiting for them on the tarmac in the tiny private airstrip just outside Jersey City. They quickly filed into the van and Quinn booted up his laptop to try and download as many of the files from the Council as he could.

Alex drove like a madman, cursing when they hit the traffic at the tunnel. They were still ahead though because if the Council arrived before them, he would have gotten a call from Alynna or Nick. Once they got through the jam, Alex stepped on the gas and didn't take his foot off until they were in the garage at Fenrir. He barely cut the engine when they filed out of the van and took the elevator straight up to the executive floor.

"They're almost here," Grant said as they entered his office. Alynna, Jade, and Sebastian were already there.

"Any luck?" Killian asked Quinn, who had quickly sat down on the couch, his eyes never leaving the screen of his laptop.

"Almost there."

"Can't you tell the Council not to come here?" Alynna asked her brother. "You're the Alpha! Rescind their invitation."

"I'm sorry, Alynna," Grant said. "It doesn't work that way."

"They can fuckin' try to take me," Sebastian gritted. "Just fuckin' try, and I'll burn them to ashes."

There was a loud commotion outside, and Meredith knew what it was. The Council had arrived.

The door opened and Jared had barely announced them

when Lljuffa Suitdottir and Rodrigo Baeles entered, followed by six burly Lycan men. They were the enforcers of the High Council, a group of highly-trained, elite fighters who protected the Council and, in cases like this, did their dirty work.

"You know why we're here," Rodrigo said, his usually friendly demeanor gone. "Hand them over, Alpha."

Lljuffa had her eyes trained directly at Grant. "Alpha, please cooperate."

"You can't!" Jade said, clutching at Sebastian's arm, her eyes glowing an eerie green. "You can't take him!"

Rodrigo nodded to one of the men, who approached Sebastian. He pointed a weapon at him, and when Jade tried to put herself in front of her mate, Sebastian's eyes changed to their burning gold color, indicating that The Beast was ready to rip out of his skin.

"Stand down!" Grant ordered.

"Take him!" Rodrigo hissed.

"Lljuffa, Rodrigo," Grant said in a warning voice. "Do you have the resources to keep Sebastian from shifting? Can you stop him from shifting and tearing this whole building apart? I keep telling you; you have no jurisdiction over him. He's not pledged to you or to me. But, if you insist on taking him, you can bet I will fight you with everything I have, not to mention his own resources. You don't want this type of war on your hands."

Lljuffa's icy eyes hardened, but she gave a short nod. Sebastian's eyes returned to normal, his body relaxing as Jade collapsed against him in relief.

Rodrigo's face fell. "Fine, but the warlock is coming with us. He must pay for his crimes against the Lycans and suffer for his collaboration with our enemy."

"No!" Meredith protested. "Alpha," she looked over at Grant, pleading to him, "don't let them take him. You know he's not a bad person!"

"He's our prisoner," Grant said.

"A prisoner?" Lljuffa asked in a mocking tone. "Then why isn't he in a cell?"

Grant's jaw tightened. "He is pledged to me—"

"Stop it, Grant!" Lljuffa cut him off. "You know that's a flimsy excuse. His pledge means nothing. He is not a Lycan. The warlock or Creed, it's your choice."

"Neither," Grant said, standing up. "If it's a war you want, it's a war you'll get, Lljuffa."

There was an audible gasp in the room, and the air went heavy until it was so thick it was like breathing molasses. Meredith was choking, her inner she-wolf begging to be let out. Everyone around her was already on the verge of shifting.

"Stop," Daric said. "There is no need for violence." He stepped forward, and Meredith grabbed onto his arm. "No, *min kjære*," he whispered. She looked up at his blue-green eyes and his handsome face. He seemed to be silently pleading with her to trust him. With a slight nod, she let go of his arm, her heart thumping against her chest. She hoped what she had read was right.

"I will come with you peacefully," Daric said, stretching his arms out. "But only if you take me personally. I will not go with your goons."

Lljuffa and Rodrigo looked at each other.

"Fine," Lljuffa relented. "Come with us, warlock."

The two Lycans reached out to him, but he grabbed them first. His fingers wrapped around each of their arms, his body stiffening as the visions flooded his mind. They didn't make sense. It was like two competing channels on a television screen. Letting go of one arm, he hoped he had picked the right person. The visions cleared again. A rooftop on a moonlit night. A man in the hat in front of him. Hands pushing him over the ledge and a desperate scream. The sound of flesh and bone hitting the pavement.

When he released the hand, he looked up slowly, tracing the path upwards to the face of the person who killed Archie Leacham. "You. You did it."

Rodrigo's eyes flashed with panic for a moment, but the Lycan composed himself. "Are you coming with us now, warlock? Or," he looked over at Meredith. "Will there be violence?"

"I'm not going anywhere, cur," Daric said in a menacing tone. "You killed Archie Leacham. Why?"

"Who?" Rodrigo asked smoothly without missing a beat. "I don't know what you're talking—Fuck!"

Meredith didn't know what came over her, but all she could think and see was red. She pounced at Rodrigo, somehow grabbing a letter opener on Grant's desk as she leaped over it on her way to the other Lycan. Bringing the slim metal tool to his neck, she twisted around so she was behind him and her other arm was around his waist. "You slimy son of bitch!" she shouted. "You killed Archie! You killed our dad!"

As the Lycan enforcers advanced towards Meredith and Rodrigo with their weapons raised, Killian and Connor hunched in on themselves, and their wolves burst from their bodies. Killian's animal was pitch dark, like his hair, with eerie turquoise-colored eyes. Connor's, on the other hand, was light gray, but a monster and feral-looking. The animal had to have been over eight feet tall on its hind legs, and his face bore the same scar as his human form. Large teeth were bared, growling at the enforcers, who were all now on the verge of shifting as well.

"Stop!" Lljuffa ordered. "No more shifting! I forbid it!"

The enforcers looked confused and backed away from Meredith and Rodrigo.

"Stand down, Killian, Connor!" Grant barked. The two wolves slunk back but remained in their Lycan forms.

"Get this crazy bitch off me," Rodrigo moaned as Meredith pressed the tip of the letter opener deeper into his skin.

"Tell us why you killed him!" she hissed.

"You all are insane! I didn't kill anyone!"

"I saw it, in my vision," Daric said. "You can't deny it."

Rodrigo looked around, "What are you waiting for? You all would take the word of a warlock and his stupid whore Lone Wolf over mine! He's lying! He didn't see anything! Why would I kill anyone's father?"

"Because he knew what you were doing," Quinn answered from where he was sitting, his voice edgy, but eerily cold. "It was you. All these years. You orchestrated everything."

"I don't—"

"Shut up!" Meredith pushed the knife harder, breaking the skin, so a drop of blood formed at the tip.

"You knew Archie. You were his contact in the Council. He came to you for help and told you what he'd discovered." Quinn stood up, taking his computer with him. He went to Lljuffa, showing her the screen. "You tried to erase his messages from your phone, but I found them. And you've also been accessing the files of the registered Lone Wolves around the world."

Lljuffa's face went pale, then her eyes grew hard as diamonds as she read from Quinn's screen. "Rodrigo... this...why?"

"Yeah, tell us," Meredith snarled. "Did you kill my biological dad? To wipe out our clans?"

"I..." He relaxed against her. "Stefan threatened me. He made me do it! Please!" he begged.

"You've been planning this for over twenty years," Quinn said. "I found your private files, traced where you copied them from the main Council server to your laptop. You have files of over thirty Lone Wolves going back for the last two decades. All of them abandoned after their families and clans were wiped away, or other clans refused them. You bribed Meredith's Alpha so she'd be sent away, didn't you? I bet I could find the payment for that."

Meredith's blood froze, and her heart beat against her ribs. "No..."

"Shut up!" Rodrigo screamed. Feeling that Meredith's grip loosened, he wrenched away from her, grabbing the knife from her hand and turning it on her.

"No!" Daric yelled.

"Uh-huh, warlock," Rodrigo warned. "Don't even think about it. My lovely Lone Wolf, why couldn't you have just let things be?" His eyes were wild, looking at everyone in the room. Lljuffa stood there in shock, while Grant remained very still. Everyone in the room remained rooted to their spot. "Archie came to me with what he had found out. That old fool. All this time he suspected something was going on and he was right. Too bad he came to me about it, thinking I was going to help him. I had to kill him of course, and made it look like a suicide. Thanks to Stefan, covering up my tracks was easy."

"Why?" Grant asked. "Why were you trying to make more Lone Wolves?"

"The Lone Wolves were going to make the perfect soldiers," Rodrigo explained. "With no clan or no Alpha ties, they would have been receptive to Stefan's mind control spell."

"Rodrigo!" Lljuffa gasped. "All this time..."

"What, you think I worked, clawed, and killed my way to becoming a High Council member for the fun of it?" He laughed. "Yes, I've been working with Stefan all this time."

"To wipe out our kind?" Grant said. "You would do that?"

"Stefan's not going to destroy all the Lycans," Rodrigo said.

"Just the ones who would refuse to bow to him once he conquers this world."

"And I suppose you were going to be his right-hand man?"

"Of course! He promised me," Rodrigo replied. "I would be Alpha and leader of all the remaining Lycans."

Daric let out a laugh. "And you believed him? Stefan is not one to share power. He would have killed you, too."

"You'll never find out now, will you?" He looked at Meredith and wrapped an arm around her waist and pulled her close. "I'm going to leave here now. If any one of you tries to stop me, I'll slit her throat." He gave her a lascivious look. "Maybe I'll keep her for a bit. She looks like she'll be fun in the sack."

"I will strip every last bit of skin from your body before I let you touch her," Daric threatened.

"Oh yeah? I don't see how—Fuck!" Rodrigo let out a pained howl as a large, gray blur leaped from behind him. He screamed in agony as a massive paw swiped at his back. Jade had shifted into her wolf form and knocked him down. Rodrigo rolled away, and the gray wolf landed on all fours, fangs bared.

Meredith sprang into action, giving her best friend silent thanks as she dove towards Rodrigo, making him shriek in pain as she landed on top of him. "Murderer!" she screamed as a fist landed on his face. Her hands curled around his neck, fingers squeezing tight, all the while it seemed like the oxygen was being sucked out of her own lungs. She couldn't breathe, and pain gripped her body. Her vision blurred around her, except for Rodrigo's face as it turned blue. The she-wolf was demanding to be let out, to rip Archie's murderer to shreds. She sent it a warning growl. No, she would have to do this. She wasn't going to let the she-wolf take over the responsibility and pain and get the blood on her paws. Not this time.

"Meredith. Meredith!" Daric's voice somehow broke through to her. "Stop. Don't kill him."

Her fingers loosened, and Rodrigo began gasping, but he was too weak to fight her off. There was something sticky on her knees, and she realized he was bleeding out fast.

"Don't do it, Meredith," Daric said softly as he knelt beside her.

"Why not?" Her fingers tightened again. "He killed Archie. He destroyed my life. All our lives."

"And he will pay for his crimes. But Archie would not have wanted you tainted with blood and guilt."

Tears began to flow down her cheeks, and Meredith looked back down at Rodrigo. No, she had to kill him. Make him pay.

"Please, Meredith," Daric said, placing a hand on her shoulder. "Killing him won't bring your father back."

She let out an agonizing sob and fell to the side. Daric caught her and embraced her, drawing her into his arms. The dam of her emotions broke and rushed out—rage, pain, regret, relief—and she continued to weep and rail at him, beating her fists on his chest.

"Let go of me!" Meredith struggled when Daric picked her up.

He ignored her and held her tighter. "I'll take care of her," Daric said to no one in particular as they left the office, and Meredith's protests grew louder.

CHAPTER TWENTY-FOUR

D aric carried Meredith all the way to his room, ignoring all the stares and looks from the people around them. He trusted that Grant and the others would be able to clean up the mess from the confrontation with Rodrigo, so he left them. Meredith was his number one priority, and she was hurting right now.

"Put me down, you brute!" she hissed. He complied, but not until they reached the shower. He dumped her into the stall and turned the shower on full blast. The cold water hit them both, making her shriek, but he remained still. She cursed and slammed her fists into him, unleashing her fury and screaming bloody murder.

"Are you done yet?" he asked when she took a pause. He switched the shower to blast them with warm water.

"No," she protested. "I want that bastard dead for what he did. Why did you stop me? I had him!"

"I didn't stop you," he said. "You stopped all by yourself. You realized I was right."

That only seemed to rile her up. "I'll kill him now. Let me out of here!" She scratched at him, but he caught her wrists.

"You won't. You can't," Daric said, slowly pushing her back against the wall.

"Oh yeah? Just you watch." She tried to go around him, but he blocked the shower door. Finally, she let out another pained cry. "Please, I have to do it. For Archie."

He shook his head. "Both you and I know that he would not have wanted you to live your life with the heavy weight of having taken a life."

"How would you know?" she bit back. "And why do you care? Don't you want to kill Stefan, too? If that was him in there, would you have stopped me? Stopped yourself from killing him?"

He let out a long sigh. "That's different. I already have blood on my hands, and let me tell you, the guilt of killing weighs on me every day. I cannot bear the thought of the same thing happening to you."

"Why?" she asked. "I'm already tainted. Archie is dead because of me, and only I could make it right!"

"You are not tainted!" he protested. "You are pure and beautiful and everything that's good in this world."

"Just let me do it! He was almost dead anyway, and the Council will probably demand he be put down for his actions. I'll save them the trouble."

"No."

"Why the hell not?"

"Because I love you," he said quietly, cupping her face in his hands. "I told you, I would give my last breath to protect you. Even from yourself."

Before she could protest or even process what he said, his head lowered to hers for a kiss. His lips caressed hers gently, and she sighed, feeling the tension leave her body. She wrapped her arms around him, bringing him down to deepen the kiss. Meredith moaned into his mouth, pressing her body against his.

"Please, Daric," she begged. "I need you."

He slowly stripped her, leaving her clothes in a wet pile on the floor. She was not as patient, ripping his T-shirt over his head and unbuckling his belt with her trembling fingers. Shoving his jeans and underwear down in one motion, she got to her knees in front of him.

"Meredith," he managed to choke out as her luscious lips wrapped around the tip of his throbbing cock. He braced himself against the tiles, pumping his hips in and out of her delectable mouth. She swallowed his length, taking as much of his cock into her until the tip hit the back of her throat, then pulling back and sucking on him until his knees trembled.

"I can't..." he growled and pulled her up, even though his dick protested at the loss. He didn't want to cum in her mouth, not this time.

"Inside me," she ordered.

He raised one of her legs, hooking it over his arm. Taking his cock in his hand, he pointed the tip at her entrance, which was already slick with her juices.

"Now. Please."

Daric grunted as he pushed into her in one motion, making her moan. She was tight and slick around him, and it took every ounce of his control not to cum inside her. He moved, slowly, taking deep breaths. She mewled in pleasure, pushing up against him as he thrust his cock deep into her. Daric reached between them, caressing her slick folds where her pussy lips gripped him. His fingers found her clit and stroked it with his thumb.

"Fuck!" she shouted as her body tensed and an orgasm washed over her. Daric felt her cunt walls constrict around him, making his cock leak. *Not yet*, he told his body. He wanted to savor this moment and make it last.

Meredith grabbed onto his shoulders and hoisted herself

higher, wrapping her legs around him, bringing him deeper into her. He let out a low, guttural sound as his cock bottomed out in her.

"God, I can feel every inch of you," she moaned. "C'mon, Daric. Fuck me. Fuck me harder."

"Fuck," he cursed softly and began to move inside her, dragging his cock along her tight passage. "You're so wet for me. Only for me. You'll only have me, only take my cock from now on."

"Yes...fuck, yes!" She pumped her hips at him, seeking out the friction that would bring her over the edge.

Daric pressed his forehead against the wall behind her. "You're mine," he growled into her ear. "Come for me. Come around me, have your pretty little cunt milk my cock."

She gripped him tight, pushing her hips forward as her orgasm blasted through her body. Unable to stop, Daric felt the wave of his orgasm pulsing through him, making his cock twitch and shoot out his cum deep into her, marking her and making her his. No, she had always been his, he knew that. From the moment they met, he knew this she-wolf was made for him.

Her ragged breath began to even out, and he disentangled her legs from him, and her feet dropped to the floor with a wet slap. She reached over and turned the water off, then looked up at him.

"Daric..." she whispered, reaching up to trace his jaw with her fingers.

"Let's get dry," he said, grabbing the towel behind him. He opened up the fluffy fabric and wrapped it around Meredith, drying her off. After using it on himself, he tossed it aside and carried her outside to the bedroom. She giggled when he picked her up, a lighthearted sound that made him smile.

As they lay down on his bed wrapped around each other,

she looked up at him with her amber eyes. "Daric...what you said earlier..."

"Yes?"

"Did you mean it?"

"Of course. I love you." He didn't anticipate those words coming out of his mouth. They just did, and he didn't regret it. "You don't have to say it back." *Yet,* he added silently.

"But—"

"I mean it," he said, kissing her forehead. "You have been through a lot today. So much has happened and you've gone through a myriad of emotions in such a short span of time. Please," he took her hand and kissed her knuckles. "Say it back only if you mean it. And only when you have had some time to think."

She sighed and nodded, and snuggled deeper into his chest.

Looking down at her made Daric's chest ache. Did he want to hear those words from her? Of course, he did. But he meant what he said. He didn't want her to say the words if she didn't feel them. And if she never said them? The thought made his insides churn. Because there was something he suspected, something his instinct had been telling him all this time.

Meredith was his True Mate.

It all made sense, and all clicked into place the first time he made love to her, though he ignored it that time.

Meredith's body grew heavy and her breathing became even as she gave in to sleep. He shifted her body, gently moving her to her side so he could press into her back. Did he dare...? His hand slipped to her front, over her belly. Flat and smooth now, but maybe, if his suspicions were correct, soon it would swell and grow with his child. Their child. Pride filled him. He had never thought he would have one of his own. Sure, Stefan had been trying to breed him, but he knew any offspring born of such a mating would have been taken away from him as he continued to stud with a suitable partner. But now, with Meredith, a spark of hope grew in him, and he pulled her closer.

He was selfish; he knew that. Stefan could take them away from him. While he lived, Daric would have no peace. And when the master mage found out how precious Meredith was to him, he would stop at nothing to try and destroy him. He kissed the top of her head. No, he wasn't going to let that happen.

———

It was morning by the time Meredith woke up. The events of yesterday, combined with the jet lag, drained her and she'd never slept so soundly. She felt better. Good enough to face the day? Maybe.

A soft knock on the door shook her out of her thoughts. Moving Daric's heavy arm off her, she stood up, slipped one of his discarded T-shirts over her head and opened the door.

"Meredith!" Jade cried as she embraced her friend. "How are you? Are you okay? How are you feeling? Did you—"

"Slow down, Jade," she said. She stepped out of the room and closed the door behind her. "Shouldn't I be the one asking questions? What are you doing here?"

"I wanted to check in on you," the other Lycan replied. "A lot has happened since yesterday."

Remembering Rodrigo, Meredith felt the anger rising in her again. "What did they do with that scumbag?"

"Don't worry," Jade said, smiling. "He's in custody. Currently, a guest in Fenrir's basement levels, but," she lowered her voice, "if he doesn't end up in the Lycan Siberian detention facility, then he might be put down."

"Good," Meredith said, gritting her teeth. She was only disappointed that she didn't get to kill him, but Daric was right.

It wouldn't have brought Archie back. "So, why else did you come up here?"

Jade bit her lip. "The Alpha asked me to come get you and Daric. We're having a meeting. Everyone, I mean."

She let out a sigh. It would have happened sooner or later. "I'll wake Daric up and get dressed. We'll be up in 20 minutes."

Jade crossed her arms over her chest and gave her a look. "Just to get dressed?"

"Fine," she said. "Fifteen."

As Jade walked away, she crept back into the room. Daric was still asleep, a sheet over his hips. Damn, he really was the hottest fucking thing she'd ever seen. She wanted to bite every inch of him, especially that delicious Adonis belt. "Stupid meeting," she growled as she walked over to him. Hmmm, she wondered if she could finish him off with a handy in five minutes. She climbed into the bed, and her hand roamed over the semi-hard bulge under the sheet.

"No..." Daric moaned.

"No?" she asked. She looked up at Daric with a frown, which quickly disappeared when she saw his eyes were closed. "Daric?"

His arm reached out into the air. "Stefan! No!"

Was Daric having a nightmare? She crawled up to him, placing her hands on his face, caressing his jaw softly. "Shhh... baby...you're having a dream."

His sea-colored eyes flew open. "Stefan."

Meredith brushed a lock of hair out of his face. "A nightmare?"

He shook his head and sat up. "No. Stefan broke down my walls and sent me a message."

"Of what?"

Daric rubbed his face with his palm. "My mother. We must talk to the Alpha now."

"Well, you're in luck, then. We've been summoned upstairs."

———

When Jade said everyone was waiting for them, she meant *everyone*. Grant, Frankie, Nick, Cady, Alynna, Alex, Sebastian, Jade, and even Liam and Lara were waiting for them in the Alpha's office. Killian, Quinn, and Connor were also there, quietly talking amongst themselves.

There were mixed reactions to Daric and Meredith walking in hand-in-hand. Nick's face was grim, but then that was his normal expression, while Cady flashed them a wary, but curious look. Frankie had a knowing smirk, while Lara and Liam seemed to be in complete shock. Meredith shrugged. They were just going to have to deal with it.

"So, now that you're all here, let's get everyone up to speed first," Grant said, eyeing Meredith and Daric. "And then we'll move on to other business. Rodrigo Baeles is now sitting in our basement detention facility. He's been stripped of his membership in the Council, as well as all privileges. As you know, he confessed to collaborating with Stefan for the last two decades. Quinn," he nodded to the other Lycan, "has given us some valuable intel from the Council servers, which, as a sign of good faith, we will return them so they can use their own resources to see how far and deep Rodrigo's treachery ran."

"From what I've seen, though," Quinn began. "Rodrigo was not only keeping tabs on the Lone Wolf population but ensuring they grew. He would find especially vulnerable children and adults, and push them into becoming Lone Wolves, whether it was through bribery, kidnapping, or murder."

Someone in the room gasped, and Meredith felt the bottom of her stomach drop. Her biological father. Was he murdered so she and her mother would have been left vulnerable? According to Quinn, Rodrigo also bribed her old Alpha to make sure no one took her in. The revelation was devastating to her and her brothers. Would their lives have been different if they had stayed in their families and clans? She glanced at Daric. Would she have known Daric? Or Jade or Lara or any of them?

"But what would he have done with the Lone Wolves?" Alynna asked.

"The spell," Lara deduced. "I bet with some modifications, Stefan could use the same spell he used with the humans to control the Lone Wolves."

"I see," Jade said. "He couldn't use it on just any Lycan because we're wired to obey an Alpha, one that we've pledged to. But Lone Wolves don't have an Alpha, and thus can be manipulated by the spell."

"The Council will be tracking down all the Lone Wolves in Rodrigo's files to make sure none of them have fallen to Stefan. And speaking of the council, Lljuffa and the rest of council have decided to leave Sebastian alone. I convinced them that Sebastian is very much in control, plus, since he's neither a Lycan or pledged to me, he's his own man."

"I don't need a pledge to protect what's mine," Sebastian said in a gruff voice. "That means all my people, not just Jade. I'll do what it takes to protect this clan."

"Good to know," Grant nodded gratefully.

"What about Daric?" Meredith said. All eyes in the room zeroed in on her. "Does the Council want him locked up?"

"We haven't gotten to that subject yet. It's still under negotiations."

"You can't let them take him," Meredith protested. "Please!"

"He needs to go." Nick's voice was as cold as ice, and his words had a deadly edge. "He can't stay here."

Meredith looked to Grant. "Gr-I mean, Alpha," she began.

"I know Daric has done a lot to all of you and I can't understand because I wasn't here before. But he's changed, and you all know that Stefan forced him to do all those things. What if it was your mother Stefan held as a prisoner?" She looked at Nick. "What if it was Cady? What would you do or wouldn't do to keep her safe?" The Beta remained quiet, but his eyes remained steely.

"Meredith," Grant said. "Daric and I have an agreement, as long as he keeps it, he'll stay here at Fenrir."

"What?" Nick's head whipped towards Grant. "You have got to be kidding. After what's happened, you'll let him stay here? No, I won't allow it."

"Nick—"

"No!" The air in the office grew thick, and Nick's eyes glowed. "It's him or me, Grant. If you let him go, that's it. I'm done."

"Nick!" Cady admonished. "You can't mean that."

"I do," Nick replied. "I'll step down as Beta if you keep him around. I want him gone by the end of the day, or I walk." Without another glance, Nick walked out the office, slamming the door behind him.

"I'll talk to Nick," Cady said apologetically to Grant. "And, if it's any consolation," she continued, looking at Daric. "I agree with you, Meredith. Daric, if you're sorry for what you've done, then you deserve a second chance."

As Cady left his office, Grant turned back to Daric and Meredith. "You two," he shook his head. "I don't even know where to begin. I knew you'd be reckless," he said to Meredith. "But, you Daric?"

"You couldn't have stopped it. She is mine," he said. "Made for me. As much as the Lupa is yours."

"What?" Grant frowned.

"She is my True Mate."

"What?" Meredith exclaimed. "I'm your freakin' what?"

Daric gave her a small smile. "Mine. My True Mate."

"Holy shitballs!" Meredith threw her hands up and began to pace. "Motherfucker!" She walked in circles, her left eye twitching. "And you knew? All this time?"

"I only suspect it, but after yesterday, I think I'm pretty sure," Daric confessed. "But even if you weren't, it doesn't matter. I'm not letting you go."

"I...I..." Meredith held a hand up, took a deep breath, and then ran to the potted plant in the corner where she threw up the meager contents of her stomach. Lara and Jade immediately ran to her, and the witch held her hair aside, and the Lycan gave her a handkerchief so she would wipe her mouth.

"Hold on, hold on," Killian said. "What the fuck is going on here? What's a True Mate and why is Meredith throwing up?"

"Er," Grant stammered. "It's kind of a long story..."

"Basically," Meredith said weakly as she walked back to the rest of the group. "As the Brits would say, I'm up the duff. Thanks to this guy," she said, jerking her thumb towards Daric. "And—Fucking hell, Connor!"

Connor lunged for Daric, sending them both toppling to the ground. Quinn, Alex, Sebastian, and Liam immediately jumped in, pulling the two men apart as best they could, which was no easy task. The huge Lycan seemed determined to keep his hands around the warlock's neck.

"You motherfucker!" Connor growled, his eyes glowing. "You fucking asshole! You got her pregnant?"

"Hooooo boy," Meredith slapped her palm on her forehead. "For God's sake, Connor, he didn't get me pregnant. I mean...I don't know yet, but if I am, I did plenty of the work to get us there, too."

"Meredith was meant to bear my child," Daric said. "We were destined to be together."

"But you're not even married!" Connor exclaimed.

"Oh, don't start, please, Connor," Meredith groaned.

"Alpha," Killian said to Grant. "I think my brothers and I should go back to our rooms. Connor will need some time to cool off."

"Of course," Grant replied. "Take as much time as you need."

"Let's go," Killian sighed. "Mer, come down as soon as you can."

"Fine. But no murdering my possibly-baby-daddy, ok, Uncle Killian?" she smiled.

Killian gave her an affectionate pat on the head. "We'll try." He gave Daric a warning look. "And you, we will be talking about this."

"Whatever you want," Daric said.

With a last nod to Grant and the others, Killian left the room with Quinn and Connor in tow.

Grant rubbed his palms over his face and looked at Frankie. "I swear, someday I'm gonna pack us up and go back to our villa in Positano where no one can find us. Is there an early retirement option for Alphas?"

Frankie laughed. "You'd get bored and start driving me crazy in two days." She kissed his cheek.

"Alpha," Daric's voice turned serious. "I have more news."

Grant groaned. "I suppose it's one of those days. All right, what is it?"

"I'm afraid in the excitement, I almost forgot to tell you that I have received a message from Stefan."

"A message?" Grant asked. "How? I thought you'd been keeping him out of your head?"

"He broke through last night, and I'm afraid..." He shook his head. "He has sent me a vision of what he plans to do. He's going to go to the New York coven compound and kill Signe if I don't go back to him."

"But how?" Lara interjected. "How does he know where she is?"

"I don't know," Daric said. "He must have figured it out."

"Grant," Liam began. "We must protect the coven. We need to go there and stop Stefan. This might be our last chance."

"Agreed," Grant said. "Alynna, let's figure out a plan."

"What about Nick?" Alynna asked.

"If he's around, let him know. Cady will talk some sense into him, and if anything she'll ask him to help if it's to protect her family."

"What if it's a trap?" Sebastian said. "You know it must be."

"Of course it is," Daric said. "Stefan's plans were very clear. He knows where she is and will do what it takes to get me back."

"Get you back?" Meredith asked. "And then what?"

"Probably kill me."

"No!" Meredith protested. "You can't!"

"But, if I don't, he'll kill her."

"I don't want you to die. Not now. Not ever," Meredith wrapped her arms around his waist.

"Meredith," he said, unwrapping her arms around. "I must do this."

"Fine, but I'm going, too," she pouted.

"No. You will stay here where it's safe."

She gave him a shove. "Are you fucking kidding me? After all that? I'm your True Mate, plus you know I'm invincible."

"That's not the point. And we're not sure yet if you are with child."

"You're such an asshole," she said, narrowing her eyes at him. "You said I was."

"I said, I suspected you were," Daric clarified. "And if you are, then you still cannot go. Stefan will find out and take you, and I can't be distracted."

"Alpha," she turned to Grant and Alynna. "You know you need me there."

"She can't go, she must stay here where it's safe," Daric interrupted. "If she's not pregnant with my child, then she's still vulnerable."

"So, I can't go because I'm possibly pregnant, but I also can't go because I might not be. I swear you make me want to hurt you sometimes!" Meredith exclaimed.

"I'm afraid Daric has a point," Grant said. "In any case, we might need you here to protect Fenrir."

"This isn't over," she said, turning on her heel. "Jade, Lara, c'mon, I need you girls."

CHAPTER TWENTY-FIVE

"So," Lara began as they entered Jade's lab. "I sure did miss a lot."

"Don't worry," Jade said dryly. "Meredith'll fill you in. She'll even act out parts of it for you. Maybe even use puppets."

"Jade, you need to start keeping some vodka in here," Meredith said as she began rooting through the cabinets.

"Mer, one sniff of alcohol will send you running to the nearest potted plant again," Lara grinned.

Jade walked to one of the freezers and took out three large cartons of ice cream. "Here you go, girls. My secret stash."

Meredith's eyes grew wide. "Jade, you've been holding out on us."

"I'll say," Lara chimed in, grabbing three spoons from the nearest drawer. "Hey, chocolate chip mint is mine."

"Hey, is your boyfriend about to walk into a trap and possibly be killed by his former boss?" Meredith asked as she hopped up on the table and hugged the carton to her chest. "Yeah, I didn't think so." She tossed the cover and dug into the cold treat.

"Is that what you call Daric?" Lara quipped. "Your boyfriend? Daric and Meredith, sitting in a tree," she singsonged.

Jade joined in. "K-I-S-S-I-N—"

"Oh, shut up," Meredith grumbled as she stuffed her mouth full of ice cream.

"Is it true? Are you and Daric True Mates?" Jade asked as swallowed a spoonful of chocolate chip cookie dough.

Meredith shrugged. "I can't be sure. I mean...do your mates smell good to you guys? Like, not just pleasant, but like, really, *really* good? I can't think when I scent him."

"Yes," Jade and Lara said in unison.

"And your wolf?" she turned to Jade. "She knew?"

"Pretty much," Jade confirmed. "And yours?"

"She practically peed on him to mark her territory," she grumbled.

"You know, there is one way to find out," Lara said.

"You are not cutting her up like you did me," Jade warned.

"It would be the fastest way," Lara countered. "And it worked, right? Do you have a scalpel around here?"

"You could also take a pregnancy test," Jade suggested. "You know we Lycans can't get pregnant so easily. I mean, it's only been a few days. You can't have had sex that much." Lara and Meredith looked at her. "Right. True Mates and all. You guys have probably been shagging every minute you can."

"You bet," Meredith sighed.

"So," Lara reached for one of the glass bottles on the table next to her. "We'll cut your arm and if you heal in two seconds—"

"Drop it, witch," Meredith warned. "There's no need to draw blood." She knew. Of course, it was true.

Our pup. We must protect our pup, her inner she-wolf warned. *And our mate. Keep them both safe.*

Her hand automatically went to her belly. Oh, baby. What the heck was she going to do?

"Meredith?" Jade whispered. "Are you ok?"

"Just..." Tears welled up in her eyes. "Oh God, stupid hormones!" She wiped her face with the back of her hands, and when she looked up, her friends were crying, too. "Stop it, both of you! Stop crying, you're making me cry!"

"Us?" Jade smiled through the tears. "You're the one making me cry."

Lara sniffed as fat tears rolled down her cheeks. "You both are the ones making me cry."

"Oh God, we're gonna be three hormonal pregnant ladies. The men around here better watch out," Meredith said as her two best friends wrapped their arms around her. "Okay, okay, get off me you two!" she said grouchily, though secretly, she was happy to be sharing this moment with her friends. "Now, what are we going to do about Daric? I can't lose him."

"You won't," Lara said. "I—" The witch frowned and then slipped her hand into her pants pocket, taking her phone out. "Sonofabitch!" she said getting up as she stared at her phone.

"What?" Jade asked.

"Liam...Arrghhh! Stupid idiot!"

"What?" Meredith repeated.

"He just sent me a text message. They left. I mean, him, Daric, and a couple of the guys. They took the Fenrir chopper and are on their way to the coven compound now."

"That dick weed!" Meredith jumped down from the table. "He just left!" The anger was rising in her. "Fucking asshole!"

She ran out of the lab, with Jade and Lara hot on her heels. Slamming her palm on the sensor of the elevator, she jabbed the button for the penthouse. She was furious. Even her she-wolf was pacing, wanting to be let out. Ankle monitor be damned, if she really was invincible, she could probably survive. Maybe even find out of if True Mate magic could regrow a limb.

She ignored Jared when he called her, and instead, burst through the door to the Alpha's office. Grant and Sebastian were at his desk, looking at his screen and discussing something in low tones.

"You let them go?" Meredith raged. "Why?"

Grant's face looked grave. "Daric got another message from Stefan while you were gone. He was on his way to the compound to take Signe. I told him to take the chopper and a few of our best guys. Hopefully, they'll get there in time, but Vivianne's been warned. She'll do her best to keep Signe safe."

"Even Liam?" Lara asked, puzzled.

"You know he would do anything to protect your parents," Grant said. "And you as well. He knew you would insist on coming."

"Ugh, men are such stubborn assholes!" Meredith growled. "I can't believe they would leave us! We're three badass pregnant ladies! We have to help them now. Sebastian, don't you have a helicopter on standby, too?" She slapped her palm on her forehead. "Fuck me, you're a freaking dragon. C'mon, go and shift into your badass beast and we'll climb on your back—"

"You ain't riding on my back," Sebastian bit out. "None of you are. You're all staying here. We're in lockdown mode."

"What?" Jade asked. "But Sebastian, we can help them."

"If it comes to that, I'll be letting The Beast out," Sebastian began. "But we can't risk anyone seeing me in broad daylight. And don't you think I'm letting you get into this, too, Jade."

"Frankie's on her way home to The Enclave to stay with Mika," he said, referring to Alynna's daughter and his niece. "Right now, no one leaves or enters Fenrir and the remaining security team is on standby."

"Nick?" Meredith asked.

The Alpha shook his head. "They're gone. According to his security detail, he took Cady and Zac, and they're headed to the Hudson mansion to visit his grandfather. I've been calling them, but he's not answering. Neither is Cady."

"Hold on," Lara frowned. "Cady's not answering her phone?" She took her phone out and dialed her cousin's number. "Hmmm...it's not working."

"You mean it's busy?" Grant asked.

"No," Lara shook her head. "I mean, her phone's out of service."

Grant's eyes flashed and began to glow. "Fuck. This is—"

The lights in the office began to flicker and a few bulbs in the overhead lights burst, showering glass down.

"Going exactly as planned."

The silence was palpable as Stefan and Victoria Chatraine materialized in the middle of the room.

"Stefan," Grant growled, and the air changed, signaling the Alpha's impending shift into his wolf form.

The master mage raised his hand, and an invisible force pushed Grant to the wall, pinning him there as he struggled.

"Don't even think about it," Victoria warned Lara, who was getting ready to use her own powers. The older witch drew her cloak open, revealing a small bundle. "Unless you want this little one hurt?"

"You bitch!" Lara cried when she saw what was in the other witch's arms. "That's your grandson! You wouldn't!"

"Wouldn't I?' Victoria drawled, tracing a long red fingernail down Zachary Vrost's soft cheek. "Want to test it out?"

"Don't hurt him!" Lara pleaded.

"No one make a move," Stefan warned them. "Think you all can take us on? Who would you choose to save? The child or the Alpha? I doubt even you four could stop us before we kill either one."

"How did you get in here?" Jade asked. "This office is protected with magic, and you've never been in here before."

Stefan laughed. "That's why I asked our dear friend Rodrigo to do me a favor," the mage explained. "First, he was wearing a small camera so I could see the inside of the room. And then, I asked him to drop a little toy of mine." He lifted his other hand, and a small, silver object floated from the floor and back into his hand. "A simple coin, infused with a spell that broke Vivianne Chatraine's protection spell."

"What do you want?" Grant choked. "Daric and Signe are not here."

"Oh, that little message I sent to that traitor?" Stefan bellowed. "I can't believe he fell for it. Or you all fell for it. There is no one going to the New York coven compound. Signe is safe." His red eyes trained on Meredith. "I've found something else more valuable."

As Stefan's bony hand pointed toward her, Meredith could feel coldness wrap around her body, seeping in through her pores as she was pulled to the mage. She struggled and dug her heels into the floor, but it was no use. She went flying across the room, landing on her knees with a loud thud in front of Stefan. The coldness wrapped around her and she couldn't move.

"Meredith!" Lara shouted. "Let her go!"

"Or what, my dear?" Stefan mocked. "When you see Daric, tell him I look forward to seeing him again. If he searches far back enough, he'll know where I am." He then looked at Sebastian. "Ah, the Creed Dragon. You're a bonus." His other hand let go of Grant, sending the Alpha slumping to the ground. Jade threw herself in front of her mate, but it was no use as Sebastian's body careened forward. As he was kneeling in front of the master mage, flames began to engulf his body.

"Uh-uh." With a tsk and snap of his fingers, Sebastian fell down, the fire around him extinguishing as if it was never there.

"Sebastian!" Jade screamed as her she-wolf tore through her body and lunged at Stefan.

Meredith looked up, watching as the large wolf leaped into the air, her paws aimed at Stefan. She held her breath, waiting for the sound of fangs and claws ripping into flesh. But the sound didn't come, and she felt the coldness wrap around her again. Grant's office began to shimmer and disappear in front of her eyes.

———

The helicopter flew over the green fields and forests of upstate New York, leaving the glittering skyline of Manhattan behind. As Daric sat in the plush seat, he wondered if he was doing the right thing. Yes, he told himself. He was doing this to protect Meredith and their child. His she-wolf would bare her fangs and claws at him, but she wouldn't stay mad forever. Well, she could stay mad forever, but at least she'd be alive.

The Fenrir helicopter was built for luxury and not for battle. It could only fit a limited amount of people, so Daric, Liam, Alex, Alynna, and two of the senior members of the security team, John Patrick and Heath Pearson, squeezed into the cabin. Sebastian and Grant stayed back to coordinate the efforts to send more forces to the coven compound just in case and to hold the fort. Of course, he knew when Meredith and Lara Chatraine found out they'd been left behind and locked down, it probably would take an Alpha and a dragon to prevent the two women from tearing Fenrir apart.

"We're almost there," Liam Henney said. The chopper slowed down and then descended into the large field behind Vivianne and Graham Chatraine's home.

As soon as the door flew open, Daric hopped out of the

chopper and began to walk towards the back porch of the house where Vivianne, Graham, and Signe were waiting.

"Mother!" he called as he picked up his pace, reaching the porch in no time. "Thank God you are safe," he said as he embraced her in a tight hug. He felt Signe stiffen in his arms, and he immediately knew something was wrong. Looking at Vivianne's ashen face and Graham's grim expression, he was certain that something bad had happened.

"What is it?" he asked. His heart thudded a frantic rhythm against his ribcage as Vivianne spoke.

"Daric...I'm sorry," Vivianne sobbed. "Grant just called us. She's been taken. Meredith."

The knot in his stomach grew, and the pressure behind his eyes made his vision blur. Vivianne was speaking, saying something about Sebastian Creed and Nick Vrost's young son but the words weren't making sense. His worst nightmare had come true. Meredith. His Meredith had been taken by Stefan.

"Is Lara alright?" Liam asked as he came up behind Daric.

"She's fine," Graham answered, and Liam visibly relaxed. "She's pretty steamed at you, son, but she's safe."

"Stefan never showed up here," Signe said. "I'm sorry. So sorry."

"It's not your fault," Daric said tersely. "It's mine. I should have known this was a trap."

"Why would Stefan kidnap Meredith?" Graham asked.

Daric looked at his mother, and she nodded in understanding. "Because Meredith is the most precious thing in the world to my son," she said, with just a hint of sadness in her voice. "She's his True Mate."

Vivianne gasped. "I suspected, but I couldn't be sure. Not like when I knew Lara and Liam were True Mates."

"We need to find her," Daric said. "Mother, do you have any idea where he could have taken her?"

"I'm afraid not," Signed shook her head. "But I know only you can find her. I've seen it. I've seen you two protect each other. All is not lost."

"But how?"

Signe's eyes strayed to the bracelet on his wrist. "You need to use your gifts. Your father's gift."

Daric nodded. He had to get the Lycans to release him so he could use his powers. If Signe had seen it, then it must be true. He looked at Liam. "We must go back to Fenrir."

After they said their goodbyes to Vivianne, Signe, and Graham, the two of them headed back to the chopper. The door was open, and Alex was waiting for them, while Alynna was talking into her phone. As soon as Daric and Liam were buckled in, the door closed and the chopper lifted into the air.

Alynna had been on the phone with Grant, who relayed what happened. It seemed Stefan had taken the opportunity to capture Sebastian Creed, as well as Nick and Cady's son. The couple had been driving to their Hudson Estate when they were ambushed by the mages' human slaves, then Victoria and Stefan took young Zachary Vrost and disappeared. They were able to call for help and were now also on their way back to Fenrir.

Daric's mind was reeling. Where would Stefan take them? The master mage wouldn't use any of the places Daric knew about, that's for sure, but he would have to check. Once the bracelet was off, it would only take him a few hours to check the two dozen or so hideouts around the world he knew of. He only prayed that he'd find them in time. *My she-wolf*, he thought, as if she could hear him. *Be brave, but be safe.*

The helicopter landed on top of the Fenrir building, and all of them swiftly made their way back to Grant's office. The tension was tangible and made the air difficult to breathe. Nick and the three Lone Wolves were standing around Grant's desk, while Lara sat on the couch, consoling a sobbing Cady and a distraught Jade.

"Grant! Nick," Alynna called as they entered the office. "Shit, I'm sorry," she said, patting Nick on the arm.

Anger rolled off the Beta like waves, his face as hard as a stone. "We're going to get him back," he said in a deadly voice, looking over at his wife. "Even if I have to tear the entire world apart."

"We will get him back, Nick," Grant vowed. "We'll get all of them back."

"What do we do now?" Liam asked. "How do we find them?"

"Daric!" Lara's eyes widened. "Stefan...he had a message for you. He said, if you 'search far back enough,' you'll find him."

Daric's brows drew together. "That could be anywhere. As far as the ends of the earth." He looked at Grant. "You must release me, Alpha. With my powers, I can find them in a few hours. And I know every hiding place Stefan keeps."

"Release you?" Nick barked, his eyes glowing. "You think we're going to trust you now? How do we know that you didn't do this? That you weren't a part of this the entire time? How did Stefan get in here? How did he know where we were so he could take my son?"

"Nick, calm down," Grant said, putting a hand on the other Lycan's chest. "I know you're angry, but you're not thinking straight. I need you, please. I need you to be Nick Vrost, Beta to the New York clan because I can't do this alone."

Nick took a deep breath, his eyes going back to their normal icy blue. "Fine," he said, shrugging Grant's hand away. "We need to get to work."

"And you," Grant said to Daric. "I know you mean well, but..."

"You still cannot trust me," Daric said, his jaw tightening.

"I'm sorry. I have to think of my people, too. I know Meredith means the world to you, but we can all work together to get them back. We don't need your powers."

"If we are too late," Daric began. "And she is lost to me, you will pay, Grant Anderson. Alpha or not."

"I'll have to take that chance," Grant said. "Meredith is one of us." He looked at Nick and Jade. "Just as Zac and Sebastian are. We will not fail them. Let's get to work."

Killian spoke up. "We'll do whatever we can, Alpha. We want her back, too." Quinn and Connor nodded in agreement.

"Good," Grant said with a grim face. "Because this is it. We are making our last stand and ending it all."

CHAPTER TWENTY-SIX

Meredith felt the darkness take over her as soon as they disappeared from Grant's office. When she woke up, she had a massive headache and was lying on a thin and musty pallet. It was also dark, and it took a moment for her enhanced vision to adjust so she could see in the room.

The walls were made of logs, and various furs were thrown on the floor, but still, it was dank and cold inside. She was sitting on the only piece of furniture in the entire room. There was a single window on one side, but it was boarded up. She walked to the door and tried to open it, but it wouldn't budge.

"They have it barred from the outside," came a gravelly voice from somewhere in the room.

She swung her head toward the source of the sound and saw a figure curled up in the corner.

"Sebastian!" she cried as she stumbled over to him. "Are you hurt?"

"No," he shook his head. "But...this thing...it burns."

Meredith looked down and saw the chains wrapped around his body. The links were small and thin, no bigger than a regular necklace, but it was long and wrapped several times around Sebastian's massive body. It felt normal to her, but as soon as she tried to remove it, he hissed in pain.

"Stop," he cried. "I've been trying to get out of this thing, but it's like the more I struggle, the more it burns."

"What is it?"

"Fuck if I know," Sebastian spat out. "It burns where it touches my skin."

"Can you get us out of here?" she asked. "Shift, I mean? You could probably bring this whole place down."

"I've been trying to call The Beast," he said and shook his head. "I can't explain it, but it's like he won't listen to me. I think it has something to do with this thing wrapped around me."

"Shit, there goes that plan," Meredith thought. "We need to think of a way out of here."

"No one's been in here to check on us or feed us, as far as I can tell," Sebastian said. "I've been awake for a while, though I can't tell for how long."

"Zac?" she asked, suddenly remembering the baby.

"Haven't seen him. But, I thought I heard some crying a couple of minutes before you woke up, so he must be around here."

Meredith's hand instinctively went to her belly, thinking of her own child.

"Don't worry," Sebastian assured her. "We'll get out of here. You know Jade and Daric will do everything they can. And once I get rid of these things," he looked down at the chains with scorn. "I'm gonna burn this fucking place to the ground."

"I don't doubt that," Meredith replied. She looked at her ankle tracking device. "Hopefully, this thing works, and someone will find us."

———

"If you were an evil mage, where would you hide out?" Alynna asked to no one in particular. When Grant gave her a smirk, she shrugged. "What? We've tried everything. For some reason, we can't track Meredith's bracelet. I thought that thing could find her anywhere in the world."

"She's either somewhere that has some sort of electrical interference," Nick stated. "Or..." He shook his head.

"She's alive, I know it," Daric stated. "Perhaps Stefan found a way to disable it."

"He would have to know how the tracking bracelet worked, right?" Jade guessed.

"If he was using my powers, yes," Daric said. "But, he has taken many powers over the years, some of which I'd never seen him use. He could be generating the electrical field himself so we can't track her."

"So, we're back at square one," Grant said glumly.

Most of them stayed in Fenrir, trying to figure out where Stefan could be hiding and a plan of attack once they knew where he was holding Meredith, Sebastian, and Zac. It had been hours, and they were all exhausted, but the tension and worry kept them working. Nick had urged Cady to go home, but she remained, saying she was going to be here as soon as they found Zac. The Beta didn't want to cause his wife further grief, and so he relented. Cady had retired to her office to sleep a while ago, while the rest of them had taken turns resting and eating as they continued to work and plan.

"I...I..." Jade opened her mouth to speak but shut it. She looked at Daric, and then to Grant. "Excuse me, Alpha, I need to retrieve something in my lab."

"Go ahead, Doctor," Grant nodded.

The Lycan took one last look at Daric and left the room. Daric's gut clenched. There was something in Dr. Cross' eyes and face that unnerved him. There was anguish there, but...

something else. A spark or a knowing look. He shook his head. Maybe it was the exhaustion that was making him see things.

"How about you, Quinn?' Grant turned his attention to the Lone Wolves. Quinn and Killian were gathered around a laptop, while Connor was a few feet away from them, pacing a hole into the carpet. No one would come near the Lycan, the barely-contained rage surrounding him like a cage.

"Sorry, Alpha," Quinn said apologetically. "I'm hooked up to all major law enforcement cameras in the world, searching for a sign of them. I've also err...borrowed a couple of satellites to see if we can ping her tracking bracelet, but if something's interfering with the signal, then there's not much I can do."

"Keep trying, that's all I ask. Daric," Grant looked to the warlock. "Do you know any other places Stefan and his cohorts might be hiding?"

"I've given you a list of all the ones I know of," he said. "Any luck looking into them?"

The Alpha shook his head. "We've used satellite photos, and I've called in every favor from every clan I know to check out the sites. Nothing."

Daric let out a breath. He wanted to ask the Alpha again to remove the bracelet, but he doubted that he would change his mind. Signe said she saw him use his powers in his vision to rescue Meredith, but how?

The activity around him continued as they exchanged ideas on how they could find Stefan's latest hideout. Daric was growing impatient. As each moment passed, who knows what Stefan could be doing to Meredith? No, he mustn't think of that. Meredith was strong, and she would survive.

Dr. Cross quietly crept back into the office, and everyone was too distracted to see her slink back inside. She closed the door behind her without making a sound and made a beeline for Daric, a determined look on her tired face.

"Dr. Cross," he began. "Perhaps you should get some rest? I'm sure Sebastian would not want you tiring yourself out. You must conserve your strength for the fight ahead."

The pretty Lycan bit her lip and looked up at him with her light green eyes. "Can you really find them?"

"What?" he looked at her quizzically.

"If you could use your powers," she said, lowering her voice. "Could you find Sebastian and Meredith and Zac?"

A glint of metal in Jade's hand caught his attention. It was a small electronic device, one that he had seen before when she removed the old bracelet to put on the new one.

"I swear," he whispered back to her. "On the life of my mother and Meredith. I will find all of them and bring them back."

"Can I trust you?" she asked.

"I love her."

Jade took a deep breath. "I'm sorry," she said loudly. "I have to do this."

"Jade?" Lara asked as she approached them. "What are you—"

"It's the only way!" Jade pressed the keyfob to Daric's wrist. The metal bracelet snapped open. "Go!" she shouted at Daric.

"Thank you," he said gratefully. "I swear, I'll get them back." As he looked up, he saw Nick, Liam, Lara, and Connor running towards him, lunging to catch him. But, they were too late. Daric called on his power and disappeared into thin air.

CHAPTER TWENTY-SEVEN

It seemed like she and Sebastian had been stuck in the cold, dark room for days, but it couldn't have been more than 12 hours. No one came in and out, but food had magically appeared three times now. Meredith helped Sebastian reposition the chains so he could at least move around, but she couldn't seem to remove it from his body.

"You have to eat more," she told him as she spooned some stew into his mouth. "You've only had three bites of each meal. I know it's not gourmet, but we need to keep our strength up."

He turned his head away. "I'm not hungry. You eat it."

"Fine." She took his food and began to eat it. God, she was still hungry. This magical baby in her was hungry all the time and—"Hey!" she stood up. "You've been giving me your food because you know I'm eating for two."

Sebastian grimaced. "If you're anything like Jade, not even both our meals are enough for you and your baby."

"But you can't starve yourself for me," she retorted.

"I was in the Marines, and I was locked up for a whole month by those monsters who took me and turned me into a beast. Believe me, I've survived on less."

"Fine, but you're going to eat at least half of the next meal, ok?"

"I'll try," he assured her.

Before Meredith could answer, the door suddenly flew open and Stefan stepped inside, followed by Victoria. She got a glimpse of the outside, but not enough to tell her where they were, only that it was dark and the ground was covered in snow. Snow at this time of the year? Where were they?

Meredith got into a defensive stance, but Stefan laughed. "What are you going to do, she-wolf? You think you can get to me before I obliterate your body into nothing?"

"You motherfucker! Touch her, and you die!" Sebastian bellowed.

Stefan let out another cackle. "Ah, the Creed Dragon. Tell me, how do you like your new jewelry? As you may have guessed, this is no ordinary chain. It's made from silver mined from the Zhobghadi mountains. Though to most people, it may seem like ordinary metal, it's quite effective at subduing dragon shifters."

"Fucking bastard!" Sebastian let out a yell and struggled against the chain, but it only made him drop to his knees in pain.

"What have you done with Zac, douchebag?" Meredith asked. She turned to Victoria. "Are you going to let this asshole kill your grandson?"

"Why would I do that?" Stefan asked. "Zachary Vrost comes from the bloodline of the most powerful witches in the world. It's a shame it was tainted with dirty Lycan blood, but I'm sure once we bring him up the proper way, he'll be useful to us."

"You monster!" Meredith cried.

"Tsk, tsk, don't worry about it, my dear," Stefan's red eyes narrowed into slits. "You won't be around to see young Zachary grow up to be my most loyal servant."

"Grant Anderson and Nick Vrost will never let that happen!" Meredith declared. "You know Nick would burn the world down to get his son back."

"They will never find you," Stefan declared. He stared at the bracelet on her ankle. "I've disabled the tracking device on your little toy. Oh, don't worry, it'll still explode if you try to remove it or change into your Lycan form, but your precious clan will never find you."

"I swear, Stefan," Sebastian said in a deadly voice. "When I get out of here, I'm going to burn you alive, you motherfucker."

"Once I figure out how to use the control spell on you," Stefan began. "You'll burn the entire New York clan alive. Including your pretty little mate."

Sebastian let out a rage-filled scream and stood up, struggling against the chains. With a wave of Stefan's hand, Sebastian disappeared into thin air.

"Where did you send him?" Meredith lunged at Stefan, but he swatted her away like a fly. Her body went flying across the room, hitting the wall.

"I don't think so, she-wolf," he sneered. "You will be my prisoner until the day you die. Should Daric or the Alpha try to rescue you, I will kill you before they can get to you. I'm going to enjoy watching my former protégé suffer as you die slowly in front of him."

Meredith felt a metallic taste in her mouth, and she spat out blood. "Not if the Lycans kill you first."

Stefan laughed. "Really now? Let's see how you feel when you see this." He opened the door of the cabin with a wave of his hand.

Meredith's eyes widened as she looked outside. The knot in her stomach grew, and though she hated to admit it, they were in serious trouble.

———

Daric cursed as he walked through the empty halls of the Spanish-style villa hidden deep in the Andorran mountains. This was the sixth hideout he'd been to in the last couple of hours, and still no sign of Stefan or the other mages. It was a long shot that the master mage would actually be in one of the places Daric knew about. But still, he had hoped that he could find at least some clue as to where Stefan would be holed up.

Regaining the use of his powers brought him some relief and satisfaction. He had missed being able to flex his magical muscles, and he had forgotten how convenient it was to simply move from place to place using his powers, or create food or drink he wanted. Right now, though, it seemed so empty. Before, his powers made him feel like a God. There was nothing in this world he couldn't have or create. But this time, he was without the one thing he really wanted—no, needed. The need to hold Meredith in his arms and know she and their child was safe was consuming him. The thoughts of what Stefan could do to her or could be doing to her was driving him mad, and he had to stop every few hours to control his emotions. No, Meredith needed him to be calm and smart. To keep searching.

He walked around the villa some more, trying to collect his thoughts. As he sat on one of the crumbling stone benches in the garden, he stared at the wildflowers that were now overtaking the once-pristine grounds. Wildflowers. If he closed his eyes, he could almost smell Meredith's scent that reminded him so much of his home.

Home.

Daric's eyes flew open. Lara Chatraine's words came back to him.

If you search far back enough, you'll find him.

Not search far enough. Search far *back* enough.

Daric shot to his feet. Stefan wasn't talking about distance. He was talking about time. Realization swept over him, and he realized what the mage meant. With a wave of his hand, his street clothes turned into a heavy winter jacket, and his leather shoes became snow boots. He closed his eyes again, imagining the long-forgotten fishing village on the fjord. A chill crept over him, and when he opened his eyes, he was standing on the hill that overlooked his childhood home.

It was twilight, even though it was early yet, as this time of the year, days were much shorter. Overhead, the spectacular northern lights began to appear, illuminating the night sky. That posed a problem. The Aurora Borealis, though beautiful, also quickly drained the powers of blessed witches and warlocks. It was one of the reasons his parents decided to move to the village. During the evenings, at least, Signe could have some rest from her visions of the future, while he and his father could still practice their magic during the day or when they stayed outside of the village. Right now, high up in the valley, he could still feel his powers working, but he knew once he went down, he would feel the effects of the Aurora Borealis like a heavy curtain covering him. It would take more concentration and strength for him to use his powers, and he could be sapped after a few spells. But why would Stefan choose such a place where he would be vulnerable during the long nights?

As Daric walked closer to the edge of the hill and peered down into the valley, he realized why. Among the rundown cottages of his old village, was Stefan's army. There were maybe a hundred or so men scattered about and even through the curtain of northern lights he could feel the dark magic controlling their minds. Stefan's top lieutenants were there, too, about twenty mages in total and Daric knew his best puppeteers would be hidden somewhere where they could see and control the humans, but not be exposed to attack. And lastly, he saw

Stefan's first line of defense—about twenty or so full-grown Lycan wolves chained up to posts around the village. Stefan must have figured out how to modify the spell that controlled the humans to work on the Lone Wolves. Being dark magic, the spell didn't seem to be affected by the northern lights, as both the human and Lycan slaves remained eerily calm and still.

Daric considered his options. He could sneak in, search the huts until he found Meredith, Sebastian, and Zachary Vrost and transport them back to Fenrir. Of course, that meant he could only go to the places he could remember in his mind—his old home and the public areas around the village, which meant he'd be spotted right away. Also, with the northern lights disrupting his powers, he wasn't sure he'd have enough magical reserves to transport everyone and fight off the mages, humans, and Lone Wolves. With dawn still a few hours away, he'd have to wait and then that would mean Stefan would also have full control and capacity of his powers. He hated to admit it, but toe-to-toe, he was no match for the master mage. Stefan had acquired too many powers and too much magic over the years and Daric had always suspected that the mage was holding back.

He knew what he had to do. It was a risk, but he had no other choice. He needed an army to fight Stefan and get Meredith back. He closed his eyes and focused on his next destination.

CHAPTER TWENTY-EIGHT

Having been to Grant Anderson's office several times now, transporting there was an easy task. He just had to make sure he picked a spot that was clear of furniture or other people, lest he accidentally appear inside a sofa or table (not the most pleasant thing in the world) or another person (definitely unpleasant and unsurvivable for both parties.) He decided that just outside the office would be best, as he guessed the Alpha's office would be filled with people.

As he appeared in the Fenrir executive offices' waiting room, Grant's admin Jared jumped out of his seat in surprise. "My apologies," he said, nodding to the frightened Lycan. He strode to the door that led into Grant's office and walked in.

He expected the different reactions, of course, and even anticipated their anger. Connor and Nick immediately attacked him, and though he was tempted to simply swat them away, he knew he deserved their anger.

"Get them off him!" Jade pleaded to the others.

Nick managed to land a punch, which was a surprise, but Daric supposed it was a long time coming. Connor, on the other hand, wrapped his gigantic arms around him, restraining him and bringing him down to his knees.

"Did you find them? Where's Sebastian?" Jade asked as she rushed to his side.

Daric raised his head slowly. "I did find them."

"And?" The Lycan's green eyes searched his face. "Are they alive? Did you get them?"

He shook his head. "I couldn't. Not by myself."

While the rest of the Lycans and witches looked on, Grant stood up from his chair and walked over to him. "Well, warlock? Did you change your mind? Did you want that bracelet back on?"

"I'm sorry for disappearing like that," he said apologetically. "I know I broke your trust, but I had no choice. Please don't punish Dr. Cross for doing what she thought was right."

"Dr. Cross has been properly chastised," Grant replied, his eyes flickering over to the Lycan scientist. "But, you said you found them? Why didn't you bring them back right away?"

"If you could kindly ask Connor to let me go, I can explain," Daric said patiently. "We have no time to lose," he added when he saw the hesitation on Grant's face.

"Let him go, Connor," Grant ordered.

The Lycan grunted but released Daric quickly. The warlock dropped to the ground unceremoniously but quickly got up. As he brushed himself off, he felt all the eyes in the room on him.

"Well?" Grant asked.

He took a deep breath. "I know where they are. Stefan has been hiding out in my old village in Norway." Daric explained to them what he had seen and what Stefan had done to ensure that Daric couldn't just sneak in and transport his prisoners away.

"We need to attack now," Nick said. "While Stefan himself is vulnerable."

"But that's why he chose that place," Lara pointed out. "He's only temporarily vulnerable. The northern lights should only affect his blessed powers. Being blood magic, the controlling spell seems to be unaffected if his puppet masters still have a hold over the humans and Lycans."

"We need to help the Lone Wolves," Killian added. "If they're under some kind of spell, then you know they're innocent."

"Daric," Jade began. "You told me that Stefan is the source of the power and puppet masters are only his conduits. Do you think he's particularly weak if he's being drained by both the controlling spell and the northern lights?"

"I did not think of that," Daric said. "But it's possible."

"Then all we have to do is kill Stefan, which may not even take a lot of effort," Jade hypothesized.

"If we can get past his army," Alynna pointed out.

"We'll need our own army, then," Grant said in a serious voice. He looked at Nick and Alynna. "Start making preparations. We're going to call every able-bodied Lycan in New York and our allies. Daric," he turned to the warlock. "How many people can you transport to your village at one time?"

Daric thought for a moment. "I suppose I could move five to six people at a time."

"Good," Grant nodded. "We need to get a move on then if we want to attack Stefan before daylight."

———

Meredith sat in the hut alone, rubbing her hands over her arms as the cold crept over her. Her Lycan metabolism had been keeping her warm, but when the direness of the situation had dawned on her, nothing could stop the chill blasting through her veins.

She realized where they were being held—it was obviously Daric and Signe's old village in Norway, where the warlock and mage first crossed paths. It was dark outside, which made it even harder to judge what time of the day it was. The eerie northern lights overhead made the entire place look creepy, like some damn horror movie, but that wasn't what made Meredith's skin crawl. It was the army of men waiting outside, standing still in the cold like a bunch of zombies. And then there were the wolves—Lycans, by the size of them—surrounding the village, tied up to the wooden posts like dogs waiting to be unleashed. Stefan was well-guarded, and even with Daric's powers and the New York Lycans, she doubted they would have enough resources to fight the mages and their army of human and Lycan slaves.

She wondered where Stefan had taken Sebastian. It was a smart move on his part, taking Sebastian away because all the Lycans needed to do was free him and unleash the dragon. Hopefully, he still wasn't under Stefan's control, but if the mages got a hold of Jade, then all bets were off. She hoped her best friend was safe somewhere. And then there was Zachary Vrost. Stefan only needed threaten the child and Nick Vrost would give everything he had to keep his son safe. For once in her life, she was truly scared.

Her she-wolf whined, trying to comfort her.

"I know," she said aloud. "I'm trying not to lose hope."

Think, think, think, the she-wolf said. *What would Archie do?*

Archie would tell her not to give up. There was always a way.

"I've given you all the tools you need, Meredith," Archie said countless times. "Think."

She was tired. Bone tired. As soon as Stefan and Victoria had left, she searched every inch of the cabin, trying to find a weak spot or anything to help her get out. But there was nothing, they made sure of that. Just the furs on the ground and the single bed in the corner. She had nothing on her except the tracking bracelet and—

"Christ on a bicycle!" Her hands crept up to her chest. *The phone!* She had forgotten she had it tucked away in her bra. Her hands trembled as she took it out and pressed the power button. "Yes!" She pumped her fist in the air as the phone turned on.

Meredith took a deep breath. She would only have one chance at this, and the battery was near dead. There was no signal, of course, but most phones had a GPS unit. Hopefully, someone at Fenrir would be monitoring signals from all their registered phones. It was a long shot, but hopefully, someone out there was listening.

CHAPTER TWENTY-NINE

It had taken another few hours or so, but the New York Lycans were able to mobilize their forces and Daric began transporting them to the same hill overlooking the fjord. Every able-bodied member of the New York clan came, which amounted to about forty in total, including the security team, trainees, and a few clan members in the area who volunteered to come. Five people from New Jersey arrived, plus Dante Muccino and Frankie Anderson. Connecticut had sent ten of their own, including their current Alpha, Logan Cooper, while Philadelphia sent six of their best Lycan fighters. That was a force of about 60, plus Vivianne, Lara, and Liam.

They were going to battle a hundred human slaves, twenty Lone Wolves, and another 20 mages who were probably armed to the teeth with various spells and potions. However, if all went as planned, then there would be no need to battle them head on. The odds weren't in their favor, but they had the element of surprise on their hands.

The Lycans set up a small camp in a clearing away from the edge of the hill. Grant stood in the middle, talking to the team.

"Have we got visual?" Grant asked Quinn.

The younger man nodded, holding his tablet PC up. "The drones have just finished their survey and will remain in the air to monitor the area. Awesome tech, by the way," Quinn grinned as he turned the screen to them. "Just as Daric said, there's about a hundred or so humans and twenty Lycans scattered around them."

Grant let out a breath. "Our main goal is to find Meredith, Sebastian, and Zac and get them out. Based on the layout, they could be in any of those huts. There are twenty homes total. Alynna, Lara and Liam's team will be split up into three for the retrieval purposes. Once the hostages have been found and retrieved, contact us through the comms. Hopefully, we'll get to them before anyone notices."

"Highly unlikely," Nick interjected. "Which is why Alex and I will be leading our team to take out the puppet masters. There's no way we can defeat all of the human slaves. There are too many of them. Our only chance is to take the puppet masters down." He pointed to the black-robed figures on the edges of the village, facing the army of slaves and their backs to the shore. "Our best fighters, led by Connor, will distract the Lone Wolves on the front lines. If we catch them by surprise, we can stop them before they can mobilize the human forces."

"And once the hostages are safe and the puppet masters have been disabled," Daric began. "I will find Stefan and end him."

"We both will," Grant said. They had planned it so Grant and Daric would be watching over the ridge, waiting for the signal that the hostages were safe. Once they were sure, Daric would transport them to wherever Stefan was, and they would end this tonight. "But we want to make sure the hostages are out of harm's way. We'll do our best not to hurt any of the innocent Lycans and people, but if push comes to shove, our people and the hostages come first."

"All right team," Grant said, checking his watch. "We have an hour until sunrise. Let's finish this."

Daric watched as the Lycans made their preparations. Killian, Connor, and Quinn walked together, talking silently. As the best fighter, Connor was joining the main team that would attack the army head on. Killian was on the retrieval team, while Quinn was going to remain behind to continuously monitor the situation and fly the drones to find Stefan. The three brothers clapped each other on the back, touching their foreheads together before they separated.

Jade was also joining the retrieval team, and she was talking to an older man with graying hair. Eric, someone had called him and based on the similar features, he guessed this was Jade's father. Frankie was talking to Grant, her arms wrapped around his waist. The Alpha's stance was tense, his back stiff, but he stroked his mate's back in a tender manner. The Lupa was staying back to coordinate the teams, as although she was invulnerable, her advancing pregnancy made it difficult to move. Nick stood by himself in the corner, his face stony and hard. Vivianne Chatraine had given Cady a potion to help her sleep, and so the Beta's mate remained at Fenrir, unaware of what was going on. Liam and Lara, on the other hand, were standing silently under a tree, hands intertwined.

This was it. He would do everything in his power to make sure Meredith and the others were safe, but the moment he saw an opportunity, he would kill Stefan.

"Alpha! Alpha!" Quinn's voice rang through the silent clearing, his footsteps hitting the snow-covered ground in a rhythmic pattern as he ran back to Grant.

"What is it?" the Alpha asked as he pulled away from his mate.

"I was running a last scan, just in case the mages were using any sort of tech to help them out." Quinn fished his phone out of his pocket and held it up to Grant's face. "Look!"

"What is it?" Grant asked, his brows drawing together.

"It's a GPS signal. From down in the village."

"What does it mean?" Frankie asked. "There's no cell signal out here."

"That's the thing." Quinn tapped on the phone. "No one's phone is working out here, I could barely get a signal from the sat phones. But, something or someone is transmitting something from down there."

Daric strode to Quinn and looked at the screen. "Meredith," he said. "She stole one of your phones," he said to Grant. "I saw her, the day after the car broke down. She didn't return the phone, but slipped it into her bra."

"That must be her," Quinn exclaimed. "Good girl."

"I know where that is," he said, pointing to the red dot on the screen. "That house is in the middle of the village. It belonged to one of our best hunters, Oskar. He was my father's best friend, and we spent a lot of time there."

"If we can locate her, then that's one less person we have to worry about."

"I can get in there," Daric said. "I know the space."

"But you won't be able to get her out," Grant pointed out. "You'd both be trapped. The northern lights--"

"I didn't say I couldn't leave," Daric retorted. "But, transporting back and forth would drain me. I could probably only do it twice or thrice in a row."

"That would mean Stefan could get away," Grant said.

If someone had asked him weeks ago to agree to such a plan, he would have laughed in their face. Stefan's demise had been his singular goal in life, but now things had changed. Protecting Meredith at all costs was his priority now. "If Meredith,

Sebastian, and Zac are there and I could take them to safety, then it would be worth it."

"I agree," Grant said. "Stefan's death is not worth the lives of anyone. We will proceed with the plan, but once you have them out of there and we can reduce casualties, then we're out of here. Let's explain the modified plan to the team and get this show on the road."

CHAPTER THIRTY

Meredith stared at the phone, watching the battery meter slowly count down the power percentage until shut down. A cry ripped from her throat as the hope died along with the phone. This was it. If no one had found her signal, then she was as good as dead.

She stood up and paced. She was out of tools. Like, literally out of them. She only had the clothes on her back, and she doubted her t-shirt and leggings would be able to help her out of this one. Meredith threw herself on the bed, sobbing into the musty pillow.

"Don't lose hope, *min kjære.*"

Meredith froze. She was dreaming. Her starving body was making her hear things. Stefan was sending her visions to drive her mad. Slowly, she got up from the bed and turned around.

Daric was standing in the middle of the room, his handsome face beaming at her. It took a second for it to register in her brain but when it all clicked, she ran toward him, leaping up into his arms and wrapping her legs around him. She grabbed his face and planted a hard kiss on his lips. God, she missed him. She couldn't believe he was really here.

"Yes, it's me," he laughed as he gently pried Meredith away from him. She untangled herself from his body and stood in front him.

"You're here," she whispered, tears streaming down her cheeks.

"I've come to rescue you and—" He staggered forward, and Meredith planted her palms on his chest to steady him,

"Daric!" she cried. "Are you all right?"

He nodded. "I'm sorry. This place..."

"It's your village, right?"

"Yes, but that's not all." He quickly explained to her how the northern lights were affecting his powers.

"It's draining you?" she asked.

"Not totally, but yes. I can only perform a few more spells before I need rest."

"Okay, then what's the plan?"

"Wait, this first." He bent down and waved his hand over her tracking bracelet. The band disappeared, and the device fell on the floor.

"Daric!" she exclaimed. "Why did you do that? Your powers!"

"A small trick," he said with a smile. "I'm conserving them as best as I can. Transporting takes the most out of me, but I can still do small things. You will need to defend yourself."

"Right." She took a deep breath. "So, now what?"

"I was hoping that Sebastian and Zachary Vrost were with you so I can take you all away."

She shook her head. "We've all been separated. They've got some special chain holding Sebastian down so he can't shift and I haven't seen Zac since we were in Fenrir, but..." She closed her eyes, trying to use her enhanced hearing to tune in. "He's been crying, poor thing, but I think I know where he is. North...no, northeast of us."

"Then we must go," he lifted his hand, but she stopped him.

"No, save it! We'll sneak out. Can you remove whatever it is that's blocking the door?"

He nodded and then walked to the front door, waving his hand. Grabbing the handle, he turned it and slowly opened the door.

Meredith peered outside. "There," she said nodding towards one of the distant cabins. There was a faint light coming from the inside. "We need to go there."

"That was our old home," Daric said through gritted teeth. Before Meredith could stop him, Daric grabbed her arm, and the coldness gripped her. A few seconds later, they reappeared inside another cabin. This one was much larger and had more furniture. A fire was blazing in the hearth, and there was a bed and a baby cot in the corner. A woman stood with her back to them, holding a bundle in her arms as she rocked back and forth.

"Stop crying," Victoria begged. "Please, baby, stop." She turned around, her eyes growing wide and her face becoming even paler as she saw Daric and Meredith. "You!" she hissed. "What are you—Master!!" she screamed.

Before Daric or Meredith could move, Stefan appeared on the opposite side of the room.

"Ah, my old protégé," the master mage mocked. "Looks like you've freed your little bitch, I see."

"Let him go, Stefan," Daric said as he raised his hand.

"Or what?" Stefan slowly walked towards the witch. "Victoria, you know what to do."

"Yes, Master." Victoria retrieved the knife strapped to her waist and pointed it at Zac. "Move, and he dies."

Victoria moved the tip of the blade closer to the bundle, pointing it straight at Zac's heart.

Daric lowered his hand. "You truly are a monster, Victoria."

"No!" Meredith yelped. "You wouldn't."

Zac let out another cry, and Meredith saw Victoria's hand shake and her face falter, just for a second. "He's your grandson," Meredith pleaded. "Cady's son. Your own flesh and blood."

"Shut up!" Victoria screeched. She pressed the tip against the baby's breastbone. "I'll do it, I swear."

Daric began to raise his hand and slowly advanced toward Stefan. "You've drained yourself, Stefan, I can see your hands shaking. You've used too many spells, haven't you? Plus, all the puppet masters have been draining more and more of your power."

"Stop stalling," Stefan bellowed at the witch.

Victoria's eyes went wild as she looked at Zac and then Stefan. "Master?"

"Kill the child, Victoria," Stefan ordered. "Now."

Victoria let out a wail and raised the knife. Meredith was about to scream for Victoria to stop, but her breath caught as she saw the witch fling the knife at Stefan. The master mage waved his hand, and the knife reversed its course, sending it straight to Victoria.

The witch twisted away, shielding the baby as the knife buried into her back with a sickening squish. She fell forward, and Meredith lunged for her, grabbing the bundle before Victoria fell.

"Tell...Cady..." Victoria choked, reaching out to Meredith with her hand.

Tears burned in her eyes as she nodded. "I will."

Victoria's hand fell back and her eyes closed.

"Pity," Stefan declared. "She was quite useful to me."

"Stefan!" Daric yelled as he flung his hand toward the mage. Stefan was caught by surprise and his body was thrown against the wall.

"Is that all you've got?" Stefan laughed as he brushed

himself off and stood up. "What were you thinking? Coming here by yourself and trying to get your Lycan whore back? My men will be here in two seconds. I've already roused the army."

"No," Daric said with a smile. "I'm not alone."

Stefan was about to open his mouth when sounds of screams and shouts from the outside made his face twist in anger. "What have you done?"

"It's over, Stefan," Daric said. "The Lycans and the witches are here."

Stefan laughed. "I don't think so."

The doors behind them suddenly burst open, and five large men filed in, all carrying rifles. Behind them, a giant black wolf padded in, fangs bared.

Meredith's inner-she wolf howled, and she set little Zac down on the baby cot. She turned and then hunched herself in as the animal burst from her skin. Her limbs and face elongated, her muscles and bones stretching, and fur sprouted all over her body. It all took a few seconds, but to Meredith, it felt like an eternity. She landed on all four paws and stood in front of the other Lycan. She heard a gasp behind her, probably Daric, and she wasn't surprised. Her wolf was magnificent—all silver white fur and red eyes. She was the only albino Lycan in the world, as far as she knew.

The she-wolf growled at the humans, ignoring them as she advanced toward the other wolf. Daric took care of them anyway, as their weapons jammed the moment they tried to use them on her. The two wolves were evenly matched, same height and weight, but Meredith had an advantage, of course. The child inside her would protect her, and she wasn't afraid of getting hurt, especially not when she was protecting those she loved. Her mate. Her clan. Her family.

The black wolf lunged first, and she sprang at him, ripping with her claws and fangs. The other wolf's claws ripped down her face, sending the blood spurting and staining her snowy fur, but she ignored the pain. Instead, she went straight for the neck, clamping her canines down on the flesh as hard as she could. The wolf let out a howl of pain and rolled away from her as soon as she released him. He limped away, dragging his body into the corner as he lay down and turned back into his human form.

"Stefan!" Daric called as the mage disappeared. "Goddamnit!" He turned to the she-wolf, who had padded over to him and was licking his hand. "I must go," he said. "Take care of them for me, she-wolf." Without another word, he disappeared.

The she-wolf whined and then turned around, running into the chaos outside. Inside her, Meredith railed and scream, begging the wolf to go and find Daric, but the wolf didn't listen. Instead, she raised her head, sniffing the air as she tried to find a distinct scent. The scent of fire and ashes.

Daric immediately knew where Stefan had disappeared to, or rather, the mage had told him, sending him a vision of where he was. As he focused on the exact place, he thought that it might be a trap. Perhaps it was, but one way or another, this would end tonight.

He appeared right on top of the cliff, the highest point overlooking their village. Here, the northern lights seemed to burn much brighter and he could feel its effect more prominently. He thought he had enough power for at least a few more spells, but he was almost tapped out.

The cliffside point also offered a view of the action below, and it seemed Stefan had used the last of his powers to bring his remaining four mages and six of his human slaves with him. They stood to the side, ready to defend their master.

"Ah, you've come," Stefan taunted as he looked at Daric. The mage struggled to get up, but he managed to get to his feet.

"Your magic is almost gone," Daric stated.

"And so is yours. Get him," Stefan ordered. One of the mages stretched his hands out and began to chant. The human slaves suddenly stood up straight and began to lumber towards Daric.

Daric lunged towards Stefan, tackling him to the ground. He would kill Stefan with his bare hands if that's what it took. The master mage screamed in protest as Daric's heavy body landed on top of him, pinning him down.

"Get him!" Stefan managed to croak out as Daric's fingers wrapped around his throat.

Daric squeezed as hard as he could, but the human slaves pulled him away before he could feel the last breath leave from Stefan's body. The six men restrained him, forcing him to his knees as the largest of them twisted his arms back before pushing him down on the ground.

Stefan heaved as he tried to get up. "It is such a pity," he rasped as he slowly stumbled to Daric. "You could have been great! Could have ruled by my side, but you throw it all away for a worthless little Lycan bitch." He looked at the man holding Daric down. "Kill him."

A meaty arm wrapped around Daric's neck and tightened, squeezing the air out of him. As spots appeared in front of his eyes, his last thoughts were of Meredith and their unborn child. He wished he could have seen her future if only to know what their offspring would look like. Probably beautiful, like Meredith.

"Stefan, you shithead!"

The sound of large wings flapping filled Daric's ears and a large rush of wind knocked over both him and the man who had him in a chokehold. They rolled around several times, and when

Daric ended up on top, he slammed his fist into the other man's face, knocking him out. Looking up, he saw a giant golden dragon flying overhead. Its wings slowed down, and the dragon swooped lower. A figure dropped to the ground, and he held his breath when he saw Meredith's body fall to the ground, transform in mid-air, and land on all fours. The magnificent white wolf stood in front of Stefan, growling and snapping, forcing the mage to retreat. Behind her, however, the remaining men advanced. One of them pulled a pistol from his pocket, and he trained it on the she-wolf.

"No!" Daric ran towards them. His magic was nearly tapped out and he couldn't do anything to stop them or get her out of harm's way. One of them shot at the wolf, and she yowled in pain. She turned around, growling and advancing towards the men. She leaped at the man with the weapon, disabling him, but the rest piled on top of her, seemingly unafraid of the giant animal. The she-wolf let out a howl and shook them off her as they tried to hang on and wrestle her to the ground.

Daric wanted to help Meredith, but Stefan stood between them. The mage raised his hand, preparing to use his last bit of magic to help his goons. "Stefan!" he called, and the mage turned around.

"Still alive? You've always been a survivor," Stefan said almost proudly. "Too bad, though, I think you've used up your magic and your luck."

Calling on the last reserves of his magic, Daric used it to transport the sword strapped to Stefan's side into his hand. "No, I think you've used up the last of yours." Daric raised the sword, pushing it straight forward into the mage's body. Stefan's eyes bulged in disbelief and his face scrunched in agony as he screamed.

"Kill them!" he ordered the remaining mages as he staggered back, blood dribbling from his mouth. "Kill them all."

The four mages turned their attention to Daric and Meredith. The she-wolf had managed to knock away one of the men, but the remaining four circled her. The mage controlling the human slaves waved his hand, and two of the men walked away from the she-wolf and trudged towards Daric. The remaining mages slipped their hands into their robes, preparing what Daric knew were various potions that could disable both him and Meredith.

"Traitor!" Stefan hissed with the last of his breath. "If I die tonight, so will you!"

The winds picked up, getting stronger and faster and Daric had to dig his heels in to keep steady. As he saw a flash of gold in the distance and heard the beating of wings, he knew what Sebastian was planning.

"Meredith!" he screamed. The white wolf's ears perked up, and with one last growl, she turned tail and dashed to Daric. When she was a few yards away, her hind legs gave one last push, and she lunged through the air to leap over Stefan's dying body and tackle Daric to the ground, rolling them away just in time as fire and lava rained from above.

The heat was unbearable, and the smoke and ashes made his lungs burn, but at least they were alive. They both were. Warm fur and heavy muscle shrank back into soft skin and supple limbs. Daric used his body to shield her, landing with a thud on his back as Meredith slammed on top of him.

"Oomph!" Meredith sputtered. She tried to look back but turned her head away. The light burning from the dragon fire was blinding, and Daric himself closed his eyes until the heat faded away.

"Is he..."

Daric opened his eyes slowly. The faint light of dawn was slowly creeping across the sky as the sun rose from behind the hills. Turning his head to the side, there was nothing but ashes by the edge of the cliff. "Yes. It is done."

Meredith let out a whoop of triumph and pumped a fist high in the air. "We did it! Hey!" She looked down and raised a brow at him. "Are you getting a victory boner?"

He laughed. "You are naked and bouncing on top of me," he pointed out.

"Right." Meredith slowly eased off him and got to her feet. She bent down to help him up, and he accepted her hand. As soon as he stood up, however, Meredith let out an indignant cry.

"Daric," she sobbed, tears filling her eyes. "You...your..."

"What is it?" he asked, running his hands over his body. "Am I injured? Should we get a doctor?"

"No," Meredith cried. "Your...hair!"

Daric frowned and touched his head, running his fingers through his hair. He realized that it must have caught some of the dragon fire, as half of his long locks had been singed off.

"Nooo!" she bawled. "Your beautiful hair!"

Daric chuckled. "*Min kjære*, it is just hair."

"Just hair?" she cried. "*Just hair*? Don't you know how much I loved that hair of yours? It'll take years to grow back."

"I'm a warlock," he reminded her. "I could learn to regrow it back if you wish."

"Really?"

"Really."

"Good," she reached up and kissed him. "Now, let's go back to the village and see what's going on."

"As much as I love seeing your delectable body," he said as he began to unbutton his shirt. "I'd rather keep the image to myself." He handed her his shirt, and she accepted, slipping it over herself.

"Thanks," she said. Suddenly, her eyes grew wide. "Speaking of naked bodies..."

Daric pivoted his head and saw Sebastian walking towards them, a scowl on his face and naked as the day he was born. He looked back at Meredith, and when he saw her eyes slowly dropping lower, he pulled her face to his chest.

"A little help?" Sebastian asked.

Daric nodded, and with the wave of his hand, the grass around Sebastian's feet floated up, swirled around his torso and the fibers changed into a pair of white boxers.

"Thanks," he said gratefully.

"Sebastian, my man! High five!" Meredith bounded to him, her hands raised. "Flying was soooo fun! Let's do it again. What do you say?"

"I'm not letting you anywhere near my dragon," Sebastian huffed.

"No more dragon rides?" she pouted.

"Never again. What the hell were you doing, tugging and pulling on my horns?"

"I was trying to steer!"

"*I* was steering, you idiot!" he growled.

"Oh, and by the way, you're welcome for the rescue! Thank God my she-wolf was smart enough to come and find you first."

"That makes one of you," Sebastian snorted.

"Did you see what you did to Daric's beautiful hair?" she countered.

"I have to go see Jade," he said, ignoring her. He looked down at his boxers. "Shit, I should have asked you to make me some stretchy pants like the Hulk. I don't want to show up buck naked in front of everyone. I'll see if I can walk back down."

"We'll follow," Daric said. "But I need a few minutes alone with Meredith."

Sebastian nodded and turned to walk away. Meredith suppressed a giggle when she saw what was printed on the back of Sebastian's boxers. It was a unicorn in bright shades of pink and purple.

"You're so bad," she whispered, swatting him playfully on the arm.

"Since you seemed to enjoy his body so much, I thought I'd give you something better to look at. And no one calls you idiot and gets away with it."

"Ha! That'll teach him." She laid her head on his chest as Daric's arms came around her. She breathed in his chocolate scent and murmured against his bare skin.

"Did you say something, *min kjære?*"

"I said," she looked up at him. "I love you, Daric."

His blue-green eyes turned from stormy to calm, and a smile tugged at his lips. "And I love you, my she-wolf."

Their lips met in a soft kiss as the sun continued to ascend, filling the valley with light. When they had enough of each other (for now, at least), they pulled away and started walking towards Sebastian, who was trying to figure out how to get down from the cliff.

"Let's go," Daric said, offering his hand to the other man. "I'll take us back."

CHAPTER THIRTY-ONE

The three of them appeared right in the middle of the village. While it was not as chaotic as it was just hours ago, the scene was certainly grim. Grant was kneeling next to a Lycan who was lying on the ground, his chest wrapped in bandages, comforting him as an older man tended to his injuries.

"You'll be fine, Patrick. Dr. Faulkner will take care of you," he said, clapping the man on the shoulder gently. "Jared will be happy to know you'll be coming home soon."

"Thank you, Primul," Patrick replied. "It's an honor to serve you."

Grant gave the man a nod and got to his feet. Beside him, Frankie helped him up and then wrapped her arm around his waist, snuggling into his side.

"Meredith! Sebastian! Daric!" Grant's face lit up. "Thank God! You..." He looked at Daric. "Is it done? He's gone?"

Daric nodded. "Yes, Alpha."

"And I made doubly sure," Sebastian added. "I don't think anyone can come back from being turned into ash."

Grant broke into a smile, and he hugged Frankie closer to

him. Tears were streaming down the Lupa's face. "It's over," she whispered, her hand slipping down to cup her growing belly. "It's finally over."

"Meredith!"

Daric saw the three Lone Wolves running towards them. Connor's strides were much longer than his brothers', so he reached Meredith first. He scooped her up into a fierce hug and kissed her forehead.

"Mer," he breathed, closing his eyes.

"Aww, Connor," Meredith said as he let her go. "I love you, too, ya big lug!"

Killian came next, and he lifted her up into his arms. "I'm so glad you're safe," he whispered into her hair.

"Hey, runt!" Quinn greeted, his face beaming. "I think if something did happen to you, I'd miss your ugly face. Owww!"

"Shut up!" Meredith said as she launched herself into his arms. "I was worried about you, too."

Quinn's face faltered for a second as he hugged Meredith. "Yeah, well, don't think I'll be around to help you next time you're in trouble." He released her and looked at Sebastian. "Jesus Christ, you really are a motherfucking dragon."

"I told you, but you wouldn't listen," Meredith said, giving him a shove.

"I thought you were joking!"

"Sonofabitch!"

All of them turned towards the source of the cry of frustration, who was stomping towards them. Alynna's face was drawn into a scowl as Alex ran behind her. He, on the other hand, looked ecstatic.

"What's wrong?" Grant asked his sister.

"What's wrong? *What's wrong?*" she fumed, opening her jacket, and showing everyone her shredded and bloody shirt.

She lifted up the torn fabric, showing the smooth, unmarred skin. "I'm pregnant. Again," she moaned.

"Hey, baby doll, don't be blue," Alex said as he came up behind her, pressing a kiss to her cheek. "Mika will love having a baby brother or sister."

"I really didn't want to spend another Christmas pregnant," Alynna whined. "Do you know how much wine I'll be missing? And eggnog? And vodka? And—" Alex kissed his wife to quiet her down.

"Sebastian!" Jade was running toward them at full speed. She launched herself at her mate, who caught her and spun her around and planted a long kiss on her mouth.

"I...I thought..." she choked, barely containing the tears and emotions.

"I'll always come back to you, darlin'," he drawled, drawing her into his arms. "Always."

Lara and Liam approached them, the witch's face grim. "Daric, Meredith," she called. "We can't find Zac. Nick's been going crazy looking for him."

Meredith looked around. "I put him down in the cot! Let's go get him."

As they walked towards his old home, Daric tensed. So many memories, so many words unspoken. As his steps faltered, Meredith threaded her fingers through his. "You can do this," she whispered.

He gripped her hand tight, and they walked inside. It was just as he remembered. His parent's bed in the corner, and his own twin bed in the other end. The cot where Zac lay sleeping was the same one his father made, with his bare hands and not with magic. "A father should be able to build things for his child," Jonas said as they put the baby cot in the storage shed in the back. "I'll teach you how to make one of these so that someday, you can make one for your son, too."

Victoria's body remained crumpled on the floor by the cot. He shook his head. Poor, misguided Victoria. Still, in the end, she did save her grandson's life. With a wave of his hand, her body disappeared. Victoria's favorite place was the gardens in Stefan's mountain retreat in Colorado, and so, he sent her remains there, burying her under an oak tree.

A soft cry drew his attention back and he looked at Meredith as she picked up Zac. He imagined her doing the same to their child and emotion welled up in him. It was real. This was all real. No more mages, no more Stefan, no more danger looming over their heads. Only Meredith from now on, and their child and many more children if he were blessed. Their love was like the sun, bringing light into the dark world he thought he would be living in until he died.

"Zac!" Nick's urgent voice knocked him out of his thoughts. "Where is he? Is he safe?"

"He's fine," Meredith said. "He just woke up."

Nick strode to Meredith, freezing as his eyes zeroed in on the squirming bundle in her arms as if he wasn't sure if it was true. As he took Zac from Meredith, his expression turned to that of relief, as if the weight of the world had lifted from his shoulder. He leaned down and took in the scent of his son, kissing the baby's chubby cheeks. "Hi there, Zac," he said, his voice shaking with emotion. "I've missed you. Mommy's missed you too. She'll be so happy to see you." Zac gurgled back happily.

Nick looked up at Meredith and then to Daric. "Thank you," he said, clearing his throat. "And...I apologize. For everything." The Beta smiled—a genuine one that Daric was sure didn't come easily to the stoic Lycan.

Daric nodded in acknowledgement and Meredith smiled. "You're welcome," she replied and then took a deep breath.

"Wait, Nick," she called as the Beta was about to leave. "There's something you need to know. About Victoria."

"What about her?" Nick asked, his voice a low growl.

"She...she saved Zac from Stefan. She asked that I tell Cady she loved her."

Nick's face was inscrutable, but he nodded. "Cady will want to know Zac is safe. I'll call her now." He pulled Zac closer to his chest and left the hut.

Meredith looked down at the empty cot, her hands running lovingly over the wood. Daric walked to her, wrapping his arms around her from behind.

"This was yours, wasn't it?" But she posed it like it was a statement, not a question.

"My father made it himself," he confirmed. He pushed her hair aside and nuzzled her neck, letting the scent of wildflowers tickle his nose.

"Can we come back here, another time?" she asked as she turned around to face him. "I'd like to explore the area. Maybe you can show me where you grew up."

"You only have to ask, *min kjære.*"

EPILOGUE

O ne month later...

"This is definitely the Disney Princess wedding to beat all Disney Princess weddings," Jade said, her eyes wide as she took in all the decorations. "Where did you find a 10-foot tall stuffed unicorn? Wait, never mind." She shook her head. "Your demented ideas and Daric's powers are a dangerous combination. I'm only glad he can't change living things. Who knows what creature you'd come up with."

"Oh, give me a break," Meredith retorted. "It's my wedding day."

"Did you really have to have me dress up like Belle?" Jade asked as she twirled in her yellow maid of honor ball gown.

"Hmmm..." Meredith narrowed her eyes as she looked at Jade. "Do you think Sebastian would mind if I had Daric whip him up a new outfit? He's getting really good at creating clothes."

"Don't even think it," Jade warned, knowing what Meredith was thinking. "Not after the last time."

There was a knock on the door, and Lara walked in, looking gorgeous in a blue Cinderella-inspired ball gown.

"At least Liam was game to dress up as Prince Charming," Meredith grumbled and turned around. "How do I look?"

"Beautiful, Mer," Lara said, her eyes shining with tears.

"Yes," Jade agreed. "You look stunning."

Although Ariel was her favorite Disney Princess, Meredith nixed the idea of copying her wedding gown. So, instead, she decided to go with an Ariel-inspired gown. It was a fitted bustier mermaid dress in white, but studded with sea-green Swarovski crystals and sequins shaped like scales. Not only did it look gorgeous, but the color reminded her of Daric's eyes.

"Thanks!" she replied, snorting back the tears threatening to spill over. "Oh dammit. Thank God for waterproof mascara." Lara and Jade, already used to crying at a drop of a hat when all of them were together, pulled out their handkerchiefs and offered it to Meredith. Once the tears were dried, the three women composed themselves. Jade helped Meredith with the veil and Lara brought over her shoes so she could slip them on.

"Ready, Meredith?" came a voice from the door. Killian peeked in, his face breaking into a smile as his gaze landed on Meredith. "You look beautiful," he beamed.

"Aww, don't get me started again," Meredith moaned as she felt the tears welling up again.

"We'll give you some privacy," Jade said, walking towards the door.

"Be ready in five, though," Lara reminded them.

Killian entered the room, moving aside so the two ladies could pass. He looked handsome in his black tux, but then again, Killian always looked striking in formal wear.

"Well, do I pass?" he asked jokingly.

"Yeah, you'll do," she answered with a smile. She walked up to her brother and touched his arm. "Are you okay, Killian?" she asked with a frown.

"Yeah, I'm good," he replied with a smile, but Meredith saw that it didn't quite reach his eyes. Something was wrong with her brother, she knew it. The leader of their little family had always been laid back, smooth, and charming, especially with the ladies. Meredith used to joke that he was James Bond in real life, and not just because of his skills. Ever since he came to New York, she could feel something was different. He hadn't even given any of the Lycan women at Fenrir a second glance, even though half of them were throwing themselves at him.

"If you need to talk about anything—"

"I'm fine, Mer," he insisted. "Let's get you hitched, okay?"

She nodded and took his arm. She wanted to know what Killian was hiding, but she knew better than to pry. He would tell her when the time was right.

"God, I can't believe you're getting *married*," Quinn moaned. He and Connor were waiting just outside the door. "Who the hell would want to tie themselves to one person? How stupid. Plus, neither of you have a last name, did you realize that?"

"Oh, shut up," Meredith replied. "I hope you fall in love with a girl who won't take your shit and make you work for her. I don't think I'll be able to stop laughing when that day comes."

"Never gonna happen."

"Sure." She turned to Connor. He looked uncomfortable in his tux, and was tugging at the collar. "You look great, Connor."

"I look stupid in this monkey suit," he growled.

Meredith laughed and walked over to him, adjusting the tie that had gone crooked. "You look amazing. The ladies'll go crazy for you."

Quinn guffawed. "Or at least you won't scare them away too much." Meredith shot him a warning look.

"Yeah, sure," Connor shrugged.

"I wish Archie were here," Meredith said quietly.

"I know," Killian added. "But I'd like to think he's around, somehow."

They buried Archie next to his wife at their family plot a few days after the confrontation with Stefan and the mages. It was a small memorial, attended only by the four Lone Wolves, Daric, and a few people from the Portland clan, including their Alpha.

"C'mon, everyone's waiting for us," Quinn said, turning around quickly, but not before Meredith noticed his eyes getting misty.

She linked arms with Connor and Killian as they followed Quinn down the end of the hallway that led to the outside lawn.

It was a beautiful day for a fall wedding in Portland. The leaves had fully turned, and the woods outside the mansion where the four Lone Wolves grew up in were bursting in golds and reds.

As the quartet began to play, Lara and Jade walked down the aisle. Guests filled up all the chairs on either side, most from New York, but a few of the Lycans from the area had been invited too.

Then, the music changed, signaling for everyone to stand. The bride came down the aisle, escorted by her three brothers and everyone clapped and cheered.

When they got to the end, Daric was waiting for them, with Sebastian and Liam standing next to him. Meredith thought he looked super hot in his gray tux and his shortly-cropped hair. After they came back from Norway, she nearly jumped out of her skin when she walked into his bathroom and saw Daric from behind, his hair newly chopped off. She joked that she thought he was someone else and that now she had a new boyfriend. When he asked her later that night if she still wanted him to regrow his hair, she giggled and said she'd think about it.

Vivianne Chatraine was waiting for them at the altar and performed a traditional witch binding ceremony and blessing. Once it was all over and she declared them man and wife, Meredith quickly wrapped her arms around Daric and pulled him down for a kiss. She didn't even stop when Quinn loudly said that she was supposed to wait for the signal that groom could kiss the bride. Daric, on the other hand, was startled, but eagerly returned his new wife's kiss. When they broke away, Daric saw Alynna in the front row fanning herself, and she gave him a wink.

The reception was in full swing, with a full band playing classic tunes and Meredith dancing with all her brothers, even Connor, who seemed strangely graceful on the dance floor. Daric took his mother for a couple of dances as well, and she beamed proudly the whole time. She also shyly introduced them to her date for the evening, a handsome older gentleman named Merrick, who was old friend of Graham and Vivianne's.

"Well, *min kjære*," Daric said as their dance ended and he guided her off the dance floor. "Did I give you the wedding of your dreams?"

"Yeah, it almost made up for your proposal," she said dryly.

"I suppose I've learned my lesson to never be romantic," he replied.

"Ha! I love that you brought me back to your village, like I asked," Meredith began.

"But now I know never to take you to exotic places when the season premiere of Game of Thrones is 'dropping'."

"At least not someplace without Wi-Fi. We're not savages," she joked as they sat down at their table, where a chocolate fountain was set up no more than an arm's length away from Meredith.

"Have you both gotten enough chocolate?" Daric said, slipping a hand over her stomach. "I swear, our child might come out made of chocolate at this point."

"Not nearly, no," she said, as she took a bite of a chocolate-covered strawberry. She offered Daric the remaining piece, and he swallowed it in one gulp.

"This is amazing, baby," she said as she looked around them, surrounded by their family and clan. Grant had given her a full pardon, as her reward for saving Zac Vrost, but as soon as he released her from her bond to the New York Clan, she pledged to them. They were now hers, as much as she was theirs.

"I'm glad you're happy," he said. He turned to the left and saw his new brothers-in-law walking towards them. "I think you're about to be even happier."

"What?" she asked. She looked at the three men approaching them and then back at her new husband. "Something going on? What did you see?"

"Nothing," he said. "Just a conversation I overheard today."

The three Lone Wolves came up to them, shaking Daric's hands and giving their sister a hug.

"Meredith, we wanted to wait until after the ceremony to tell you something," Killian began.

"What is it?"

Her brother could hardly contain his smile. "Sebastian offered us all jobs. Back in New York."

"What?" she asked incredulously. She looked at Connor and Quinn, who both nodded.

"We'll be running an offshoot of his company. We'll be doing special ops for Creed Security, using our skills to help his clients."

"And, when we're not going on ops for him, we'll be helping

those Lone Wolves find their families," Quinn added. "And make sure it doesn't happen again. To anyone."

"Oh my God!" Meredith cried, hugging all her brothers. "That means you'll be living in New York?"

"The Alpha is granting us special permission to stay in the city," Killian continued.

"Yeah, well, we can't miss our first nephew or niece's birth, can we?" Quinn said.

Connor nodded. "We gotta make sure he or she has all the right skills."

"Not that you'll need our help raising the pup. You'll both be great parents." Killian's face softened, and Meredith didn't miss the hitch in his voice.

"Aww...you guys!"

"Ow, Mer!" Quinn complained when she hugged them again. "Watch the suit. I got ladies I gotta go meet!"

"Ha!" she laughed. "Fine. Go then. I guess I'll be seeing more of your ugly faces soon."

With a last nod to Daric, the three men left.

Meredith turned back to her new husband. "I hope you're okay with them staying."

"What? Of course, I am. If it makes you happy, it makes me happy. Besides, I think Connor doesn't hate me as much now that I've made an honest woman of you."

"Right," she giggled. "And are you happy?" she asked quietly.

"Of course." He drew her onto his lap and pressed his lips to her neck, making her moan. "I once thought that you would be a weakness, a distraction."

"And now?"

"Now, you are my world."

"Daric," she whispered. "I love you."

"I love you too, Meredith."

EXTENDED EPILOGUE

FIVE YEARS LATER...

"Oh my God," Alynna exclaimed as her eyes grew wide and her gaze landed at the women in front of her. "None of you breathe on me. I swear, if I have to spend another Christmas pregnant, I'm going to scream. Dr. Faulkner has come up with some sort of Lycan True Mate birth control. STAT." She put down her youngest, 6-month-old Knox, in the bassinet beside the couch.

Daric laughed, and Meredith giggled as he rubbed her growing belly. Beside them, Jade was talking to Lara over video chat on her phone. The Lycan scientist was about five months along with her third child, while Lara was in the hospital, already in labor with her and Liam's second. Cady was patiently waiting for her turn on the phone with Lara, sitting comfortably on the couch with a plate of half-eaten cake on her very pregnant stomach. She would be giving birth any day now too, to her and Nick's fourth baby. The twins came after Zachary, and now everyone was betting that Lara would be having twins as well. Meredith *may or may not* have had a little bit of help from her husband when she placed her bet.

It was a long summer weekend, and as such, they all ventured out to the Anderson mansion on Long Island for a barbecue. Daric enjoyed weekends like this when he could just relax and spend time with his family. His work with Jade in the lab at Fenrir was satisfying and kept him busy, but he wanted nothing more than to just spend time with his wife and their two children (soon to be three). Meredith was now one of Grant's head lieutenants, effectively 2nd in command of the Lycan security force, after Nick Vrost.

"What's wrong, Alynna?" Grant asked as he and Frankie sat down next to Cady on the couch. The Lupa was the only other female currently not pregnant. She and Grant already had three of their own, twins and a young daughter who was two-and-a-half years old. "Aren't you happy to be doing your duty to the Lycan race?"

"Oh, I've done my duty alright, I've done it four times!" she exclaimed, referring to her and Alex's four children.

"Four times?" Alex interjected as he joined them. He was sweaty from playing with the children who were now being watched over by Sebastian. "I think we've done it more than that." He bent down to kiss his wife. "Not that I'm counting."

"Not that, pervert!"

Grant groaned. "I don't want to hear this."

"Grant, your sister is a married woman with four kids," Frankie said playfully. "You know she has sex. Lots of down and dirty sex with her hot husband. This can't be a mystery to you after all this time."

"La la la," Grant stuck his fingers in his ears. "Not listening."

"Oh yeah, Mr. and Mrs. Super Alpha Lycan Pheromones?" Alynna quipped. "I would say half the time, you guys trigger us and," she nodded to her kids, "at least two of those are a result."

"And maybe this," Nick said as he came over, rubbing Cady's belly affectionately.

"Hey, we got those special seals installed in our apartment

and Grant's office after we got married!" Frankie said. "You guys," she said pointedly at Alex and Nick, "did that on your own."

"I'm hungry, baby," Meredith said to Daric, her eyes pleading.

"You're always hungry," he retorted. When Meredith gave him a pout, he kissed her forehead. "I'll get you some burgers."

"Yay!" she said, raising her fist in triumph. "With mayo and ketchup—"

"And extra pickles," Daric finished. "I know." He stood up and walked over to the grill, where the burgers and hotdogs were keeping warm. As he piled a plate with food, something hit him on the ankle. Looking down, he saw a red ball by his feet.

"Oh, hello Zac," he greeted the young boy as he bent down.

Little Zachary Vrost looked up at him and smiled. "Hiya, Unca Daric," he greeted, his light blue eyes sparkling and chubby little cheeks pink from running.

Daric picked up the ball and held it out to Zac. As he reached for his toy, the little boy tumbled forward, and Daric quickly caught him before he hit the ground. As his hands touched Zac, he was taken aback by the vision that came to him. A tall, handsome man with ice blue eyes dressed in a tux. A young woman with long blonde hair and amber eyes in a white gown. The man whispered something in the woman's ear as they danced under fairy lights and her face broke into a familiar smile. He couldn't hear what the man said, but he caught one word. A name. Her name.

"Hey, you alright, bud?" Nick said as he stood over them. "Sorry about that," the Beta said sheepishly. "I swear, you can't take your eyes off them for a second, right?"

Having two boys of his own, Daric agreed. "Yes, indeed." He picked up Zac and then handed him to his father.

"Thanks," Nick said as he took Zac. He gave Daric a

grateful nod before walking away to join the rest of the children, who were now piling on top of Sebastian as they played their favorite game, catch the dragon.

Daric wasn't close friends with Nick and Cady, but over the years, they had come to some peace and understanding, and they all treated each other with respect and kindness. He accepted that there would always be some distance between him and Vrosts, but he didn't mind because he was plenty happy with his family and circle of friends. He wondered what the Beta would think if he knew what Daric had seen in little Zac's future.

"Hey, what took you so long?" Meredith asked as he sat down.

"Sorry, *min kjære*," he apologized. "I had to make sure I got all your condiments."

"Oohhh!" She made grabby hands at him, and he gave her the plate. Grabbing the hamburger, she took a big bite. "Hmmm...so...hmmm good..."

"Slow down," he laughed. "I don't want you to choke."

"Oh yeah, tell that to your son or daughter," she said through a mouthful of food. With one last gulp, she devoured the entire burger.

Daric sat down next to her and took the empty plate, placing it aside. He put a hand on her stomach. "I've thought of a name."

"Really?" she asked. "Boy or girl?"

"Girl."

"How do you know?" Meredith asked, her eyes widening. While she loved their sons, Daric always knew she longed for a little girl to spoil and introduce to Disney Princess movies. "Is this one different from the boys? Can you see her future?"

He shook his head. "No, I'm still unable to see visions from you or our children," he said. "But I have a good feeling about this one."

"So, what's the name?"

"Astrid."

Meredith thought for a moment. "Hmmm...I like it. What does it mean?"

"It's a traditional Scandinavian name," Daric explained. "It means godly strength or divine beauty." He had no doubt of the beauty part, but, the strength would be something she would need.

"It's settled then," she said. "If it's a girl, I mean."

Daric drew her closer, and she laid her head on his shoulders, enjoying the cool summer breeze and the laughter of children around them.

The End

The True Mates series continues with a spinoff :
The Lone Wolf Defenders
Available in select online retailers

Do want to read a (**hot, sexy and explicit**) extended scene from this book featuring Daric's proposal, as well as an **alternate scene** that never made it?

Then subscribe to my newsletter - it's free and you can opt out any time, plus you get **ALL my bonus content** including a FREE Book - The Last Blackstone Dragon.

Subscribe online here: http://aliciamontgomeryauthor.com/mailing-list/

THE LONE WOLF DEFENDERS

STANDALONE SPINOFF TRUE MATES SERIES

Killian's Secret

Loving Quinn

All for Connor

Available at select online retailers

AUTHOR'S NOTES

WRITTEN ON MAY 3, 2017

As the last book in the series, writing Tempting the Wolf was a special challenge. Daric, so far, has had the longest story arc in the series and Meredith's was pretty long, too. I wanted to make this book amazing, for them and for you readers who have been on this journey with me.

Also, Taming the Beast was a hard act to follow. You all loved Sebastian and Jade so much, and I could tell that story was going to be special. So when I sat down to write Tempting the Wolf, there was some apprehension and a lot of doubt. After a few days of struggling with writer's block, I sat down with my music teacher and we talked about the difficulties I'd been having with my voice breaking and her advice was just to work through it - keep singing and vocalizing until you work through the problem. And I thought well, that's what I should do with Daric and Meredith. So I sat down the next day and worked through it. And you know what? It worked. The words flowed out. The ideas came and I was struggling this time, to write them down so I don't forget them. I'm still sad I was unable to incorporate all the scenes and jokes I wanted to include (hence the alternate scene at Muccino's, which you can read by signing up for my newsletter).

When I first introduced Meredith in Witch's Mate, I already had an idea of her background and her old mentor, Archie Leacham (did you "catch" that reference?). Daric's background was a little more fluid, but from the moment I wrote him, I knew he would need someone special to match him and challenge him.

I sure hope I did Meredith and Daric's story justice, and I'd really love to hear what you think, so email me at alicia@alici-montgomeryauthor.com for your thoughts or all other comments. I do my best to reply to each and every email I get (even if it sometimes takes me a while). Can I just say, it's been such a pleasure writing these stories for you.

Still here? How about I tell you more about the background of this series...

I actually started writing the True Mates series back in 2014, though the idea came to me earlier than that. In 2011-2013, I was been living in China with my then-boyfriend (now husband), JT who was teaching English there. Now, you may be wondering, "What does China have to do with werewolf shifters?" Well, bear with me...

As you may or may not know, China has had the one-child policy in effect since 1979. Many of the friends I met there had no brothers and sisters. The people who were my age were the first of their generation to grow up in households without siblings. Growing up with several siblings of my own, the idea seemed even stranger. At this time, I was also voraciously reading a lot of paranormal romance stories because we didn't have good Internet out in the sticks were we lived. So, one day, it just struck me: what if there was a group of people (or in this case, Lycans) who could have only one or no children at all? And well, the idea just kind of evolved into the True Mates Series.

Fun fact: Blood Moon (Cady and Nick's book) was going to be the first story in the series, but I had a hard time trying to put the lore together and have to explain what the Blood Moon is, as well as True Mates pregnancies. (They were also going to be stuck in an avalanche in the first draft, but that's another story). So, I realized I needed to first set up the world and use an outsider (Alynna) who would be seeing the world of the Lycans for the first time.

So I began writing in 2014, first I made outlines and tried to put the world together. I adore world-building and I had so much fun. I wrote the first six chapters and then real life happened - I got engaged. We also moved to two different countries and I had couldn't get to my half-finished manuscript. Finally, a year after our wedding, I decided to go back to the manuscript and I published Fated Mates (originally titled, Finding the Pack) in August 2016.

And here we are, six books later and I'm still here. And you're still here! From the bottom of my heart, thank you! I'm going to keep writing as long as you keep reading. Oh, and reviewing too! Please consider leaving me an honest review (and any other authors you follow) - it really helps me, not only with sales, but also tells me what you want and how I can improve (and I'm always trying to improve).

So, as you have seen in the previous page, True Mates isn't over yet (not this generation anyway). Killian, Quinn, and Connor's stories are still waiting to be written, and I'm excited to bring them all to you. If you've been a longtime fan, you know I try to plant my characters in advanced. Did you happen to see that little clues I left you about their stories and the special ladies who'll be coming into their lives? Oh, and for all you

Dante fans (and I know you're out there), I'm listening and you'll just have to wait for the *right season* for our favorite chef's story.

Ok, I've rambled on enough. But let me just tell you thank you again, it's been my honor to tell you these stories and I have also enjoyed getting to know you through your reviews, email, messages, tweets, and Facebook comments. You all inspire me and you're the reason why I do this.

All the best,

Alicia